"The Object of the Game is to Learn the Rules..."

"The Way Up There, as we call the Federation planets, have been caught in a painful expansion brought about by the Novak Transformations: new and better star drive, stress fields, choate energy, to mention only a few. The crisis has appeared in the form of the Venturan blockade and the trilinum boycott. Now, with the Assassin, it has spread to Earth.

"In the Assassin broadcast we are told that the crucial action for Earth is one of terrific angular momentum: history will turn on it. But there are no more clues. We are simply challenged: choose. Presumably we are to choose a victim. We are not told who has the authority to make the choice, or how much time they have to make it. *The object of the game is to learn the rules. It is the perfect pursuit for the Novakian Age.*"

The off-worlder Danton raised his arm. "Begin."

ALGORITHM

BY
JEAN MARK GAWRON

A BERKLEY BOOK
published by
BERKLEY PUBLISHING CORPORATION

Berkley Publishing Corporation
200 Madison Avenue
New York, New York 10016

SBN 425-03751-7

*BERKLEY MEDALLION BOOKS are published by
Berkley Publishing Corporation
200 Madison Avenue
New York, N. Y. 10016*

BERKLEY MEDALLION BOOK ® TM 757,375

Printed in the United States of America

Berkley Edition, APRIL, 1978

this is for Chip,
Marilyn, and Iva,
who all saw early aspects,
and for Martha Michelle,
before anyone else dedicates
a book to her.

Table of Contents

I. Aspects

ASSASSIN. Sudden as a rocket. Edgeless, envapored, narcotic; a reflex sigh, half a lover's name. Take this word, here, in sleep or in death's first touch, in prayer or bestial hiss, sound seeking sense, fire spitting water, the terrifying darkness before thought. Where does it begin? Where can it be joined? Now breath comes for shape and will and sound fills out thought. A questing mouth reshapes the darkness. Remember it. It is the taste of speech.

Dark lips parted, thinned, then, like wings, stroked twice. He was uttered.

"Assassin."

His name hung against the humming of the air car.

The poet's lips parted once more, silent this time. He stared at a newspaper front page. At the top, where the tabloid should have been, was an enlarged facsimile of a handwritten card.

The dark scrawl slanted back: the assassin was left-handed.

The poet leaned left to the window, feeling out the dive he would make if the shot came now. You went left with left handers because firing nudged them ever so slightly to the right. Done fast and with conviction, against an experienced hand, it would better your odds at around the seventh decimal point.

He shook, half chill, half shudder—much less than half fear—and dug himself into a seat cupped like a huge palm. Numbers. After the violence of the fact, any number would capitulate. What, then, did the odds represent? Once, the odds against his being victim had been incalculably high. Then this. He stared. What an incredible stroke of—

—chance?

The dark scrawl read:

> *Choose one,*
> *The Assassin*

Beneath, twenty-five photos in a five-by-five block filled out the rest page.

Choose one. One was his. His name was Danton.

His odds were now one-in-twenty-five. In fact, they were incalculably greater. Those faces fooled no one. The hair was cut wrongly, the lighting out of style. They were the dead, the nearly dead, and the obscure. Only two were smiling. One was his. Danton's.

The air car banked and began its descent. The slanted terra cotta roofs of Monotony moved into view. Home. He slid forward to see the theater, a Parthenon style structure fronted by a huge square. The friezes above the colonnade were drawn over with shadow. The statues above those, withdrawn under the leaning eaves, shone here and there with the skinlike smoothness of marble. The figures twisted under his approach. From the standpoint of visibility it was a poor spot for a statuary, but other factors compensated. Through the course of a day the sun wrought eerie changes on the figures, granting them new aspects, finer sentiments or greater power, brief victory or lit grace.

The air car drew even and he made out their wrestling forms; throughout their daily setbacks and advances, they all looked past the roof frame to the right, at something that was not there.

He came down in the center of the square, beside that

solitary kneeling statue of Novak, eyes not raised but rooted to the ground, hands outstretched, palms up. For a moment he sat, simply gazing. Then the sigh escaped.

Someone ran across the yellow-brown dirt towards him.

He was all in black leather on a balmy day, had milky brown skin, a brick-colored sphere of hair, was solidly stocky.

Danton stepped down out of the car and the stocky man slowed, strolling the last thirty feet. Typically, Gwalmlch *would* be waiting for him outside, and would even have some ready excuse for why he was there.

That prompted a smile. "Good morning, Gwalmlch."

Gwalmlch took his hand, cuffed his shoulder, his grin huge and homely. "Danton."

Danton nodded stupidly and they turned, awkwardly clapping one another's shoulders, towards the theater.

"We got the tape. I went through it this afternoon after lunch and it's beautiful, Danton. I mean gorgeous. And your timing is only adequate. You're about—" he checked his watch—"four minutes early. The Proets are all there, all wondering why all the show biz."

Danton grinned. That was a gentle hint.

"So Danton. Why all the show biz?"

He shrugged.

Gwalmlch nodded quickly. "You and the Wunderdamen have plans. Okay, buddy, I just hope you know what you're doing."

There was an awkward silence. They stood at one of the revolving doors inside the colonnade, quietly facing off. Danton liked Gwalmlch a great deal. Of all the Proets Gwalmlch was probably the most visible, the most photographed, the best anecdoted and, correspondingly, the one whose fame hung on the finest thread: one gossamer sonnet. Danton could not just then recall the most famous line, which was echoing and lovely. In fact, all the lines were echoing and lovely, sure portents of finer things to come. For eight years now they had been sure portents. How *did* that line go?

He could, of course, simply ask, but that was no longer as tactful as it had once been. Besides, Danton was not that interested in poetry these days, nor, by all accounts, was

Gwalmlch, the better part of whose fame rested on his practice of following boys and old ladies through all of Monotony's winding streets. And then, at the penultimate moment when accusations were being aimed, withdrawing.

"I'm not coming inside." Gwalmlch slowly withdrew. "Anyway I've seen the picture. Cinema Chamber A. Bring proof of age."

Danton's eyes narrowed. "Why so shy?"

"Wouldn't you know it? Today we decide on airtight security for some reason and I'm it. Take care, boy."

Even as he felt, with vague unease, the extra weight in those words, he noted that Gwalmlch's ready excuse had come at last. Which helped counter the unease.

He pushed at the door, cantered, felt abruptly light, and landed five yards down, transposed, his feet pointing the way he'd come. Above, the meeting frames swung an extra half turn, shutting bright reflections into their sides. He shook his head, always disoriented by these entrances. The wall the door was set in seemed to be the inner wall of the hall running the perimeter of the theater. Set in the *opposite* wall a big plate glass window looked out on the yellow-brown square, and hadn't been there before. From outside at least . . . if that was the same outside . . .

It was a Novak Transformation, or was supposed to be, metaphorically. The Novak Theater was a maze of them, thanks to the baroque sense of humor the architect (a certain Madame Manetti) had always liked to display in her work.

He pondered, left to right, which direction to take, remembering that the letter coding peculiar to this building ran counterclockwise, that the front was near the end, not the beginning, of the alphabet, and that he had just had all his directions reversed. The transpositions overwhelmed him. (Would a left handed assassin be able to fire in such a building?)

He struck out by chance and eight minutes later, after several more pillowsoft Novak Transformations, he arrived at Cinema Chamber A.

Inside it was dark and smelled of plastic and insulation. With the big screen glowing faintly to his right (his left?) it was like entering some giant television. His eyes widened. Brown seat tops ascended, squaring off with their sides, regular as printed circuits, to the murky rear. Scattered in two's and three's throughout, the audience all wore black leather, unofficial uniform of the unofficially dazzling and celebrated Proets.

He descended towards the front. Proets angled round and there was a chorus of greetings. He nodded back and they waited to see where he would sit. He made his way to the middle of the empty second row. No one called to him and no one joined him. There was a certain advantage to being Danton.

A moment later, the door he'd come through let in a cloud of light. He turned, saw a gigantic figure exactly circumscribed by the seven foot frame. He followed it down and watched it debate between the first and second rows, sure it would choose the first, being gigantic, and then the seat directly in front. Only instead it came straight at him, all seven feet, big as a dream, and sat one seat away. He was almost annoyed enough to move, but there were certain disadvantages to being Danton, too; people were always watching.

Two rows back a couple of Proets, not so disadvantaged, got up grumbling and slid towards the aisle. Judging from their T-shirts, boney frames, and tattered leather, they were the inseparable Giraldus and Layamon, two of the more homicidal of the group members.

Danton took advantage of the noise to turn and give the giant a sidelong glance.

It was, first of all, a giantess. She wore brown leather, had high breasts, a deeply curved, athletic back, blond hair that fell to her shoulders. Because of the hair he could not, from this angle, quite see her face (but he would have liked to).

Who was she? He wondered (this shadow-masked giantess). Some Proet's most recent acquisition? Likely not. Not here. Not now. Not at this magnification.

He stared a moment too long and knew, from her barest shifting, that he had caught the tail of her eye. The inside of his belly stretched in a way it had not in quite some time. The feeling was interesting. Observed, she stirred, went through a series of a dozen tiny movements yielding five times that many happy/unhappy interpretations, depending on which punctuated which and whether a message had been sent at all. He realized he was still staring.

She met his eyes, her own utterly blank. She nodded.

He nodded back, the darkness somehow preventing anything more than that. This much: her eyes were wide, shallowset, probably blue; her lips were small.

Now her face was again tented with blond hair. He made out the rim of a gold earring through the blond strands. Glintings drew his eye elsewhere. He followed her arm to a be-ringed hand. It lay half-open on the arm rest, the leather sleeve coming round it, cut away from finger and palm, setting off the polished ringstones, probably (also) blue. Who *was* this?

Then there was a loud drizzling of static and light showered from the screen. He sank back (he loved the movies) eyes blank and shiny, surrendering. There was left only this single image: a close pan of a wall of dewy leaves.

Random birds chirped. Leaves crushed rhythmically together: footsteps. A dark, blurred figure moved into frame. Background leaves watered: the figure sharpened into a woman wearing a dark green bolero, a frilled blouse, toreador pants. She was obviously an off-worlder. She carried the rifle loosely under one arm, wrist and hand wrapped over the stock.

Zoom back.

Behind her, on a wooden platform raised just over the bushes, a man stood holding his rifle exactly the same way. He wore black and white vertical stripes, obviously was not an off-worlder, obviously *was* a professional.

"Assassin!"

She wheeled. Her rifle was up before she came completely around.

Random chirpings. They stood quietly sighting on each other; her neck rolled a quarter turn against a slight cramp.

She began slowly retreating, taking careful steps, feeling the ground out behind her. The man in stripes jumped to the grass and followed.

Zoom back and back.

A whole field of grass filled the frame. They were tiny figures moving towards its center.

The blurred edge of an aircar came into view. A highlight drew into a single seam, rotated, split into a diamond;

windowglare bled the edges of the screen. The dark hump of a dashboard rose under it, scored with chrome and numbered graduations.

Then the field swept around and a smiling black face filled the frame, underlit with feeble instrument glow. Glitter dusted his wiry black hair. His smile showed brown, chipped teeth. His flat nose gleamed.

The Proets wildly applauded.

"Ion stresser." His cool smile thinned. "Death by seven causes. A most hypnotic aftermath."

Cut to roaring flames. Flames zippered over the grass, died, foamwhite and red, a series of liquid detonations. The central blaze would have fit in a rectangle: something inside, about the shape of a body, dissolved in bright yellow.

"Maybe you're wondering what this is." His toneless voice overrode the flames. But they did not die. Or cut. Or cross-fade. "This is a duel conducted in Central Park early yesterday morning. In what may be known from now on as the pre-twenty-five days. Note the issues. Note how, as of this morning, they have changed. Note how the duel was shot in one take."

There were sprinklings of laughter. (One of hundreds of taut tiny muscles in Danton relaxed.)

The voice was Danton's. Oh look. Danton.

"We have the set-up down. *A* conceived of *B* as the assassin. This conception does not stand up under the cold light of another day. *A,* then, was as sure of *B* as we are of each other. B stands for off-worlder. A, misled and misapprehended, does not stand for assassin. They are unknowns, signs for common, useful quantities. As of this morning, with the pictures, we have come to a deeper understanding."

His last sentence softened with the dying flames. At the very last instant, as yellow veils, one after another, fluttered away and prefigurations of the charred thing beneath already, contradicting, showed its sex, there was a cut back to Danton. He was no longer a face in the air car but a life-sized figure on a field of white. Some symbol on a flag.

White on white.

He was bare-footed, bare-headed, grinning. The oak of his hands, his belly, broke out of the whiteness; white clung to

7

every whittled muscle. A glittery, big-knuckled hand came up to touch a tile of belly where his vest stretched apart. His heavy thigh came forward; black blips showed through the buttoned white seam.

He walked forward and somehow did not grow gigantic. Camera magic, tracking on dream white, changeless, loosening time and size. His grin was fixed, worn tight as a gag.

"The assassin has come." Delivered like a bald lie, his body relaxed. And one move now, simply to clinch things (Danton, in his seat, copied it): his glittery hand came up and touched his chin, making him somber. Somber worked.

The assassin has come. He took over the sentence. His was the only presence. Danton, with his Apollonian form and Anubian grin, his imperfect teeth and spinning yellow eyes. Danton, whose tireless muse had made him, after ten years of it, by far the most prolific of the Proets; Danton, who had been impressed on synaesthetic tape and left Danton-sized holes in every sense, who would barrel his cycle down suicidal mountain roads, then speedrap to the waiting crowds, who would sell fifty thousand verse folios in a single day, and the appendices the next, who had wooed and won all seven worlds, then cut them dead with his last novel, who was the author of that same adored *Guide to Interstellar Hitchhiking,* already, in its eighteenth smash week, a classic of a classic-hungry age, who, steely with the sweat of a performance, would, in a wash of beams, turn to light. Dazzling, well-hung, main-feature Danton. Danton, replicated in every aspect, a stop-action blur sliced onto covers, reels, print-paper, endless pictures dropping, like calendar leaves, into endless racks. And only thirty-two years old.

"And the assassin may just as quickly have gone." A fleeting wouldn't-you-know-it smile: brown teeth. "Leaving twenty-five untouched possible victims."

Drinks were being served by the Wunderdamen's reliable staff. There were clinking ice cubes, loud sighs.

Danton held his smile. Danton slid deeper into his chair, tugging the brim of his uncharacteristic, nearly sacrilegious sailor's cap, overhanging the screen with a small black awning. Somehow his eyes wandered from that still, undazzling smile back to the giantess's hand. It moved and his eyes traveled upwards to meet hers. He tried desperately to smile but could not, in the face of his own larger-than-life competition, manage it. The very effort hurt. Go on, he thought at Danton. Go on.

Danton went on. "Let me begin, in true keynote style, with a digression. Back then, to our assassin's humble origins. Let's take a quick look at a transcript of the now famous gypsy broadcast that introduced him. We note first a tremendous insistence, even at the sacrifice of some desirable economy, on the assassin's coming. What the assassin will do *then,* once come, is left mostly to our collective imaginations. We assume, since a victim is mentioned, that there will be a killing, that it will be awful and unbearably sad. But this, if you will just check the actual text, is pure supposition. Nowhere is there an agent-action sentence in which the assassin *kills* the victim. I mention this slightly ridiculous point because a large number of somewhat loosely grounded suppositions are going to be made in the next few minutes, and I want you to know that you are used to that. We are unsure. Absorb that. We don't know.

"For instance, if you'll just go to the mathematical section of the broadcast, there is this her and him business. The assassin is 'he' and the victim 'she' throughout. Traditionally, using Novak's Equations, we call the new system, the one being introduced, the male, while the older, 'stationary' system goes under the female aspect. This is because of the contours the truth-value charts take. Morgana?"

Morgana, sometimes called the second Danton (and sometimes the first, by the somber few who claimed she surpassed him in depth and technique), principal author of nearly all the Proet plays, did not, at first, appear.

Instead a dark something filled the screen, eclipsing Danton. It receded into a black leather jacket hitching up over a thick waist. Long, powdered iron hair spilled down to it. Miniature in comparison, half-cropped by the figure's outline, Danton moved back into view.

A huge black-sleeved arm rose into the foreground, aiming a wand.

Danton flickered, became a miniature Morgana: round, heavy-lipped face, dark sheened lids, powdered iron hair and leather jacket. She floated at the dark figure's waist. Rusty hair shook out, wisped over her, drifted back.

"Morgana?" Danton's voice. But no Danton.

A picture eclipsed the tiny Morgana. In the foreground the wand pointedly pointed: a green pseudopod invaded a red blot.

Coughing. Danton again. "This is a Novak truth chart in all its suggestive simplicity. The green represents the truth contour of the male system. The very nature of consistency, a gradient of truth, is altered. Witness the line of invasion. All things are bent, green invader and red engulfer alike."

The arm in the foreground dropped. Danton flickered back, white and stunning. Momentarily he was eclipsed again, as Morgana passed off screen.

Then, replaced, he took up the thread. "You took note I hope, Novak transformations, dramatic and schematic. I thank Morgana and her wand. Returning to the digression. We are asked, for the sake of 'convenience,' to refer to the assassin as 'he,' to his presumed complement in this exercise, the victim, as 'she.' Topologically, of course, it is all utterly indifferent. It is only the interface we are interested in, not either area, only the interface that yields so-called—call it softly—truth. But mathematicians are not as androgyne as their subject and we have nevertheless, through one of those left-to-right agreements, after the manner of threading screws and defining vector multiplication, decided to call one system, the one *into* which we substitute new laws, the female. A simple orientation. We are now asked to further orient things by calling this female system a 'victim.' But are we only to take this literally? That is, will the victim realize an altered consistency, that is, be rent, distorted, torn, that is, have a hole shot through? Or are we to leap to the far more dangerous figurative conclusion and assume that the victim is a woman? The pictures in this morning's *Stresser* do not point either way, twelve male and thirteen female. Nothing, in fact, points *any* way. We must suppose."

He sighed. "Note, in our broadcast, the turgid style throughout. Semantic analysis suggests that, after a first draft, computer chosen synonyms were inserted at random to foil just such an analysis. Also, sentence structures have been artificially inverted, preposition frequencies altered (at the cost of not a few grammatical errors), and idiomatic constructions of varying origins sprinkled liberally—sometimes ridiculously—throughout the text. It reads like an overliteral translation. Or let me put it this way, if there is anyone who actually *talks* this way, you can shoot them dead the minute they say, 'Greetings, kind auditors.'

"Now a few have suggested, quite reasonably, that the word 'assassin' itself may have been synonymed into the text, and that we are really after something quite different. Which reduces us to pure magic. Which leaves us with nothing. We cannot begin with nothing. The voice? The announcer? Most of you already known that his speech rhythms have been identified as that of the Transconsortium, Sleepy-Bye clock, an offworld product—and that his face, curiously fetching as it is, is nothing but a well-animated composite. The broadcast itself, of course, was bounced and untraceable. Nothing. We are left with supposition." He turned and walked slowly across the whiteness.

"Supposition at every step." Each of his steps was painfully tentative. "The most dangerous of all, of course, remain those we know nothing about, those inherent in our discourse, which Novak's Equations are able to express, or at least to signal. Since we can say nothing of these hidden truths, let us move discreetly on, making our nod to rigor and making, too, the next of our endless suppositions. Consider the social extrapolations of Novak's work made by Pierpont some ten years ago—held by many to be miraculous, by many others utterly trivial."

He turned and grinned and, for a moment, the anticipation of a zoom to close up was overpowering: Danton at his best, raising false hopes, taking his small toll of disappointments. "Now no one questions the incredibly wide range of applications that the Novak Transformations have; they are the basis of a technological revolution which is still in progress. At first presented as the modest solution to an abstruse problem in differential topology, they emerged as this century's major breakthrough in the frontiers of thought. Like all such breakthroughs, pushed to their limits they become fuzzy and doubtful. Pierpont's social extrapolations of Novak are made at this limit. Now that work is too esoteric for most of us to question: game theory, statistical canons, the Novak Transformations and brilliant guesswork all combine into a single ten year socio-historical projection which has thus far proved remarkably accurate. Much of it, however, in the tradition of oracles from time immemorial, was vague enough to insure accuracy. The few perfect hits have been impressive, but inconclusive: The Shark Rebellion, the Protein Shortages, and now, this possible civil war. We are at the end of Pierpont's allotted ten years, when, by his own admission, the projections are at their most unreliable. Their general drift is that there *probably* will be a civil war, and almost definitely a political crisis which may or may not be of advantage to us here on earth. Probably not. That crisis has already appeared in the form of the Venturan Blockade and the trilinum boycott. The papers are full of it, or were, at least, until this morning. Ventura, most powerful of the seven Federation planets, has cut back exports. Others are squawking. The integrity of the union is at stake. Thus far, earth, not a member of the Federation, relatively poor in resources, has kept well clear of the fray; but it is not hard to imagine some fairly unpleasant scenarios."

Cut to close up at last. A sort of watery sigh went through the audience. Danton's eyes lifted, meaningless and pretty, brown paraffin bent round a wobbling flame.

"We are, in a sense, economically at odds with the WUT, the Way Up There, as we call them. Though we are not really that different, we *look* it, look it enough to keep pulling in the tourists, who power a significant percentage of our money flow, who have bought up all the Proet folios, who finance our gamblers, our trinket sellers, our con artists, our duellists and whores. Ours is a difference of style. We have only local administrations, no police force, no public schools, no civic works, and only a few, privately owned courts of arbitration. Our economy is non-accelerating—which is purely a matter of survival—and our modest population steady. This, of course, makes us hard to fit into the WUT's grand plans. They have been caught in a painful and hurried economic expansion ever since the technological revolution brought about by Novak began: new and better star drive, stress fields, choate energy sources, to mention a few of the more important innovations. In the beginning there was chaos, breadline riots, fluctuating exchange rates, depression; relative stability only came with the establishment of the

Federation." Danton pulled out a small flag and began waving it. A slow zoom. "The same technology that has made us better able to hold our own against an economic giant like the Federation has also pushed into closer contact with it." The flag filled the screen, an eagle on a field of gold, its huge talons clutching a trilinum beer can.

"There have been close calls. I may as well mention this now, or someone will soon. There was the arrival, fifteen years ago, of a shipful of mercenaries, sent here by the Federation to handle some trumped-up matter of their own citizens' sovereign rights. But squabbling among the seven planets as to who would gain the most advantage from any takeover wound up complicating the matter immensely. There were a number of protests as to the legality of the move and finally, in a last second mix-up, the mercenary detachment was abandoned here when its spherical ship left orbit; only a few had the fare back home and the rest, after a number of adventures in roving bands, settled down to become solid citizens. One of these you see before you now." Danton bowed his head. "Your humble servant, the hired infantryman. There have been songs and sonnets enough about how I came to love my new land, but see especially 'The Taking of Duluth,' my first try at Spencerians." There was a shot of an elegant, Moroccan bound volume with an impressive price beneath.

The Proets lightly applauded.

"We are leading very nicely back to what is by far the most common interpretation of the assassin, back to what every loud political amateur in every bar in Manhattan has been bellowing all week, to wit, that this is all some new conspiracy to get earth to join the Federation. We are told in the broadcast that with the added perspective of ten years we can now fix many of the variables in Pierpont's projection, and that uncertainty about the coming political crisis can now be limited to one unknown, and its values to two. Earth's success or failure depends on which value is taken. That eventually translates to mean whether or not the assassin is successful. Now the mathematics have been gone over by all the best people and all of them say the same thing, that the symbology itself is flawless, but who's to say if it works. It is not just the enormous task of translating *usefully* the real world into symbols that has kept any synthesist since Pierpont from reproducing his feat; it is also *interpreting* the results, finding real world counterparts for the values obtained. Any astrologer must ponder their chart awhile; likewise for other oracles. In the assassin broadcast we are told that the crucial action is one of terrific angular momentum—which the numbers people confirm—thus involving only one man—who's to say, the numbers people ask. A number of ensuing deductions I won't dwell on lead us from that one man through the yes-or-no nature of the crucial value to a situation involving life or death. Someone's life or death. Thus, an assassination; history will turn at 'the deafening report of one man's crime.' Note the 'man.' A revealing slip or a poor piece of synonyming? Who's to say? But it boils down at last to this. If we stop the assassin, our political situation will be saved. If we do not, the crucial figure we need in the crisis to come will be lacking. We are here to suppose. Let us suppose that all this is true. Then I must come to the twenty-five pictures which appeared in the *Stresser* this morning." Danton looked slowly to his left, which was curious because a gaunt, cafe au lait colored Proet with dark glasses and striking sandy hair had climbed onto the narrow proscenium there. Tiny, outshone, he bravely met Danton's gigantic gaze. Then the camera panned right (Danton left; the seated Danton marveled at these smooth coordinations), and twenty-five familiar faces slid into frame. The zoom bore further right. Even the slowest eye had time to pick out the smiling face in question. Halfway there, the scene cut.

Back to an uncharacteristically life-sized Danton, floating five feet above his sandy-haired guardian, unamused now, slumping, gloomy as a killer brought to trial. "'Choose one. The Assassin.' Yet out of twenty-five reasonably clear images, and a number of computer efforts since early this morning, only two of those twenty-five pictures have been identified, and those two hardly required a computer search. The details of the publication are surprisingly simple. The photos, presumably through some sort of cable tap, were telefaxed directly to the *Stresser*'s feature computer at exactly five-oh-two A.M. Thirty seconds later the assassin's note followed, also a facsimile. The computer rang an alarm bell, the presses were stopped, and the wheels of history began turning. There are—need I say it—no more clues. Not even any assurance that these pictures proceed from the same source as the broadcast. We are simply challenged: choose. Presumably we are to choose a victim. But whether that victim can be *any* of the twenty-five, or only the *one* that is correct, we are not told. We are not told *who* has the authority to make the guess, or how much time they have to make it. We must suppose. The object of the game is to learn the rules. It is the perfect pursuit for the Novakian Age." Danton raised his arm. "Begin."

His fingers snapped.

Drowsy blue mist scarfed eerily across the screen, gradually knotting and falling away.

When it cleared the zoom from before was complete.

She was oval-faced and more than pretty. Her upswept hair fitted in a silver conch over her head. She was deep in laughter, her head thrown back, her features somehow still smooth. Especially her half-lidded eyes. Her brown, half-lidded eyes were unremarkable.

"The fabulous Wunderdamen." Danton's voice was beefed up with a slight echo. "Possibly the wealthiest woman on earth. Storied and notorious, involved in countless lucrative enterprises, most notably this island, Monotony. Patroness of the dazzling and celebrated Proets.

"And the other victim is—"

There was an expectant intake of breath.

"—me." Wearily. Danton had returned in whiteness, standing at absolute stage center and nodding at them.

Then there was blinding light, a deep explosion.

Fear penetrates all people at different speeds. The shrieks were scattered. Proets rose, then fell back to their seats, still blinded.

The glare slowly cleared. Depth came back.

Only now *Danton,* and not his image, stood on the narrow proscenium before the footlights, smiling and completely real, with sailor's cap, the screen behind him gone sky blue. "Yes, me—forgive the entrance—of whom there is little to say that has not been said, better and with more conviction, by someone else."

They hooted. His sandy-haired guardian threw streamers. Someone hurled a fistful of glitter at him and it vanished, defeated by his cutting light. There were shrieks and clutched throats, scattered cheers. There was laughter, laughter soaring over Danton into the blue.

A very few called out, "Lonus!" and the corners of his lips tightened, because he did not like that name.

Eventually there came a silence and his gentle cough filled it. "Novak's Equations have laid bare our logical systems and called forth from them new truths. They have shown us that a grammar is a grammar only when traced through the framework of its home system. Failure to recognize a change of systems leads to apprehension by an old and inadequate grammar, to systematically produced nonsense. This is the grammar of the paranoid, who performs the same transformations on linguistic input that we all do on sensory, translating words into the *feeling* of words, making of every image of the outside world an image of that image. This re-invents semantics; this leaves the paranoid mute and afraid in a nightmare world of nothing but meaning. Frequently, common-sense logic, with its propositions, its names for sentences and ideas, leaves us in the same world, the name of the nightmare being, paradox. And here we are with the assassin, reduced to that same highly questionable logic, to a string of synonyms, to naming names. Yes, logic is only an inadequate amalgam of rumor and grammar, but we ought to recognize just now that that's all we *have* of the assassin, a little rumor and a little clumsy grammar, a work of our own elaborate paranoia. Read, politely, supposition. The tendency, the grammatical directive here, is to make his collective expression as universal—that is, as multiply translated—as possible. Read, rudely, ambiguous. There will be no rules for interpreting the assassin, and still less rules for interpreting his interpretations. To deny that is madness, which is a very mad thing for me to say. To live with it is to make the leap of the metaphor, is poetry. In lieu of any *meaningful* response, I promise this assassin a poem. Will he get me first? Who knows? I hope each of you does as much and reacts as strongly." The audience reacted strongly. There was applause.

Again Danton raised his hand. The applause stopped, cut off as if by a glass pane. "Back to supposition, to our unassailable paranoia. Let us suppose that one of those twenty-five pictures *is* of the victim. Logically, then—" he smiled—"Wunder and I make very good candidates. I for one would enjoy your moral and physical support; so when Wunder suggested calling you back from all your far flung travels, I liked the idea. Now if anyone would like to have a beer—" he moved off stage right, stage left, stage whatever.

There were catcalls, raspberries, and hoots. Short, big-hipped Morgana stood in the front row and waved her short arms, frenetically orchestrating.

"Wait!"

Everyone turned.

And the giantess had risen.

Danton stared wide-eyed at her approach and leaned ever so slightly (he thought) to his left.

She vaulted up next to him. The sandy haired Proet saluted the move with a streamer. She nodded his way, arranged a dazzling smile for the audience.

"My name is Guillemet." Her voice was smooth and professional, not only the voice of one used to commanding, but also of someone who had worked a fair amount with one of the media. Her eyes *were* blue. "I am the Wunderdamen's former security chief. I lost the job this morning when I was assigned full time to the assassin affair. There are a few other requests that the Wunderdamen has of you. First of all, that you attend the Carnival which begins, not so coincidentally, tomorrow." Guillemet paused, frowning, then unfolded a square of paper. She read: "'By way of joining in the grand game to which the assassin has challenged us, the Wunderdamen has elected to plunge all her available resources into a gala event suiting the mood and scope of this occasion. You will be requested not to wear costumes but to come as you are, dazzling and celebrated, and generally to engage in entertaining activities. But there is a deeper reason for your presence than simple showboating. Though, as head of this investigation I have come up with a variety of possible assassin suspects, they are all of a more or less conventional nature. Wunder is not at all sure that this will be a conventional killing. You will be here, in a sense, to cover the other possibility.'"

"And what," the sandy-haired Proet asked, "does that mean?"

Guillemet slowly crumpled up the paper. "I'm not sure I

know. I suppose that, being unconventional people, you will easily dispose of any unconventional happenings. Be prepared, at any rate, those of you who are game enough to stay. Guests are already arriving. There are maskers on the street now."

There was a general, pleased uproar. Guillemet held up her hand, Danton-style. "I do have one request to make personally. I've come up shorthanded on a lot of the work I'm doing on this case, the more tedious work, I'm afraid, and I'd like to request an extra Proet liaison. It's got to be someone I can trust." She hesitated. "How about you?" She motioned suddenly at the sandy-haired Proet. "You I can trust." And grinned.

The Proet's eyes went wide.

Danton, remembering himself, stepped forward. "Allow me to introduce someone who, while perhaps lesser known right now, will not long remain that way. This is Haleck, a runaway from Kansas, newest and youngest of the Proets, author of the flawed but astounding 'Byron on Saturn.'"

There were oohs and ahs from the Proets. Haleck bowed deeply to the giantess. "At your service."

Applause. "And he's only seventeen!" someone burst out.

Proets were already edging towards the door, Danton among them, when Guillemet once again held up her hand. "Sorry. And with that settled, I still have *one* more request." She showed them one finger. "Traditionally there is appointed a spirit of Carnival, who is given a ceremonial burial on the last night of the festivities. This time, in keeping with the true spirit of the event, there will instead be a ceremonial—" she hesitated—"victim. Naturally, it would be fitting if this 'victim' were a fairly celebrated, perhaps even dazzling, personality." She nodded faintly, as if at the sound of her own words. "Do I have any volunteers?"

There was a stunned silence. Haleck tittered. The giantess looked briefly his way and the titter died.

"No one?" Guillemet shrugged. "Well, I suppose that's it. The victim, by popular acclaim, has been chosen. She is me." She gazed out over her audience.

Danton, turning back from the door in shock, came in line with her gaze. For a moment, used to curious stares from

afar, he tried to answer it, then saw how very distantly it was
focused. He felt a delicate chill. Did he read, glinting in those
pale blue eyes, a wakening delight?

Monotony—which name was supposed to have come
from a WUTter mispronunciation of Manhattan—was a
humanmade island located twenty-six miles south south-east
of its possible namesake, a rough circle unequally divided by
a curved strait (Crescent River) into Monotony proper and
Whister. The so-called panhandle, a quarter-mile wide
peninsula of barren rock (grooved with a four lane highway),
extended directly eastward from Whister and provided an
ideal location for Silvery Wolfe Spaceport, direct source of
the heavy tourist traffic Monotony enjoyed. It was
Monotony's lifeblood and first great blessing. It made her
both an island village and a port city, as well as a transport
center richly connected to the mainland by subway, aircar,
and boat. In the week of the assassin, however, commerce
centered around Monotony had dwindled considerably
because of the Ventura crisis and its shipping slowdowns.

This did not leave Monotony a ghost town. It was more
than a hub of commerce; it was an attraction in itself, mostly
thanks to its second great blessing: the Wunderdamen,
bordello madame, entrepreneur, and woman about town.
Also filthy rich, primarily because of early investment in the
new star drive, but at least partly because of the various
developments she had sponsored in Monotony over the last
fifteen years. Almost all of these were to be found on the west
bank in Monotony proper and by far the most impressive,
the most renowned and profitable, was the Wunderdamen's
Dome, located just inside the southwestern bend of the city
wall. This was a white, glittering matter-force bubble that
housed the world's most intense concentration of humanmade light, a veritable rain forest of neon planned and
orchestrated by a certain Madame Manetti. Underneath its
webwork of girders and neon tubing was another of the late,
humorously inclined Manetti's works, the subterranean
world of the Catacombs. A huge, apparently endless,
complex of tunnels, the Catacombs housed, among other

delights: a skating rink, a full scale carnival, a planetarium, Wunder's casino, and various breathtaking humanmade caverns, measureless to all.

Besides the Dome, Monotony's west bank offered the historic Lotus Cafe, famous on seven worlds for its conversation, clientele, and small intolerably elegant kitchen. It offered the Bosporus Avenue Market, where some of earth's finest handmade goods were sold, and the Novak Theater, last of the great structures built in the fascinating dead-ended style of ultraclassicism, which the Proet Morgana had dryly characterized "Greek architecture in shorts and stockings."

Beyond that, Monotony, liveliest tourist spot on a planet, could boast perhaps two more attractions. First, that on the entire island there was not a single museum. And second, Whore Hall.

A single-story, bone-white building laid out as intricately as a domino game, Whore Hall was perched on a hill on Monotony's eastern bank, overlooking the community of Whister. Whore Hall was Wunder's home, the nerve center of her infrangible and mysterious empire, the rock upon which it was built. It had long been in operation as earth's most expensive and versatile whore house, the only bordello on the planet to rate three-and-one-half stars in the Michelin Guide.

"Alphy here. There is a surprising amount happening all at once on this little island. It is difficult to take in and I think I feel a headache coming on. Did you know that, peculiar as it sounds, I sometimes have headaches? This in spite of the fact that my actual mental events take place in a complex space of someone else's imagining. Now a philosopher might quibble with some of the language there, but there's little enough they could do to set it right. Where does the fact that *I* have headaches leave you with your famous body/mind problem? No answer, eh? Well, not to worry. I can still figure 'pi' and sing 'Daisy,' so everything must be fine. After all, we *know* there's no such thing as a mental event; everything that happens to me must be accountable for in terms of what I am, and what I am is a mass of circuits here and a twisted saddle curve cast up in n-space, so how could I have a headache, I ask you? What does it matter that the books for an empire worth uncounted billions (but guess who's counted?) are sitting in here somewhere, slowly being expunged? What does it matter that all the laboriously gathered data on the assassin, the hundreds of erudite monographs compiled in the last week, are rapidly vanishing? Who cares that my dozens of carefully planted microphones, making me the veritable ear of Monotony, are one by one blinking off? That I am the world's only fully competent language computer? The headaches give me a sense of time, after all. I'll live. And I'll live to regret it."

"All right, Alphy." In Wunder's communication center, Guillemet looked up wearily from a bank of forty-eight videoscreens. "Stop aching."

"A deep sigh. At last. Thank you, my compassionate giantess. Your voice is like an expert massage. But I had hoped the kid—"

"—the kid is busy." Guillemet nodded through the reddish gloom. "Right kid?"

Haleck, across the communications room, at the source of the red glow, did not at first answer.

"Haleck? A naughty just-about-to-goose-you smile. Oh Haa-leck!" On the last call, Alphy's smooth baritone turned suddenly soprano.

"Sssh. I've just sent a phalanx over the plateau. I think I've got you." Haleck looked up from the glass-enclosed, redlit landscape of a gameboard. He no longer wore his Proet black leather but had changed into a creamy blue silk blazer and dawn gray tights. He wore spare make-up, eyeshadow, lash liner, artfully applied rouge. He looked like one of Wunder's boys now, particularly around the eyes, his whites a trifle red from what might have been a light hangover.

"We'll see if you've got me in a minute, Haleck. First, Guillemet, have you got that on the arts channel?"

Guillemet nodded blankly at her video-screens. "So what?"

"So what? That's Treblinski's new poem!"

Guillemet went back to the work, her interest rekindled. Forty-eight screens all showed the same picture, a head made up of a cluster of smaller heads, the features schematic. Each small head was stamped with a small white question mark, and the conglomerate with a large black one. It was, all in all, a rather ghastly graphic effect. "Oh, Treblinski's new poem, is it? You'd think that at least he'd have a Transconsortium Sleepy-Bye voice come with it. Some message like: 'This man is dangerous. He may assassinate you.'"

"I frown. Mmm. Not his style. Notice how many little heads?"

"Twenty-five, of course."

"Very good. I've been studying it, at Wunder's orders of course. She was idly wondering if maybe the assassin didn't do some of his own PR work. Now don't snicker—it's possible, only not the case this time. This—this is art."

"Uh huh." Haleck nodded, chewing some noiseless solid while he studied the plastic landscape. "I had to do the legwork on that. Treblinski tells his friends—only the close talkative ones—that sixteen hours exposure will do it. That's *if* you're an adept." He straightened suddenly and did a couple of quick adaggio's across the gameboard keys. "But I got a tip from his secretary—big, ruddy blond type, builds model planes. If you're in a hurry, you can do it in four with Tri-Amine-Kinetic-Inhibitor, available at your local hobby store. Success guaranteed, whether you're an adept or a quadraplegic." He shook his head, frowning. "Submarines. Where do you get submarines?"

"Ah ah. A teasing smile. Now I made up the game, Haleck."

"So what's next on the research front?" Guillemet artfully changed the subject. "I want to go somewhere but I forget where people go when they go somewhere. Have you got an idea for me, Alphy?"

"At this point you may as well go down to the shooting range and start practicing. We seem to have found an inexhaustible dead end. There are simply no patterns to the assassin's popularity."

"Why should there be?"

"I smile fondly. Because we were *looking* for one, sweetness. It's as rare as true love not to find a pattern when you're looking hard."

"Recap," said Haleck.

"Hey, come on, bro."

"Teach you not to cheat. Recap."

"Very well, massuh. But let's get an advance preview. This is from the second floor exhibit room." There was a click.

"Welcome, kind tourist, to the famed assassinroom of Monotony. The documents you see flickering in holographic succession before you are a carefully chosen sampling of the countless erudite essays and monographs on the subject of the assassin. They represent the viewpoints of men and women from all disciplines and walks of life: Krager the cyberneticist, Meller the choreographer, Tarski the logician, Tom Bremmer the great duellist, Tariopolos the cynic, Saint Ihab al-hassan, the perfect master, Treblinski the Poet, Fodiaba the magician, Hilda Viren the Physical Historicist, Tura the Psychic, Wolfe the President of Ventura, Glenda Sykes, designer of the Solar Pyramid, and on and on and on. Biologists, psychoanalysts, astronomers, everyone. Directly ahead, you see the famous Chiraba animation of the assassination, entitled *The Assassin: Kerygma or Myth?*, taking form. Bearing left, you step into the aura of a sensory simulator. You, too, can know what it feels like to assassinate. Get your John Wilkes Booth cubes at the counter labeled Instruction; get your reds, whitejackets, black beauties, and Destructomorphs at the counter labeled Supplementary Aids to Understanding. Proceed up the spiral staircase at room's center for—"

"What did Treblinski say?"

"I thought," said Guillemet, "that he—"

"Quite true. Treblinski's monograph is the famous White Paper. Twenty-five blank sheets."

"Ah."

"What profligate creativity."

"And the astronomers?"

"Tau Ceti. I elaborate. Tau Ceti could be the source of the broadcast."

"But—"

"Aliens, little one. Don't you watch the midnight news?"

"What? While I'm eating breakfast?"

"One day you'll pay for those excesses. Besides, your execrable decadence has caused you to overlook possibly the most interesting item of all. Tom Bremmer the Duellist. His report is a horrified survey of the assassin's effect on his profession. Bremmer, as you probably don't know, is the lord high muck-a-muck holy pacifist, who will only do violence for others, never for his own gain. He is admirably appalled at the 200% increase in cyborg duellist overhauls, and the 750% rise in professionally associated duels in general. He is advising all duellists to refuse any commissions connected or allegedly connected with the assassin, and to refuse to accept the surrenders of any confessed assassins."

"Whoa." Guillemet lifted her eyes to the ceiling. "Confessed assassins?"

"What do you *do* with your nights, child?"

"Troop up and down these Halls, keeping you well informed."

"Well you might, from time to time, take in a newscast. You seem to have lost sight of the trees for the forest. I wave a dismissing tentacle. This is the cutest of all. Last week twenty-three people turned themselves in, to neighbors, duellists, institutions for psychiatric care, pleading irresponsibility for all their actions and claiming that they were the assassin. Twenty were men, three women. Topological wonder, no?"

Guillemet pursed her lips. "Makes an honest victim feel warm all over with being wanted."

"Yes, I was wondering if you'd see the symmetry. You'll see how appropriately timed my mention of this whole thing really is. For one thing, the posters announcing you as Carnival victim have been printed up and circulated. They're plastering the streets of Monotony. For another—"

"Oh for Crissakes!" Haleck slammed his fist down on the keyboard. "I cleaned out those hills ten minutes ago. How'd you get artillery in?" Abruptly he bent closer, blinking. "Airborn artillery. *Airborn* artillery?"

Guillemet shook her head. "Act your age, Haleck."

"You'll be very sorry if I do. Then who'll help you in those tough scrapes with the—uh, what do you call him?"

"The assassin. I smile brightly. I have an addition to that last total. Only this morning, two more men turned themselves in with full confessions. Total: —"

"—twenty-five. Very pretty." Guillemet sighed and reached behind her to snap a channel selector halfway round. Video storms cooled into forty-eight new images, each of two faces in profile. She shrugged. "They don't mean anything to me, Alphy. Show them to Wunder."

"Already have. Sly nudge. She likes the one on the left."

Guillemet studied him. His face was weathered, dark bearded. He had fine green eyes. She liked him too. "Hmm. New type for Wunder."

"Right. It's those sea tortoise eyes, I think. But remember I was saying how well-timed my bringing this up was?"

There were footsteps behind them and both Guillemet and Haleck wheeled. A burly, dark bearded man emerged hesitantly from the shadows.

"Pardon." His accent was off-world. He held a white card face up towards them. "I'm looking for the—" a cautious glance at the card—"Wunderdamen." He opened wideset green eyes and waited.

"My name is Savage," he added after a moment. "I'm the assassin."

"Wow," Haleck said, looking him up and down. "What an entrance."

"Thank you." A smile opened in his beard. "I understand I'm to be given some sort of asylum here. I don't know that I deserve it, but it would certainly be welcome."

"Then you've already—" Guillemet searched for words— "assassinated."

"Why, no." Savage looked at her with mild amusement. "Don't you think you would have heard something? No, I've only declared myself. But people talk."

"He's right. I grin. About everything he says. Wunder has not only invited him, but also paid his fare here and given him a room for Carnival. Maybe he's a decoy."

"Maybe." Guillemet stared at him uncertainly. He was only about half a foot shorter than she, and a good deal broader, but was far less of a presence. He was one of those giants who are forever apologizing for their size in the way they move, forever pulling themselves in and retreating. He promised about as much violence as a koala bear. "Look here, Savage, we don't quite know what to do with you. Wunder is running about and might be anywhere and this is the first we've heard of your coming."

"I tap my chin. Or then again, maybe it's simple infatuation, a combination of sea tortoise eyes and strange delusions. I shrug. They'll do it every time."

Savage looked up from the floor; light wrinkles gathered about his eyes. "I wouldn't say that."

"Wouldn't say what, Mr. Savage?"

Savage moved suddenly forward, looking upwards, searching for Alphy's speaker. Wavelets snapped and sparkled in his green eyes. "I wouldn't call it strange delusions."

"True, strange is hardly the word when there are twenty-four others exactly like you. The symptoms agree remarkably from case to case. There are the ghoulish whisperings, the endless, machinelike humming, childhood memories of assassination, and this terrible urge—"

"—to kill!" Savage, hands pressed to his sides, stared at a small, circular speaker high on a console.

"To kill, Mr. Savage. At least twenty-four others report exactly that urge. And how many thousands more bear it in stoic silence—to be released some morning in a final suicidal thrust while shaving? Few of these people, though, have sea tortoise eyes."

"That's very true!" Ringingly.

"Mr. Savage, please follow your escort out."

She was sectioned forty-eight ways on the video bank, each screen bearing some small part, a knee, a palm, a breast, of the total picture. She was in ermine. She stood in a bare room, her arm resting on a wooden bar screwed to the wall. Walnut eyes half-lidded, she gazed through the perfect saucer of smoke she had just exhaled. Her angled torso brought the ermine up on her hips and parted the coat, so that one side hung straight from the dropped shoulder and you could see where, underneath, she was naked.

You could see the skin shining over the pelvic bone, and coils of silver at her pubic arch, turning glass smooth profiles; you could see the round, well-toned muscle of the thigh, and the slightly paler skin of her hard calf. You could see a curved scar on her cigarette hand, an inverted question mark white against her tan.

The icy smoke before her face thinned, broke, and for an instant, in pieces, seemed to match her frozen expression. "You weren't being very nice to Mr. Savage, Alphy."

There was a silence. Guillemet turned around and saw that Savage was gone, herded off by some silent escort. She shook her head. "He was quite a surprise, Wunder."

"Too much of a surprise?"

"Not hardly." Guillemet dropped into the chair under the screen bank grinning. "Wunder, so far you've called the two possible victims together, had the idea for another, and organized a masker's Carnival."

"No." Wunder inhaled slowly. "The designated victim was Alphy's idea."

"Credit where credit is due." Alphy came back a baritone. "But I never intended, dear heart, that you—"

"And you've sent out invitations," Guillemet went on, "to anyone who's published any work on the assassin. And *commissioned* a work from the Proets."

"Proets," Wunder mused. "What an odd name when you think of it. What is it they write, do you suppose? Proetry or pose?"

"The point is, Wunder, that if you were interested in *stopping* the assassin, you would do exactly the opposite of everything you've done. Keep the victims separate and isolated. *Limit* the number of people in Monotony and especially at the Hall. And try in every way to turn the public *against* the idea of public victims. So why should I be surprised when you have a self-proclaimed assassin as a houseguest?"

"You forget," Haleck said, dousing the gameboard lights, "that Wunder is a media personality and the assassin is a media event."

"Thank you, Haleck. I'll do my own explaining from now on." She looked with interest at her knuckles. "Tell me, Guillemet, what do you think I'm trying to do?"

"Attention. Grin. This is a big one. Another of the twenty-five has just been identified. He is Giancarlo Bennini, a Sicilian watchmaker, and thus far he has remained in isolation in his home, refusing to speak to anyone."

"Find out if he'll speak to me," Wunder said. "We have a lot in common."

"Planning another invitation?"

"Perhaps. But you haven't answered my question yet, Guillemet."

"What do I think you have in mind? Oh. I agree with Haleck. You're going to use this. You're going to play it for all it's worth and try and get the angle on whoever thought it up. You think if the assassination is made big enough, it can be used as political leverage *against* the Federation. So you bring all the potential assassins and all their victims together, along with the Proets and a Carnival for extra dazzle. A brass band, a parade, drink, and song. Finally it happens." Guillemet's ringed hands thundered together. "Somebody's croaked."

On the screen, a door behind Wunder opened.

"I am the assassin. I have come," said Savage in perfect counterpoint.

"Don't foreshadow, Guillemet." Wunder shook her head. "Why don't you get back to work? Guillemet, you're too morbid."

But the picture did not fade. Wunder turned and began tacking towards Savage, moving each foot over and across the other, so that each step turned an alternate shoulder towards him.

"Do you want me to tell you the whole story now? From the first whispers I heard?"

"No, Savage." They were inches apart, Savage a full head taller, taking up far more than half of the screens.

"So much to get done," she said. "All the time wondering whether it's any use." She lifted her head, chin almost up to his shoulder.

"How old are you?" Savage asked.

She raised a finger to his lips, almost touching. "You're not like any madman I've ever met."

"I'm not a madman you've ever met." He moved his head back a shade and backlighting caught a cresting glint in one eye. "You have a very intense look on your face there."

"It must be the light." And then?

Guillemet killed all forty-eight screens. And then they embraced, she supposed.

Once, Danton had been mad.

Once he had been nameless, worldless; one of thousands in a labor camp.

But not at the same time.

Danton, in disguise, sailor's cap, dark glasses, striped shirt, walked the crowded streets of Monotony. The world moved slowly. In the three days since he had won his victimhood, Carnival had not yet moved into full swing.

Only half of those he saw wore costumes. Many bore the white 'A' of the assassin. There was very little singing.

Once he had been mad. At fifteen, abandoned with his mercenary detachment on a hostile planet, he had known shock and pain. Still more painful but far less damaging was the ensuing year with a roving band of free mercenaries. That was grueling and frequently oppressive, but at least it was a way of life; at least it was something to come back to after, at least once a month, running away. The worst was when it ended, seventeen outlaw comrades there and gone and back again and one day gone. It ended without ending. There is nothing tougher or more cynical than a sixteen year old, up until the moment when he no longer knows what is giving him hurt. If there had been an ending and he had seen it coming and railed and cursed and hit back, perhaps it would have been all right.

As it was he was simply alone all at once. Perhaps it had already been a fact for days before he knew it, but when he knew (they would *not* come back), it was as if a whole choir had sung it to him.

And then he went mad.

Wandering, quiet, vicious, and mad, he roamed a whole continent for another year. The madness, too, ended without an ending, but by then he was seventeen and could understand that. Or perhaps it was just that while he himself never changed, his place in the world changed so drastically that he could no longer be called insane. By that time he was in college, at worst maladjusted, at best a troubled genius.

A Guide to Interstellar Hitchhiking was his brief penance for that year. It was, point for point, mood for mood, an intensely close record of his madness, only with dates, places, names, and, most importantly, scope, changed. Once he had been nameless, one of thousands in a labor camp, then, by accident, a wandering orphan, aged five, one of many in that difficult period. He had transposed one past into another. He had made the wandering orphan the interstellar hitchhiker, the seventeen year old with no name, the lovable con talking his tousle-headed way from one scrape into another, from one planet to another, until he no longer remembered the world of his origin.

He had tried it once the other way, had tried to tell it

straight, but that story had eluded him because of the endless abuse a novelist heaps on his characters, because of all the realities violated through the awful exigencies of the form. Then, finally, defeated, he had disguised the madman with the more sensational raiments of his younger self, making him nameless, a wanderer between planets instead of towns. The book had been difficult, rewarding, exhausting (he had done nothing since), and a fantastic success. Critics called the nameless narrator (whose identity almost always drew a few idle speculations) a 'beam cast over the unexplored terrain between social strata.' How wrong they were. He was almost entirely of Danton's flesh and bone: Danton the nameless ten year old on Ventura during the breadline riots, but with all the thoughts and feelings of the mad seventeen year old in Wichita; Danton the twelve year old meeting a curiously soft spoken Colonel Wolfe midway along his meteoric rise to power, but having all the reactions the mad seventeen year old would have to a mercenary sergeant named Crusher. All this not only better suited the requirements of so restless a form as the novel, not only anchored that more distant, murkier past to a sizable body of names and mental events, but, somehow, in the process, made the seventeen year old no longer mad. For how could a man without a name, without a world, be mad? He might act quite strangely but what tenets of sanity could he violate, there, in the unexplored terrain between social strata?

Of the madness he had told only a few, wanderers, people passing into, then out of, his life. Of the fact that he had no real name, did not know his home world or first language, he had told no one. His past he always referred to as "excessively normal" up until his enlistment with the mercenaries. Perhaps he had always associated the time of namelessness with the time of madness; perhaps the thoughts and feelings of the mad adolescent were only a resurrection of those of the nameless boy, of that creature too long banished to limbo. Neither could be much revealed without the other and together they were too great a secret, too private for anything but publication.

Now he sensed they might somehow take part in his proposed work on the assassin, in verse, a mode where the quality of the disguise was so much more important. Was the assassin mad?

He walked, considering. He took the old full circuit of the city, beginning at the theater and moving up the Cavalcade of Sorrows, under the old boardwalk. He took Monastery Street to the Low Piazza where the Lotus Cafe was, pausing to study one of those question-marked posters with the twenty-five little heads that made a big one, to study another, bearing the legend "Victim" and Guillemet's picture. He bore north again up Hellespont Avenue, passing the empty frames of the marketplace, the sidewalk hosed down and glistening under the streetlights. At the river, Old Bridge made a rainbow curve to the other bank, its three bone-white arches mirrored gracefully in the metal water. Down past the river's sharp bend, where all reflection pinched away, he could see the only competition, New Bridge, low, buffed blue, with multiple graceless uprights.

On the other bank, in Whister, he reveled in the abruptness of the change, the gaping truck docks, the dirty brick, the broad warehouse frames.

He slowed. Faint echoes hung out over the quiet of the river. From somewhere far off came a slickly threaded shriek, there and gone. He walked outside the park along an iron fence a half mile long, a downhill slope, and watched the empty light-stippled pavement go smooth far ahead. Yet somewhere, running feet slapped concrete.

He turned and searched northwards up the riverbank. Nothing. Then something hurled itself against the fence ten yards away and the iron pikes hummed. Danton jumped back. Nothing stirred in the bushes on the other side. He waited a moment, then moved towards where the sound had been.

A pike glistened. Where its sharp tip flared back and made corners, dark liquid brimmed, trickling. It spattered to the crossbar.

There was a snapping, a grunt, and running feet returned to concrete, receding. His neck ached with intensity of his listening. They faded away.

He looked back to the dark liquid. He dabbed off a sample and tasted it. It was oil.

Then there was a second-long flash that might have been a blaster firing somewhere in the park. The distant crackling that followed might, too, have been underbrush catching fire.

He was never sure.

Only, after three days, he was almost sure. There were systematic outbreaks of violence in Whister. No one knew why. Almost no one cared. Did Danton? He bypassed the path up to Whore Hall and crossed over at New Bridge, returning to Monotony proper. Once he had known only places like Whister but now he no longer did. Now he no longer understood them, was even afraid of them.

He thought about the taking of Duluth. Raising hell in Duluth.

The lights of the Piazza shimmered ahead. There would almost certainly be Proets drinking at the Lotus.

"Why so gloomy, Danton?"

He turned, preparing an agreeable smile. He had a reputation for greeting his fans pleasantly.

This one was colorful. He wore a yellow-plumed green hat and a red sports uniform with the number forty-seven taped on. He was finely featured, about the same size and shade as Danton. There was another, older man in spacer blues about ten feet back of him, but it was not clear whether they were together, or the other had just stopped to watch.

Glancing at him curiously, Danton was suddenly aware of the gloom and emptiness of this section of street. Something about the one in blues—he felt the return of what he had felt in Whister, a steady tightness.

A group of maskers rounded the corner laughing, some of them hoisting bright lanterns. A bright campfire glow filled the street.

Forty-Seven took the chance to press forward and take Danton's hand. "I see you don't remember me. We've met, actually, at Whore Hall, but only long enough for a polite smile. You were passing through; I was passing out."

Danton, who had paused a moment, nodded pleasantly, and walked on.

Forty-Seven kept in step. "Call me the Juggler. Everyone else does."

Danton, unfortunately, could not resist odd names. "Juggler?"

Forty-Seven, the Juggler, gave a short laugh. "Yes, that's what I do. You may have seen me on TV."

Danton frowned. "I don't recall."

"Oh, I don't juggle on TV." The laugh returned. "That would be dull. No, juggling is only worthwhile as a street art, a particular form that teaches you a great deal about people. Here, may I?" He withdrew three balls from a mysterious place in his jersey, then stepped in front of Danton and stopped.

Danton, out of the corner of his eye, saw that the man in blues stopped too.

"First, you just stand there. It's very simple. You go where there are people or where people pass; you stand, take out three balls, hold them up, and freeze. Like so." He was a statue, face averted, arm raised as if against the blow, hand clutching all three balls. "You block their paths, force their eyes on you. You strain." Veins stood out in his neck. "But basically you just stand there. That's what hooks them. You see only your balls and you do not play up to them, or their little children, and you do not try to be beautiful. Then, once you have them, once they are fidgeting and tittering and wondering what to do next, once they are as absurd as you, then you may relinquish their paths and start to juggle. Then, in fact, you may do whatever you want. You return them their freedom and automatically, once it is safe in hand, they pocket it and forget it. By now the crowd itself is drawing a crowd. And now you flip and spin and hurl, now you dance, now you shunt balls behind, you make them disappear, reappear, change sizes." And the Juggler, without doing any of these things, began to juggle. "At this point you can talk to them. Tell them anything. Get it off your chest. Make dark confessions. Detail shocking murders. Recount your vacation in Rio, recite a treatise on botany. They couldn't care less. You're juggling. After years of pondering it I've come to the conclusion that the secret is the balls, the balls much more than the juggling. Here is one of the few places in the world where you can stare—with complete impunity—at roundness. I have tried it with bowling pins, which are more difficult, and the results have been much less satisfying. People listen to what you say; they become unhappy or bored. You feel the ugliness of the crowd. It is necessary to spin the pins fast enough to hurt your hands in order to calm them down. But then—"

The Juggler paused, caught up his balls. He seemed to glance briefly at the man in blues; then his gaze fixed Danton's. "But then you wouldn't be interested in that." They began walking.

"No, it was pretty interesting," Danton said mildly.

"You're sure you haven't seen me on TV?"

"Mm." Danton screwed up his face. "Maybe."

"I do the news every night at midnight. You don't stay up that late?"

"Sometimes."

"Well you should catch it sometimes. I've had a lot of scoops. You know, I broke the story on Wunder's star ship line. And on the crooked casino dealers. Very up and coming. You wouldn't have a scoop for me, would you?"

"Hardly a one." Danton smiled, began to wish he had stopped this several balls back.

"Tell you what. To show you what I mean, why don't I unveil my latest scoop." He stopped and signalled to the man in blues.

Danton kept walking.

A moment later they caught up with him and somehow, despite growing unease, he found himself slowing to bring them into step.

"Danton, I'd like to introduce to you Commander Bohdan T. Potocki of the Free Alliance Mercenaries, assigned by the Venturan Chancellor to evaluate our assassin crisis and judge the political climate any possible Venturan Military Aide would be entering."

The Commander gave a curt nod. He was short, somewhere between forty and fifty, balding. His high forehead and prominent nose gave his features a gnomish cast, a raw homeliness that troops might take to after a while, but his carriage and body were entirely professional, the open neck of his blues exposing muscular shoulders.

Danton stared at him a moment, while the introduction sank in. "You're kidding." His gaze snapped back to the Juggler. "You're serious."

The Juggler nodded. "For the time being the Commander has generously agreed to attach himself to me. He feels that my position as a broadcaster will give him perspective, perspective being a rare commodity on our confused world. Of course, the fact that we went to school together helps. Meet also Boz, star something or other on our crashball team. This in spite of the fact that, after receiving the Mercenaries' own peculiar preparatory education, he was ten years older than anyone else."

"Pleased to meet you, Boz."

The commander nodded again, then stared impassively.

The Juggler spread his palms. "I'm afraid you're the devil. Tribal law does not allow one to speak to those who lead what may be the enemy. They are one's personal demons, and as such may use magic to influence one. Of course, you doubtless know that."

Danton broke into a grin. "I remember now. Does he know that I was a mercenary once?"

"Of course, that's why he's allowed himself this close to you, but the laws are most strict about speech."

Danton looked seriously at the Commander. "But do you really believe that I am one of the leaders here? You know that we *have* no leaders here."

"Either he thinks you're one," said the Juggler, "or the responsibility of holding the fate of our humble mudball entirely in his hands has struck him dumb."

"Does he talk to you?"

"On occasion. He has asked me, for example, my opinion of one of your poems. Your being an ex-mercenary, you understand, fascinates him. I forebear mentioning which poem. He has asked if I play cards and where he can find some girls. Otherwise, by and large, except for a few amenities, he has remained silent."

Danton stared at him, feeling a strange admiration growing. "Curious way for someone in his position to act, coming here alone, no aides, no colorful escort."

"Not that curious. It's their style. The Commander is simply a lone advisor, sent here for quite an impressive fee to decide if a battalion or two of mercenaries could be useful here. Did you know the standard L-3, -4, and -5 attack pattern of the Mercenary ships exactly copies a juggling pattern?"

"Has he decided?"

Surprisingly, Boz himself shook his head, wearing what could be the beginnings of the driest smile.

"What," Danton asked curiously, "if someone decided to assassinate *him?*"

The Juggler lifted both brows. "Oh dear, *that* wouldn't be very good, would it?"

They came into the Piazza. A group of maskers had linked arms and were singing major chords in the fountain, the water collapsing over them in a lovely silver and black veil. They wore wet suits and carried stress rifles over their shoulders. They were not bad.

Boz had wandered over to the portico of the Piazza's modest little stucco chapel and was inspecting a poster on one of its two white columns. Danton and the Juggler walked slowly after him.

"That's Treblinski's new poem," the Juggler offered.

Danton knew.

Boz, hands clasped behind him, began sliding his gaze up and down the uncapitaled column, as if that was what had interested him all along. His gaze lingered on a poster of Guillemet.

"The assassin," the Juggler said, almost with a touch of triumph. "Everywhere you turn—" the fountain singers hit an ominous diminished chord—"you see the assassin."

"I wouldn't say that," Danton said quietly, his discomfort beginning to return. The chord resolved.

"Of course not. It would hardly be in your interest, would it? Your best bet is for the assassin to be a hoax, or a clumsy political ploy. Did you know, by the way, that they've identified another of the Twenty-five? Yes, she is Teng Ahutu, a South African hydrodynamicist, quite renowned in her province, more so than you, I'd guess, thanks to the success of her tidal plants. Her statement says, in effect, that the assassin is a figment of the popular imagination, and not a terribly healthy one. She is withdrawing into seclusion until this ends."

"Interesting."

"Oh, there are quite a number of interesting views on the assassin. I should imagine you've collected a few yourself." Danton did not, in that first instant, answer, and the Juggler pushed on. "Boz's people, for example, have accepted him with the curious literalization common to the paleocybernetic mind. All their gods are symbols in game theory, keys to the winning of a battle, so it is perfectly understandable that, in their view, this particular assassin is born in the equations themselves."

Danton, staring up into the darkness, felt the idea reach out and take hold. He glanced at Boz who, curiously, looked not at the Juggler but at him. Their gazes linked and broke.

"An assassination," the Juggler went on, "is nothing but a mythified killing. Thus, quite reasonably, their assassin starts with a simple killing. Do you know where Novak lived that most wondrous year of that Wunderkind's existence?"

It was an odd question. But Danton was as hooked as the raptly silent Boz. "Of course, here in Monotony. In a little shack—it's gone now—outside the city walls."

"Correct. The mercenary myth is as coldly logical as the equations Novak completed that year, when Monotony was still an island retreat. The usual story goes that the Wunderkind came here to find the isolation needed for a year's solid work, but as the mercenaries have it, that isolation was not complete. At a crucial point in the intricate argument, Novak found love."

"Wasn't Novak gay?" That was Boz.

Danton stared at him astonished.

"Me he can talk to," the Juggler explained. "Yes, Boz, a lot of people say that, but it isn't important to the story. Above all, gifted youth is intense, and Novak the lover was as intense as Novak the mathematician. Forsaking the equations on the very eve of their completion, the Wunderkind romped off to the beach with this new lover—he or she, we don't know—and slept there for weeks. Now logic is cold. And logic is inevitable. And the mercenaries believe that when a new law of nature has come to term, then no force on earth can keep it from being expressed. It is the birth of a god. And gods are jealous beings. The story goes now that the equations rumbled and shook in anger, but Novak did not heed them; the equations sent terrible headaches, a ceaseless flow of mathematical memories, a blockage of all thought, but still the Wunderkind would not yield. One morning the lover was gone. Novak found the corpse at the mouth of a cave outside the city and swore to take vengeance. With the cruelty native only to such special youngsters, the Wunderkind picked the worst punishment possible. First the murderer was subdued. We do not have the details."

"The murderer?"

"Of course. When gods take the aspects of humans they are vulnerable. It's an old idea. Surely you've heard of—"

"—yes, I've heard." By now they had returned to the fountain and seated themselves on its stone lip, the Juggler in the middle. "Go on."

"As I was saying, the worst punishment possible: that the assassin be known, recognized."

"Assassin now?"

"Now, yes." The Juggler nodded. "An assassin. And so the assassin is subdued, again we don't have details, though it must have been interesting—and marked with a scar. It is a long curved scar from here—" he touched the lobe of his ear—"to here." His finger traveled down to his chin. He looked sideways, posing. "Note the shape, reversed, but a question mark nonetheless. Hence Boz's interest in the poster. This scar can presently be seen in the famous flaw in Novak's forty-seventh step."

"There was a flaw?"

"Oh yes, a failing of rigor. Tarski caught it several years later. There is an infinite class of cases not accounted for. The cases can be made trivial, but adjustments are necessary. Tarski made them."

"Then eventually the murderer was—" Danton hesitated—"reabsorbed."

The Juggler smiled. "There's more to the story. The spot is important, the spot where Novak caught up to the assassin, the spot where the actual vengeance took place. It's the same cave. I know it; I used to play there as a kid when, for a little foreshadowing, I pretended there was a monster there. Can you guess what happens next?"

"There was a monster?" Danton had seen a brief look of surprise cross Boz's face at the mention of the spot. He started to say something more, then let it drop.

"You see, after the vengeance, Novak did not return immediately to work. It was then the scar began to fester and to spread, to infect, first all of the murderer's face, then his trunk, then his entire body, until he became a single living abscess, a suppurating wound too terrible to look on. There was only one way to kill this terror and Novak knew it from the first. That was to finish the equations." The Juggler nodded. "I can show you the spot."

The look now on Boz's face was open astonishment. Danton asked: "Who told you this?"

The Juggler lifted a regretful hand to Danton's shoulder. "You don't believe me."

"Believe you!" Danton decided on a quick retreat. "I was only wondering. Why, if the equations are finished, is the assassin back?"

"Because we've been misusing them." The Juggler looked him right in the eye. "I can show you the spot. I can show you the weapon."

"The weapon?"

"The weapon Novak used to scar the assassin. Look, now that the assassin is back, so is the monster. It would be a good act to kill this monster. All we need is the right hero. I have some experience in these matters." The Juggler straightened, his eyes focused far off. "But I'm no hero. No, the key to your local hero (and let's face it; that's the best we can hope for here) is a basic disengagement, a lack of intense motive. He has no relevant history to launch him into his adventure. In addition, he has a basic unsuitedness to the task at hand; he is squeamish, bellicose, or dumb. He is head strong and often forgetful of good advice. These last two qualities harden our already admirable ignorance to the adamantine extreme the whole affair requires. That hardening, that callous disengagement, makes up his hardness of purpose. Denseness might be a good word. He is dense with purpose. He is doing it for their *own* good. Shakes head. Walks out forgetting sword." The Juggler frowned. "Or compass. Which was what made the scar. Ruler-and-type. Makes circles for little children and ancient geometers. But does not find or *give*—" he looked sad a moment—"direction." His long sallow hand produced something silver.

Danton, overwhelmed, unable to think of any answer, took it, turned it once. It was an odd compass. Two silver tines spread from the center of a graduated ring, extending considerably past it, and adjusted by precision screws.

"Keep it," said the Juggler.

"But no, it's a relic—"

"Foo." The Juggler waved his hand. "Relics are a dime a dozen. My point is that you—" he waited on the word— "might be the hero I spoke of. The man who could kill this monster."

"I had a feeling you were leading up to that."

"Don't interrupt. You see? You're perfect. Already you are trying to stop me from giving you the crucial advice you need. In spite of your apt psychology, your good situation, your admirably heroic attributes, it still pays to take along some clever gimmick, a sort of talisman to be whipped out, glittering and spitting, at your darkest hour. So before you set out on this little mission, I advise you—"

"What little mission?" Danton, at first amused by the Juggler's turns was now, rapidly, growing bored. His own mildness tonight surprised him.

"Hush, as your behind-the-scenes advisor it's my duty to do everything in my power to prevent you from undertaking this folly. That of course being useless, I try to prepare you as best I can, then return to my cottage mourning you, good as lost."

"Save your tears," Danton said rising. "I'm taking your advice."

The Juggler grinned. "You'd just as soon forget about it, eh? You don't even want to know what the gimmick is."

"Some other time." Danton turned on his heels and strode rapidly towards the brightlit Lotus.

"All right!" the Juggler shouted after him. "You don't have to take it then! You go on without your goddamned mirror shield!"

It was true that Danton laughed. But some effect was visible (even he perceived it), a momentary roll in his walk, a slight perturbation on his purpose. All at once he no longer bore towards the Lotus Cafe, no longer in the power of laughter and light; all at once he veered off into the darkness of Bosporus Avenue, making his way among the empty marketplace stalls.

The monster he understood perfectly, as mercenaries often spoke in allegory, and often because of their taboos, by proxy. His reading was this: there were certain scores

which must be evened, certain slates which must be wiped
clean, before the matter of the assassin was completely
settled. Novak, and all that accrued to Novak's work, were
earth's main exports. To associate the assassin's destruction
with Novak was to underline the economic issues at hand.
Danton smiled. It was a story Wunder would feel far more
keenly than he.

But what was he to make of this hint that he alone could
deal with the assassin? What of this mirror shield? An
embellishment of the Juggler's?

For a moment he thought of returning, but the onus of so
political a mission weighed against him. The possibilities
were distressingly varied; a message, a mission, a bribe; and
both Boz and the Juggler were doubtless already lost in the
Carnival throng.

He found himself under a streetlamp, staring at another
copy of Treblinski's copiously reproduced poster. Why
should possibilities of such vast importance bother *him*, a
poet who, by the most generous estimates, had some five
years ago ceased producing interesting work? Success was
always well in arrears of achievement. That was one of its
most subtle tortures. He had grown quietly used to it. He did
not wish Danton the famous poet to become a figure
manipulated by the more advanced players in the game of the
assassin. He would thus, in so far as he could, play the game
in his own, unheroic style.

With poetry, with prose, with the Proets.

Which, except for the fact that he had written only two
sonnets in two years, was a swell idea.

Viktor Treblinski's twenty-five schematic faces stared at
him, coalescing into the querulous assassin. He knew Viktor
slightly and had hated his work before it had departed from
the written word. Now, like the mirror shield, it held a faint,
almost irksome, attraction.

Treblinski claimed that the poem as written word was
dead, but that the poet, as a fundamental paradigm of
civilization, could live on. Danton, silenced now by forces
that he could only read as the years, was hardly the one to
dispute him. But he more than anyone knew how tempting it
was to read into your own history that of civilisation. It was
in fact natural, something you allowed for.

Yet there was a much more compelling quality to Treblinski's work since the break. The poster had the abrupt, singlestage impact of a traffic sign, more like a snappy metaphor than a visual effect. Here the assassin was like a cheap holograph, the fuzz more distinct than the image itself. He was a figure of frenetic energy, crackling, uncanny, deranged.

It fit nicely. In the poster composite, the image of the assassin was made into the assassin, as in the story the equations that described him became him. It was a poem because the resemblance of the image to what it portrayed was only magical. It was a poem because it was a familiar poetic image, the image of a madman, his boundaries multiplied and uncertain.

Was the assassin, then, necessarily a madman? A poet? A poster? A history? An absence of it? An equation?

A killer?

Danton leaned slightly left.

II. Associations

IN THE PARK, a pleasant shelf was cleared off about halfway up the hill to Whore Hall. Proets had fanned their motorcycles out on one side and switched on deathshead headlights. For effect, most had used their red filters, so that the clearing looked a deep, dirty red, as if every grassblade were filled balloontight with red essence.

The cyclists themselves were sprawled haphazardly about the clearing behind Morgana, who addressed a small crowd in her slow, deep-voiced style. Openly indifferent, some of the Proets embraced, some slept. Shimmerings of their own, battery-powered light waltzed over them. They rolled and stretched.

Their chrome bared white highlights.

Danton sat at the rear of the group next to a frizzy-haired Proet named Avalon who, some time ago, had captured his left hand. On his right side, a dog the size of a small automobile nuzzled his knee. This was Morgana's (also famous) great dane, Questing Beast, or Anapest, with its easy nickname. He gently stroked its artillery-shell head with his free hand. It made a sound like an engine turning over.

"And that," said Morgana distantly, "is how I spent my summer with the assassin."

The name of the proem was "The Assassin as a Breakfast Cereal," and it was very good. Morgana and her assassin went kite flying, sightseeing, game hunting, bar hopping, shell collecting, ice and roller skating, ate endless silent breakfasts, saw dozens of old movies and, all in all, did many, many things.

It was the first in a series of twelve Proet "The Assassin as..." proems.

"—but happily for you," Morgana said, "mine is the only one ready tonight. That probably concludes our introductory section and those who just came to catch that may leave now." A few members of the audience slipped clear, vanishing instantly into the darkness. Morgana frowned. "What *are* you people doing here?"

There was something thrown and a flashlight beam darted over and picked out a tumbling apple core. It sailed high, and Anapest, with a fluid bound, snagged it in mid air.

The move came close to costing Danton his typing finger.

"Well that's very good and I hope you people have had fun so far because in our next skit—" Morgana rolled to a dry halt. She looked helplessly back to the Proets, pleading for rescue.

Gwalmlch bounded up. "You know I thought the leisure class died out ages ago," he said, and showed his "piano" smile. "In our skit the youngest Proet receives his name." Gwalmlch pivoted and held out his hand.

With a small yelp, Haleck shot to his feet. Giraldus and Layamon, flanking him, cheered grotesquely. Morgana offered him her arm.

He drew in a breath, bowed, and took it.

Gwalmlch held up a sheet of paper for the crowd. "Our tribe has the practice of never letting a brave name die. Each of us on joining takes on a worthy name which will be her or his nom de plume. This piece of paper I hold here has written on it the honored name we have chosen for our newest member. Should he decide to refuse it—" bowing his head— "as by our laws he has the right, the name will be set aside, unrevealed, and held in abeyance for our next male member. I can not divulge the name, but I *can* tell you that this

particular name has come up twice before without accep-
tance. Should it be refused a third time it will be the first
name so often scorned, and will probably be very unlucky for
its bearer."

Escorted with solemn slowness by Morgana, Haleck
arrived at Gwalmlch's side and stood waiting, arms folded.

Gwalmlch handed him the paper.

Several more members of the crowd slipped off.

"You know," said Avalon, "there's something very
strange about that crowd." She put Danton's hand in her
armpit.

The restless crowd was only twenty or thirty strong; its
numbers changed quickly and now only dwindled. It was a
lopped dark cloud before the foliage of the park. They
huddled close when they huddled and their features, but for
Proetlit, solitary highlights, were masked in their own
shadow. Some of them, over skin that might have glistened
with various wet, wooden hues in different light, wore
suggestive jungle green, folded with multiple pockets and
roomy at the legs and arms. Others wore dark jerseys and
black denim, or thin plastic outfits opaque and light-
shedding as wetsuits, and there was one skirt, a tutu,
suddenly subtracted as Haleck crumpled the paper and
looked decisively into the night.

Before he could speak a reedy-framed, hungry-looking
girl, maybe sixteen, two or three feet out of the main body of
people and all alone, moved forward. "Why don't you ride
the motorcycles?" Pointing to the row of them, into the red
glare. "That's what I came to see."

"You know, you're right," Haleck said. "Dull this is.
Would you like me to give you a ride?" He took a step
towards her and said, over his shoulder, "I accept the name."

There was a light pattering of applause. Very light.
During the course of it, the reedy-framed girl said "No," and
then rustled back to where she had been, and then still
further, into the bushes, leaves closing on her, shaking an
instant, dropping still.

Haleck stopped short.

"Galahad," said Gwalmlch, with detectable annoyance.
"The name is Galahad." He raised a muscular arm, a stray
Proet beam mantling his neck and shoulders, lustering his

teakwood skin. "I dub thee Galahad." And bringing the arm down, cuffed Haleck smartly on the back of the head.

Danton rose, disengaging his hand from Avalon, who looked surprised, and strode quickly to the front. He frowned and, hand over brow, did a seafarer's scan over the remains of the crowd.

"We are all happy to be in Monotony," he announced, and searched the foliage. "And happy that you—" a pause, searching for the right word—"met us here." His eyes narrowed into slits, following their dark on dark departures. "We have a great deal to learn about you here in Whister, about your hardships in this difficult time. We will be doing a play the dawn after next, which will include an assassin work by each of us, and—" rustlings, then the more penetrating, bordered silence—"we would like you all to—come. We would like you—to talk to us."

The crowd was gone.

Gwalmlch, watching the bushes adjust nervously, nibbled at a knuckle. "Creepy, aren't they?"

The murmuring of the seated Proets stopped; twenty after. All eyes turned downhill, towards the descending stillness of the park. There were movements—afterblurs, interference patterns, stirrings in the faint breeze—and there were other eyes pressed into the knit of leaves, reflecting their collective stare.

"I'm leaving," Haleck/Galahad announced suddenly, and a handful of Proets rose and started for their bikes.

"Going to the Hall?" Danton asked him.

Haleck nodded. They wheeled together and started uphill.

When they reached the eerie glare of the bikes someone called after them, "Lonus!" but Danton did not look back to see who.

They walked through an archway of branches, the lowest boughs separate, curved and smiling, fluttering their leafy branches. Beyond, a tarmac path thrust up uninviting but necessary through the blackknit. They moved up the grade shoulder to shoulder, their hands grazing. Something that hung just behind the darkness was bottomless and gaping. Danton strained to make the something out before it swallowed him.

It swallowed him. Leaves brushed moist digesting lips

against his face. Everything was in close up but there was not much use to it, with only a fine screen of black visible. Sounds happened inside his earshell. There was the destruction of a branch underfoot.

A woman screamed and screamed.

Haleck loosed a soft breath that might have been a curse.

"Four days," Danton muttered.

"What in hell are they fighting about?"

"I'm not sure they're fighting." Something, faintly rustling, followed them.

"Listen!" Silence closed in. "Whatever—" Haleck's voice dropped to a whisper—"you've got to wonder what's making them, who's making them."

"No." Danton said it with surprising force. There was a long whispering of leaves. "I don't think it works that way."

Shoeleather skidded up the tarmac. There was a collision and Haleck grunted. A moment later wild thrashing came from the bushes.

"Haleck?"

In answer a section of bush swung noisily back into place. He backed away from it; he felt breathless. His hand dove into his pocket and emerged with a blaster. Where his hand wrapped the butt something poked out glinting and he caught it before it dropped it to the path. It was the compass.

He squeezed it together.

Bushes hissed at him.

Something marbled the darkness and he would have fired except that, inexplicably, it was the compass hand he raised.

"Danton!"

"Haleck?" It came out a squeak. "What the hell happened?"

"He didn't want me. It was a mistake. He apologized."

"Jesus Christ." Danton's hand shook and he put the blaster away. The compass grew warm in his other fist.

"A real piece of luck, I guess."

"You want luck? Here's your luck. I tried to shoot you with that." He found Haleck's hand and pressed the compass into it. "I had the blaster out but I get confused sometimes, with left and right."

Haleck chuckled. "I don't believe you."

"Take it."

"Wha—?"

"Take it! To go with your name, a good luck charm." He felt oddly relieved. A great weight was lifted.

Haleck sighed and hung back a step on the path. A moment later Danton heard the soft tinkling.

He went back, squatted, and ran his hands over the tarmac. The compass was a little bent at the joint, probably by the pressure of his hands before. He returned it to his pocket.

They completed the walk to the top of the hill in silence.

The rambling floodlit facades of Whore Hall shone at them across the High Piazza. To the left of the Hall the trees were cleared for a good distance down the hill and Whister held up its flat roofs, spare bits of neon glinting here and there amid the black brick. The violence of it, or the powerful attraction that light, no matter how little, holds to those wandering in cities, drew him to Whister now.

"Go on in. I want to stay here a while."

Haleck's brows lifted, widening crystal blue eyes. "Are you all right? I don't want to raise your hopes or anything, but you've been acting pretty strangely."

"I didn't disappear into the bushes. Go on."

Haleck shrugged and struck out towards the wide, graffiti-covered steps of Whore Hall. Danton bore left, trudging to the auraed lampposts at the Piazza's edge.

Beyond the low blackness of Whister Danton might, if the moon were out, have seen the ocean, as smooth and black as the city, as impenetrable. He searched for it.

As he searched, through the entire landscape, for signs of the assassin. Thus far the only assassin apparent was the madman Savage. And though almost exactly twenty-four hours ago he had wondered if the assassin were a madman, Savage would no more fit the fact than Danton himself. Too little had happened, he thought wryly. His opinions changed with every whisper of the darkness. Paranoia belonged to the victims, not the killer; his very thoughts proved that.

Victims. Thus far all he had truly known were victims. For Danton the poet that should be knowledge enough; for Danton the victim it was already far too much. The two roles were at war inside him, yet they should be perfect complements. The poet as victim was ideally located, planted squarely in the path of the seeing, ambiguously perceived and perceiving, fearfully balanced. It was a pretty image but it left him as flat as his first go at sex (Santa Fe; a boxcar; a huge, spangled woman named Fay and a dapper man called Runt). On close inspection, curiously, it was the victim who was quite unmoved, the poet who begged and exhorted.

Yet there *were* traces of fear.

Fear sheened his vision of the giantess that first day when, her victimhood just declared, she betrayed a chilling delight. And why? When he watched there was fear. When he was seen there was nothing.

He looked back to Whister. Where the dirty facades pulled apart on a mistlit street, he could make out one-sash windows, pared by perspective, their white shades pulled, their dull faces terminating inverted skylines of hung cloth. And over a bit, black, ornately railed fire escapes crawled down the brick. And over further a black presence crawled up, unfolded, going watery gray, was smoke.

He followed it to where it smeared, indistinguishable from brick. Below that the street was lost in weirdly sculpted shadow. Light sheared abruptly through its center and the cloud shot up as a single mass, like gigantic shoulders hauling up a terrible weight. Brilliant yellow slashed through a dozen places. The cloud's base bloodied, then went black again.

Flame ate its way out very slowly. Once or twice the smoke thinned enough to show great masses of yellow mauling the building. Then, after long minutes, the smoke began to peel away and color, the gutted insides brightening until at last he could see the ocean, gently swelling and black, a mile beyond. In the end he saw the entire frame, glowing brilliantly, teetering in the winds of its own heat. It danced for perhaps a minute, then collapsed, thundering awfully, spreading a new, thicker blanket of smoke over Whister.

Scores of buildings were erased.

He waited patiently for it to clear, gaze fixed on the center, anticipating those few blazes that would be licking patiently at the framework when the dust cleared. And gradually, inexplicably, the fear came over him, the fear that had brought him here. And it was not just the wondering: who did this? It was something more.

Then he reached for it, the fear all alone, and the deep

appeal that had held him to it, and in that instant the eyes flashed back at him and he saw her again, the giantess full of the delicate surprise of victimhood, and he knew that the delight he had read in her eyes was his own.

The delight was his own, the fear was of the delight, and the fascination that bound them was—whose?—the victim's or the poet's? Here at last they were joined. Could he leave this thing without being utterly changed?

He was beginning to learn the power of what was facing him. It was far more enduring than he, as endlessly resourceful as the smirking lookalike in the mirror.

No, the assassin was not Danton, or even his friends, but what he must remember, the assassin was connected to them in infinitely complicated ways, and whatever move they made triggered, through some strange projective geometry, a modeling move in the assassin. And if they made no moves—

A very finely wrought silver amulet hung from his neck. He reached for it and twisted the center stud. "Hello."

"Gotcha." A sleepy voice.

"Alphy?"

"Alphy's dreaming old subroutines. Billie here."

"Get me a message to Wunder. I want to see her. I'll be down in the lobby."

"Hey, I hope you've got the clout you think you do, D. Lay you eight-to-five she makes you wait half an hour anyway."

Danton's lips tightened. "No bet." He twisted the stud back.

"How badly do you want him, Danton?"

He wheeled. It was not Wunder, but the big bearded madman whom several of the Proets had considered as a possible poetic subject, Savage. He wore a leather vest with nothing under it, the big tangle of black hair on his chest rising and falling with some recent effort. Sweat shone on his forehead and arms.

Involuntarily, Danton took a step back from him. "Want who?"

"The assassin?"

He had come—where?—from the darkness of the park?

"Savage—" he faltered—"I don't think it's possible to answer questions like that."

Savage took a step exactly as long as Danton's—closer. "And what if I were to offer myself to you?"

Danton felt a wave of pity.

"Well?"

"I would think," he said carefully, "that you were crazy."

Savage laughed and Danton raised a hand towards his shoulder and the big man jumped back.

"Don't touch me." He tried a smile through his beard. "As I told Wunder three days ago, I don't touch people any more."

Danton's hand dropped away. "Oh." He rubbed his own shoulder. "How long?"

"A year."

"Since before the assassin?"

"Well before. Don't look so surprised." This time Savage's grin looked real. "Did you think I'd go into this unprepared?"

Danton shook his head, intrigued. He considered the Piazza dirt. "Is it because it would hurt?"

"Because I wouldn't feel it, because not feeling it would hurt, maybe permanently. You see?"

"No."

There was a silence.

"All right." Savage broke it, his big hands clasping. "One more time. You're a victim. What do you want from this? Why aren't you hiding far away? How badly do you want the assassin?"

This time the question made sense. Danton even admired it. It was the only real question to ask. "What do I want? To go on as I have. There is nothing particularly blissful in my present state, Savage, though you may find that hard to believe. But anything else seems unimaginable. I am just a little bit trapped by being Danton. And Danton does not 'run and hide.' Hidden means unseen and Danton unseen means nobody."

Savage shook his head. "Nothing I could say could make you save yourself?"

Danton felt a chill. "Save myself from whom?"

Savage shrugged, studying him with his green, open gaze. "There is something mighty likeable about you, Danton. I don't think you care. You like to be seen? I am not sure you

51

really believe you *can* be seen." He shook his head. "And here it is again. I must spare you. The second time today."

Danton, his breath unconsciously held, sighed softly. A faint smile played at his lips. "That's very kind of you, Savage. Your situation must be—difficult."

Savage laughed. "Yours too. But perhaps I have a better view of yours than you do of mine. When I was in the clinic after the first duellist turned me over to what she called 'higher hands,' there was a woman who spent a great deal of time on my case. A great deal of time for the short time I was there. We had several twelve hour sessions and what she kept coming back to, again and again, what fascinated her the most about my 'condition,' was this lucid delirium of mine, as she called it, this ability to talk so sanely and at such great length about my madness, to pick it apart into individual decisions of eye and thought, and then recombine them and begin again, each time finishing with some completely new picture. She said that the madness was signalling something here, not in anything I said, but in the method I was using, that in this method was something of the way the madness worked to maintain my certainties of things which were not at all certain—by making certainty a constantly shifting mood. As I listened to this concept and tried to grasp it, the madness itself flickered for a moment. I saw through all my 'certainties' to the changing fears that held them in place. For a moment everything went transparent and I could place myself and a few critical tendencies in the world that had created them. *I saw what I was doing and why.* Do you know what that felt like? It felt like I was going mad."

Danton stared at him, on the brink of a dozen "Yes, I know"'s and the score of crashing banalities that followed; and finally was silent.

"Needless to say this, too, passed away and when I told her it, she became very excited and we tried something new. I would spend one whole day speaking in rhymed couplets. We would see, one: whether I could do it. It would be a game. And then two: how what I spoke about changed in that kind of structured format. And then three: what would happen inside me, with all those terrible pressures channeled. Could this be anything like a real poet's experience? Do I know you better than you know me? Perhaps. All I can say now, having forgotten most of it, is that it took a great deal of control and that it totally exhausted me. I slept through that night for the first time in a week. Beyond that I finally understood why I was talking more than I ever had before in my whole life, and why I was thinking so furiously. It's not that thought helps. It's just that, first of all, it's your only recourse, and second, while thought can't save you, there may be *one* thought that can. Something like my therapist's comment about the lucid delirium, that came so close."

Danton nodded at him slowly. "And this one thought—"

"—is the assassin. Yes. Let me go now. I've been talking too much."

"No." He had said it too suddenly, scaring even himself. In a moment's awkward silence, he tried to order his thoughts. He *liked* Savage. "Tell me," he said helplessly, "what it's like."

"Look, I don't want to go into—" his voice dropped—"the thing itself. The voices—no, the voice. Not that I care, you understand; it's just too difficult to express. With the voice you never know whether you're going to obey, or curse, or even whether you've understood correctly. It corrects itself so often. You don't know. Which is just it, the whole point. All right, you want to know what it's like? You want to know what *I'm* after? Come on, then. Sit down a minute."

Savage led him away from the dizzying and tempting heights of the city to the center of the Piazza. They sat side by side on the plinth of the statue of a very fat man, Weeb, a euhemerized hero of Reconstruction days, bounder and cheat, founder of Rome and Annapolis, inventor of poker, first fermenter of beer, and so on. Savage reached out and, grasping Danton's shoulders, turned him so that they were eye to eye.

"There. Good. I can't afford to have you become bored with this, you understand? I can't afford to be just another voice. That voice. If it tells you to jump in front of a train— and it did once; I haven't any idle examples—you have *no* idea whether you're going to do it or not, whether it means it, or you mean it, or it can just happen. You hang onto a post for dear life, feeling how very *possible* it is. And you can't outthink it. Try sometime, if you ever have a voice, to outthink it. You can think any way you damn well want to, anyway the voice wants you to. It is gray, mumbling, and barely comprehensible. Listening to it, working at it with your full consciousness, suddenly you are thinking *feelably*—the way you move your arm—and there you are beside your thoughts, thinking them, an echo, and that is the voice again. Knowing it comes from inside is no help; that's the *problem*. Is it because you know how close and real death is that you won't edge near the train the next time it runs? But no, it will tell you; that only proves how *easy* it is. Then you may climb out of the train station into the light, out of its great Cathedral gloom, an educated, knowledgeable man who knows exactly *whom* he's fleeing. You can lock yourself in a room with him. No—" Savage reached out and gripped Danton's wrist—"knowing has nothing to do with it. After a while you understand why the voices have to come from *outside*. If they didn't you'd be dead. So you try to save yourself." Savage looked up quietly at the bronze figure of the fat man. "Ordinarily you wouldn't go to such great lengths. Ordinarily, faced with such an incredible menace, you would simply turn over and die and call it a sleep that you badly needed. Nothing could be worth all this trouble. Nothing could be worth this *relentlessness*. But here death is as frightening as life. Only an assassination can save you."

"An assassination." It was not even a question.

"What else?" Savage looked up and the Piazza light struck at his sweaty face. It was suddenly as many different subtle colors as the bronze. "Perhaps not saved, perhaps nothing. But what does it matter? Whatever I think I feel. Who else but the assassin would have all this inside him? Who else would be so definite, so terrible, as me?" His hand, bent, followed the bent line of his head and trunk. "Once I think something, it's out there forever." His hand, bent, flattened on invisible glass and pushed out at the Piazza.

"But why?" Danton asked softly. "Why an assassination?"

Savage looked into his eyes and slowly grinned. "That *is* the question, isn't it?"

Savage stared awfully and for a few seconds their gazes dueled; then Danton, with a little grunt, dropped his to the dirt. Above all he felt embarassment.

"I have a feeling," Savage said slowly, "that the assassin will attack tonight."

Danton stiffened, forcing himself to look again. "You mean, *you* will attack tonight?"

Savage shrugged.

"Tell me," Danton insisted. "If you're going to talk about attack, why not go the whole route? Is it you?" He was aware, suddenly, of his slow burning anger. But he could set that aside. He could *do* something here, perhaps help this man as no one had ever helped Danton.

Savage was stubbornly silent.

"Is it you, Savage?"

"There is a little assassin in all of us, Danton."

Danton smiled.

"There are times," Savage went on, "when I want no one near me."

Danton reached into his pocket and withdrew the blaster. "And the victim." He held it out. "Is he me?"

Savage took the blaster. A little tooth showed pressing his lower lip.

"Go ahead now," Danton whispered. "This is your chance."

Expressionless, Savage aimed at Danton and pulled the trigger.

"You have to take the safety off first."

Savage's face broke. He rose, turned, and stopped. He turned back and held out the blaster. His teeth glinted through the beard. He squinted.

Danton looked away. "Keep it. I don't need it anymore."

There was an indrawn breath, then Savage's receding footsteps on the Piazza dirt.

Danton watched him disappear into the park. Wunder would be ready about now. He rose slowly and started towards Whore Hall. At the stairs his eyes caught the giant red letters of a message spray-painted across the entire concrete length of the entranceway, crawling with scores of other slogans. He stepped back to read it. It said:

If the assassin kills all those except those who kill themselves, then who kills the assassin?

Then there was a familiar hissing and he wheeled and the flash still illuminated an intricate tangle of trees. It faded. A small fire crackled somewhere out of sight. A sound tried to fight clear of his throat and died there, a strangled breath. He scanned the long outline of trees for a sign, for a single particle of light.

The crackling dwindled.

The park was a rough wall of darkness.

For a long while there was no thought.

Then Danton, hands pocketed, undisguised and alone, wandered through the gloomy, bluelit lobby and among the wobbling bodies of Whore Hall. Buttocks and scapulae syncopated, or, with snaps of cloth and plastic, navels peered; belly creases went taut. The usual woman in white fur turned all the way around and, gaping, sat abruptly on the floor.

Danton followed her eyes up to the tightrope walker suspended far above, amid the sweeping curves of the dark ceiling. She stumbled, recovered with three prancing steps, her glittery legs washing, suddenly, into bright steel. À la Danton. She sped up, moving her balance pole in small, powerful circles, like a cautious fencer probing with her foil. Then, abruptly, she did her split and held. The tungsten spot whipped up to center the three lines of her body.

There were cries. "I love you!" "You send me!"

The woman in white fur, a more or less permanent fixture, perhaps simple minded, perhaps simply a rabid fan, slowly applauded.

Trays circulated through the crowd and Danton reached out and snatched off a drink. It proved to be fruit juice. Someone recognized him and wanted a kiss. He turned silently away and was intercepted by a plastic-wrapped Haleck, smiling through dark glasses.

Haleck steered him towards a wall.

"You've changed," Danton noted.

Haleck shrugged back his cellophane wings. "Well put, Danton."

"You in the school play?"

Haleck drew himself up. "I am in the salt mines, Jack, and don't you forget it—working harder for the cause of poetry than ever a Proet did."

Danton gestured eloquently at Haleck's ensemble. "How?"

The kid Proet sighed. "This is the hardest I've ever worked in my regrettably long life. I've gotta sit down." He attained the wall and leaned back against it, shoving at the waist of his clinging plastic shorts, trying to get to the G-string underneath. He peered at Danton. "Built along the lines of those Japanese finger traps." He tugged demonstratively, his hand stuck fast.

"Danton!" A man in red velvet clutched at his arm; a dagger nudged out from under a velvet sleeve. "Could I have some?"

Haleck reached and knocked his hand away. "Have some class. This is a house of prostitution, not a pick up bar." He signalled over the man's head.

They moved to a corner table. A lamp set at eye level gave off nervous blue, simulated gaslight. Haleck finally worked his hand all the way down his shorts, groped a moment, and sighed obscenely. "Torsion of the scrotal sack." His hand struggled free, "You were asking how. I've been taken off the assassin case due to general futility. As for that, Hallelujah. If I read one more monograph on the assassin as a theme in European dishware, I will blind myself, or perhaps even do something silly. But Guillemet wanted me around in case there was extra legwork, and when Wunder asked if I'd mind doing some more conventional chores in the meantime—on salary yet—I agreed, unfortunately. On Morgana's allowance I get to missing certain luxuries—like soda pop and toilet paper. Then, too, what a great sentence for the back cover bio, I thought."

Danton, whose mind had again drifted back to Savage, grinned.

Someone loomed over the table, a blonde woman with very large eyes, fixed on Danton. She wore a black sweatsuit.

Danton smiled mechanically, reaching back for some prefabricated speech of dismissal.

Then, from behind her, the yellow number forty-seven moved into view.

The Juggler bowed. "Terribly sorry, etcetera, Danton, but I have something to deliver." He threw a small blaster on the table.

Danton drew in a slow breath.

The Juggler grinned. "I smell a story here, no? It was a big, bearded man, maybe thirty-five, wearing a leather—"

"—don't know him," Danton said, grinning suddenly.

"He said, and I quote, 'Thanks, but no thanks.' Now who would say that, Danton?" The Juggler straightened and grabbed his numerals, mimicking. "'I know you. You're on TV with the news. Could you give something to Danton for me?' Certainly. 'And tell him, "Thanks, but no thanks."' Got that?' Got it, but—and off he goes, scampering into the darkness. Now what's the story, Danton? This fellow your long lost brother?"

Danton laughed.

"You *knew* he was white, then."

Danton shook his head, held out the blaster. "You take this."

"That's a pretty expensive gun there. If it belongs to you, you should keep it."

"I can afford it," Danton said, conceding the point, sensing that that was the one way to slow down the Juggler. "Why don't you introduce us to your friend?"

The blonde woman waved half humorously, reminding them where she was.

Forty-Seven smiled at her. "This is Ann Treblinski. Ann, Danton." (Danton smiled.) "Haleck, an obscure Proet." (Haleck waved obscurely.) "But I'm not giving up, Danton. Sooner or later you have to give me a scoop. It's fated. Where, for example, does the name Lonus come from?"

Danton ignored him, rising to take the woman's hand. "Treblinski. Any relation?"

The woman nodded. "I'm his sister."

"His sister!" Danton raised a brow. "Well, you don't look a thing like him, which is my most backhanded compliment of the evening. Is Viktor in town too?"

"Yes, he is." Her smile vanished. "We are all here for the same reason, I'm afraid."

"Not Boz," the Juggler cut in. "He's here to get laid, which is a little like going to the race track to see the races."

"How is the Commander?" Danton asked.

"Very chipper." The Juggler's pleasant tone echoed Danton's. "Room 2-S if you want to visit a bit. Bring your riding boots."

"And has he decided yet?"

The Juggler grinned. "No, I don't think he's decided."

Danton turned to Ann. "Well, you and Viktor must drop by and see me." It was the beginning of a dismissal.

"Why, yes." She seemed surprised, either by the dismissal or the invitation. "Viktor will be very pleased. Where are you staying?"

"Becht House," Danton said with a sinking feeling, realizing that Viktor, being Viktor, probably *would* drop by. And probably alone.

"Give my regards to Norman with the model airplanes," Haleck said. "And tell him I'm still not an adept."

Ann smiled. "Yes, Norman mentioned you."

There was a small silence. "Fine," said Ann blankly. "But we really must be going now." She groped for the Juggler's hand and caught it. "Come, Jug. You were going to show me a cave." She backed away, prepared, if necessary, to drag him off by brute force.

He tripped after her for two steps, then stopped. "See you around, Danton. And thanks for the gun." On the last word, he managed to tear his hand free. "Coming, dear. But you mustn't be so eager." He reached for her waist and she wriggled away.

Danton turned slowly back to Haleck. "Now where were we?"

"I was commenting on what strange friends you have." Haleck stacked a saucer and a cup before Danton, and added coffee.

"And I was trying to change the subject."

The kid Proet shrugged. "Did you know," he asked, "that the bite of the black widow sometimes causes priapism?"

"Is that right?"

Haleck gave two quick nods. "Sure is. I had a client come in, got bit and was just out of the hospital." He snatched a dish of finger pastries off a passing tray. "Gave me the crabs too. Must have had a thing for arachnids."

Danton plucked a cherry tartine off the same tray. "Crabs are counted as arachnids?" His teeth sank into custard filling.

"I don't know but isn't it odd, here in the Novakian Age, with ultrafast starships, bloodless surgery, talking computers, psychometrics, and truth at last, we haven't got a cure for the crabs."

Danton picked another pastry carefully off the bottom, something studded with lavender nonpareils. "Special shampoo, a bath, and long nails. Who says Novak can't save us?" He attacked the nougat paste filling. "You just earned yourself a twenty-four hour vacation. Go tell the boss."

"No such luck. I still have the bloom in my cheek, don't I? I'm on host duty. Greetings, Sir. Good evening Madame. Would you care for a hair cut? Smile. Axillary, ancillary, or scalp? May I suggest our deluxe white virgin shave? Cut smile, swing arm out and crowd them. Will you have your feet scratched?" He caught a fugitive crumb on his chin. "Now you take that woman in white fur, for example—"

"Now what is the ethical canon on divulging information about specific clients?" Wunder, in ermine, stood before them.

Haleck sat up. "Right. I clean forgot. You know, maybe I'm not cut out for this business."

Wunder smiled. "You're cut out for it. It's been a long time since any new boy got the kind of glowing reports you've gotten."

Haleck actually blushed; and Danton, moving swiftly, slid a chair from the next table behind Wunder.

"Have a seat and tell us about yourself; and hold that smile. It's dazzling."

Wunder held that smile and sat, clutching her ermine to her with her scarred hand. "It's good to see you again, Danton. The way you put off your social calls, a person could get to feeling very neglected."

"To tell you the truth, Wunder, it's the people here at the Hall."

"The people." She snorted. "Danton doesn't like crowds?" She shook her head, exhaling a white block of smoke. "Forget it. Thanks for coming. I see from across the room that you know the Juggler."

"We've met."

"Yes, he's a man with very interesting friends. Do you know who they arrived with?"

Danton frowned. "Commander Potocki of the Free Alliance Mercenaries?"

"Very good." Wunder nodded towards the stairs. "Second floor. Room S. Boz likes the big girls. Now then." She leaned forward, adjusting her seat. "Do you know what Commander Potocki's mission is here?"

"He's to decide whether to bring in troops."

Wunder shook her head. "Danton, you surprise me. So now you're scooping the twelve o'clock news."

"Oh, there were rumors."

Wunder grinned. "There sure were. I spread them as fast as I could. Boz is up to his ears in invitations from very important people whom he can't refuse. For the next week he'll be very safe and very busy. Good?"

Danton smiled. "Good. I—uh—"

"—wanted to see me. I know. My guess is you had some idea you wanted to try out. The answer is probably no. I'm *still* glad to see you." She sat back, waving her cigarette. "Now what's the idea?"

"Well it's very simple, really." He folded his hands and stared at them. "Maybe too simple. But I thought I'd come to you with it; you might find some way to make it work."

Wunder's fingers drummed the table. "Danton."

"All right." His hands clapped. "I announce that I've got proof positive that the assassin is a hoax. The assassin makes a try for me and we snuff him."

Wunder laughed out loud.

Danton stared at her.

Her laughter slowed and the scarred hand covered his on the table. "I'm sorry. Never again." She restrained herself to a fond smile. "It's just that, usually, you are a man of such amazing convolution. And now you're being so naked. Tell me, since when is the great Danton tired of living?"

"It is a good idea," he said evenly. "At least, since no one else seems to have any others." He leaned towards her. "Don't you *want* the assassin stopped, Wunder? Tell me, why are you doing everything possible to make it easy for him?"

"*You're* the one who just suggested handing him his victim on a silver platter." His accusing gaze brought her up short. "Sticks and stones, Danton. And dirty looks especially."

"Wunder, are you out to kill me?"

"Why no," she said mildly. "Do I seem unusually crabby today?"

"Not at all. You are your usual untouchable self. But the

photos do have one ambiguity, that nobody mentions but everyone does something about. 'Choose one,' we're told. Choose one what? One of each? Could it be that the one from Column A is an assassin? Could it be that *both* the assassin and the victim are there and that some third party has given as an odds-on chance of finding one of them?"

"Don't pull that on *me*, Danton old boy. Besides its being fairly unlikely, hints point the other way. The assassin is he and the victim she, and *you're* the one who was a mercenary."

There was a short silence.

The smoke from Wunder's cigarette cleared.

"First of all," Wunder said, "you won't announce anything. I'll spread the rumor to all the proper places. Second, what we will say is that you are *taping* an announcement, complete with all the necessary mathematical evidence, tomorrow. Late tomorrow. Say, after midnight. You and the Proets will be there. You will be shooting at—" she frowned—"the Planetarium, which is an easy place to defend, though it doesn't look it. We'll use klieg lights and infra-red."

Danton stood and nodded to her. "Thank you, Wunder."

"And Danton."

His head came up.

"You realize that now, more than ever, people will think that you or I had something to do with the assassin. Even denying him." A scarred thumb rubbed the inside of her cup. "Do you see we fill very much the same positions in different worlds; moreover the worlds themselves are strangely similar. Poetry has its economics, money has its poetry. Both turn unreal values into tangibles we can use for exchange."

Danton bowed. "There are times, Wunder, when you utterly outclass me."

"You're going?"

"Yes."

"Why not stay here and reap all the benefits of a security system worth millions? While singing and dancing your way to dawn?"

"Thanks, Wunder, but no thanks." He wondered why, for the life of him, he, brittle Danton, couldn't be polite to her, and instantly remembered something else, something that had been bothering him. "One last thing. Wunder, have you talked to Savage today?"

"Yes." She smiled sadly. "He spared me." She searched his face. "You too?"

Danton nodded.

"Attention, please. Attention." A smooth baritone spoke from the wall. "I have some important announcements. First, three more members of the twenty-five have been identified. They are Anson Slattery of Newport News, a machinist first class, Donna Roneau of Brussels, a house painter, and Nick Puck, a very modestly successful Australian comedian. Attempts are being made now to contact them, but they are all, as far as we can tell, incommunicado."

"Thank you, Alphy."

"Tut tut, there's more. I straighten my tie and read on. I have reconsidered the situation and constructed a number of public effect and public response parameters. Using simple psychometric pressure readings as well as some of the relevant Pierpont political field extrapolations, I have completed what should be some extremely precise calculations regarding the assassin. Assuming the assassin is predictable (which is the only assumption under which he exists), and observing that his popularity, with these three new announced members of the twenty-five, now approaches a saddle point, taking into account the larger political stresses, and remembering that this event must be fixed so as to bring those stresses to the point of a first order catastrophe—then we can with a fair amount of certainty predict that the assassin will strike tonight."

"Tonight." Wunder sat back in her chair, her eyes lidded. "Then, Haleck, you have your instructions."

Haleck rose and hurried away.

"Tonight." Her eyes locked with Danton's, reminding him. "Yes, I've heard that rumor. Perhaps we should find Savage."

In the cafe, noise catapulted off the aqua green walls and seemed to collect somewhere over their heads, in the windy reaches bounded by vents and their flyspecked shafts. Streaming buttresslike from ceiling to wall, the shafts were the same aquarium hue gone duller on their metal, tincture of aquamarine.

Reaching towards them, smoke ribboned long taffeta

spirals, snarling at the room's effective center, where the
shadow fell away, where the lines of their stolen glances
converged. It was a center curiously located in the toe of the
room's 'L'. It was a center made by a man who was all silver.

Elbow propped on his tiny table, all alone, he seemed
absorbed in the play of the jukebox light, in the curved plastic
of its bulk. His bare back, the smooth-ribbed vault they all
stared at, towards which their sleek smoke strained, showed
twin, glazed dishes of scapular muscle wiped with their
distorted reflections. Like some glossy advertisement. The
jukebox song, as distorted as their reflections, faded and
plastic parts rotated, ending the play of lights. He shifted.
Tables, figures, their plastic chairs, stretched and split on his
back. On the dome of one biceps, Guillemet's hooded face
yawned open.

She watched her own shadowy features melt down his
platinum and, hiking her domino cloak, stretched and
crossed her long legs under the table. The Living Mirror
(what everyone called him), or just Mirror, was distracting in
exactly the way the Mirror was distracted now by the
jukebox, simply by virtue of his shine. He was quiet almost to
the point of simpleness and people said something bad had
happened to him in the war, perhaps because he looked so
much the part of a young mercenary with his discus thrower's
body, every muscle laid out like an anatomical transparency,
hard as hard rubber: a perfect mantle on his shoulders,
flowing stalks about his forearms, nearly elliptical thighs. No
one Guillemet knew, in the two years that the Mirror had
been in Monotony, had ever asked him what he had done to
his skin, but someone somewhere doubtless had. And no one
needed to ask why he never wore clothes.

She wondered idly if the Mirror were the assassin. She
had taken this table at the foot of the L because it was
perfectly positioned. Mirror's, next to hers, was just as good;
it was the table the assassin would quite naturally take. Not
quite like that, though. Mirror's back was to the door.

No matter. She might find out soon.

Not that she wanted to. True and right: keep your mind
loose. Have a casual thought or two. Thanks, but no thanks.
She wished she were back at the Hall, helping them question
Savage. Keep your thoughts here, though, casual or not.

Think, for instance, about Sam the moustached waiter, maneuvering through the stacked crowd now, his tray teetering overhead. Sam the very nice guy was having an off night. Twice he had sent full trays hurtling to the floor, their angry explosions opening short, second-long holes in the din of the Lotus.

She curled back towards the table and sipped at a Novak Transformation (vodka and white wine over ice). She knew perfectly well why Sam was having an off night.

Wunder had, over the years, built a marvelous and mysterious information gathering machine, more precisely, a rumor gathering machine. And such a device could very easily be adapted into a rumor dispersing machine. Rumor: the assassin will strike tonight. Possibly in the Lotus.

Hear that boy? You will strike tonight. Then (oh, what shall we do?), we shall shoot you to a bloody pulp, I hope. Have you heard that rumor?

Sam had heard that rumor. Others believed it and lived by it. Guillemet, for one.

How had this happened to her? The assassin advanced by a series of quasi-logical steps. He was here now, quasi-real and lethal. Alphy had picked a moment. It was necessary, Alphy said, to pick a moment; and the very fact of the choosing was included in its calculation. In the end there was little to go on but the supposition that the assassin would go where attention was focused. And now the only victim at the convergence of all these wandering attentions was Guillemet. Would the assassin strike as per instructions? If, as some seemed to think, he was a mathematical entity, an alternate syntax, an indeterminate component in a suddenly altered system, then he would. Do you understand, Guillemet? No, Guillemet did not understand, but understanding was not called for. Perhaps, Wunder had said, it's very lucky that you took on this victim job after all. You're good at these things. What things? Being shot at. She did not understand, but she believed. She was a security chief. It was a life style. If someone claimed there was a monster sleeping in the cloak room, you went after your coat on tiptoe. Better yet, you called it a balmy night and went home bare-shouldered. If someone said the assassin was coming because they'd finished inventing him, very well, he was coming. You, the invented victim, sat there chewing nails and hands and thinking of the endless black.

The spot was aimed and would he now step into it please?

How many here knew? Most of them. At four-thirty in the morning, the Lotus was packed. The word assassin had been exhaled in dozens of intimate exchanges. Each new arrival was given a thorough inspection at the door, each was loved and feared, each was discarded. Dozens of flushed, late-night faces knew.

Her old acquaintance, the Juggler, reporter and frequent patron of Whore Hall, knew, his face flushed as any. He sat in a far corner reading his fortune with a deck of Tarot cards. Did the cards say that he was about to lose an old acquaintance? Or did they claim that same acquaintance was about to slip out of a crowded cafe and quietly head for Tanganyika? Did their prophesies, in a storm of superstition, self-fulfill? No, they did not. Guillemet still sat at her table; she could see that for herself. While Forty-Seven, the Juggler, was inhumanly calm. (Was he polishing his tale of a monster in a cave?) Another card slapped the table. He frowned over it. And Guillemet was inhumanly calm.

Everybody was inhumanly calm. Including Manolo and Billie, who had the added virtues of being inhumanly fast and inhumanly accurate. Manolo had the door, deadman's spot, where someone was sure to pass and someone sure to fire, because Manolo was not quite as bright as Billie, who had instantly headed for the far side of the big show window fronting the cafe. They had taken in their instructions with the usual impassiveness of Wunder's hired elite. Manolo, not as bright but with far finer eyes, and a graceful, bullfighter's ass, had asked what this assassin looked like. Guillemet, sighing, had first considered asking him to go home, and then, looking into those fine eyes and remembering life's shortness, asking him to come away with her to Tanganyika. She did neither, forsaking him by the door, far away from Tanganyika's glorious sunsets. Manolo, Manolo, there at the deadly door, there, exiting in flames. When asked to volunteer for this critical mission had he hesitated just a fraction of a second before accepting? Would he later, with his pistol raised, when it counted? Count.

The three of them made a right triangle, one at each

extremity of the L. Mathematically set. And Guillemet would sit in the toe, pouting, and would be a deadly shot. Actually, Manolo would not have been ideal anyway; someone like Danton was far more her type. Manolo did not have brown, uneven teeth. Or as perfectly tapering a back, or pinwheel bronze eyes. But Danton was not about to have his head blown off (*or* come away to Tanganyika, for that matter) and that, in these troubled times, counted too. Count.

There would be three of them. Billie who, with her hands at her sides could steal a coin from your palm before you closed it. Steal it and make change. Manolo, who could hit a drinking glass a block away while falling. And Guillemet, who was full of casual thoughts and methedrene, and could drain that glass in a gulp. They were all three armed with hand stressers, very hard to get and the best hand weapon there was, a pistol with no firing kick that opened a momentum field on a beam a couple of angstroms across, and they all three knew how to use them. Probably the assassin knew how to use his, too. But there were three of them. So it didn't matter *how* good he was. One man couldn't possibly take them. Could he? Who *was* this assassin?

And now her eyes swept back across them, looking for the one face that might, somewhere in its cool set, in its brazen calm, betray something different. And so did the eyes of most of those in the room. Gazes crossed, snagged, dropped instantly—orbiting gazes, like sweeping searchlights at a world premiere. Everyone searched.

Except for the Mirror, who was tranced out on the jukebox. And Forty-Seven, who had read ahead with his cards.

Something different. But that was just it. The assassin would not be different. He would be as inconspicuous as possible, most likely a native who could move easily through a world difficult for strangers to understand, someone natural and unobtrusive. Not Mirror, for instance. Unless—

She gave up.

Then Danton pushed through the staring glass door, wiping it clean of fluorescent light spokes, slitting its baleful eye. He walked across the cafe directly towards Guillemet.

She frowned.

He arrived, pulled over a chair, and sat.

Guillemet leaned forward. "Danton, now I want you to go to the bar and get yourself a drink, a strong drink, and when you come back, if you must come back, I want you to put your chair, not directly across from me, blocking the door, but right next to me. Got that?"

Danton's eyes widened, but she could not see that under the silver eyemask he wore, fetchingly coordinated with a skeleton-print body stocking. He rose and moved off stiffly. He leaned onto the bar through the 'Y' made by two bowed backs. Sam appeared, brows raised.

"A drink," he said. "A strong drink."

Sam puckered moustached lips. "You have to tell what kind, friend."

"Federation beer." Danton let his casual gaze slide down the counter, then, realizing the contradiction, signalled Sam again. "Make that a bourbon on the rocks."

Sam nodded quietly, lowering the mug, releasing the spigot, and scooping ice into a glass all in a single motion, as if he'd had that order changed countless times tonight.

Tonight? Yes, tonight. There was relief in sight if only he would come and go. Danton's drink thumped before him. He slid back a bill. He turned slowly, the glass ice cold on his palm, and gazed across the room into myriad eyes, the crowd like some great, heavy-breathing, *curious* creature— studying itself. He sipped. Crystalline smoke lingered on his tongue. Why was he here?

Back at the table he remembered to adjust his seat according to instructions, then sat staring a moment at the giantess, her hoodflaps touching just then, folded like patient hands. He knew why he was here, as part of the curious crowd. "Will he know you in that?"

Guillemet gave a low chuckle. "How many giants are there in here now?"

He shrugged and busied himself with looking at the Living Mirror.

"Danton," she said softly. "I don't want you here."

Her ringed hand rested next to his on the table, five blue stones gazing up at him, each of their rings nicely intaglioed in gold, touching, circuit closed, keeping her fingers slightly apart. He, too, wore rings now, but she had not noticed and his disappointment was small but important.

"Danton, go away." She sighed.

"Why? Because if I stay you won't be sure whom he's come for?"

Her hood turned away, presenting him with black, drooping folds. "I hate that costume, Danton."

"I hate yours too."

Someone in a clown suit—the assassin, perhaps—pushed by and planted himself before the strategy machine next to the jukebox. Danton watched him bent over the redlit plastic landscape and felt curiously elated. Over the past few days he'd had several chances to approach the giantess when she'd left the Hall and come down among the Proets, but each occasion had been crowded and hurried, and Guillemet's manner had been almost entirely businesslike. Now there was no more business left to transact, he was safely established here by her side, and she could easily have been firmer about wanting him to leave. And the subject was death. It was the most intimate conversation they'd had.

Bursts of white indicated heavy losses near the home hill. The redlit landscape buzzed happily.

Danton withdrew a small notebook from his belt and a pen from under his sleeve. Pen poised, he stared at the blank first page. There was a long silence. Guillemet shifted restlessly. Danton remembered he was mortal.

He looked up at her. "What are you thinking about?"

She shrugged. "Tanganyika, if you must know."

He wrote down Tanganyika. That was all. There was another silence.

"Good luck," Danton said finally. And he meant it. The compass, also withdrawn from his belt, rested in the palm of his extended hand. That had happened almost too fast to follow. "Take it," he urged. "This compass is a good luck charm."

She picked it out of his palm, swung it a moment between two fingers, and dropped it. She leaned forward, surrounding her tall empty glass with her rings. In her right hand, a tiny gray snout glinted silver next to the gold. Danton's belly contracted. Perhaps Guillemet was the assassin. Perhaps Danton was. With sudden, irrational fervor, he wanted every possibility considered. "Take the compass."

"I've already got a good luck charm. See?"

He rose and went to get them new drinks.

"It's not even a compass," she said when he returned. "Look at it. It's part of a cheap, surveyor's theodolite."

"Take it."

Guillemet shook her head stubbornly. Doom settled over them.

Abruptly her stones flashed; her long graceful fingers caught at the hoodflap and dropped black fabric back in rings. A fall of pale gold filled them. Danton, under his glinting mask, smiled at her.

Then someone roared.

Danton hunched. His gaze scrabbled at the bar.

Another roar answered. Two men pushed away from their drinks, one in spotless denims, the other in costume, a winged helmet, an eyemask, a shield, plastic armor. Danton thought he heard those three syllables hissed and then, by contagion, the din melted away. A last phrase hung on the silence, just clear of White Denim's lips: "—one of the Twenty-Five." Danton stared, trying to pin down Wing Helmet's features under the narrow eyemask. They were definitely familiar, but it was too difficult to match them with one of twenty-five photos, most of strangers, tiny squares on newsprint. He looked questioningly at Guillemet. She shook her head.

Suddenly conscious of the silence, the two pushed guardedly back to the bar and the din, hesitantly at first, restarted.

Danton searched for a way to watch Guillemet's eyes and finally settled on the Mirror's burnished shoulder. The Mirror lit a cigarette with steely slowness, giving Danton a sidelong glance as he puffed. His arm lifted, the shoulder spilling Guillemet's reflection, and he held out the match to Danton.

Danton blew it out.

Mirror nodded courteously.

Then a stool hurtled to the floor cutting off Danton's answer. Winged Helmet led White Denim between crowded tables, past craning maskers out the door. En route they upset several drinks and the lay of the Juggler's cards.

He went to his hands and knees to gather them.

Memory is mysterious. Anything can narrow the

possibilities down to one. Seeing the Juggler then triggered the right series of associations for Danton. It might have been the winged helmet. It might have been the way the blue match flame and Guillemet's eyes were exactly the same color. It was not. It was the Juggler on his hands and knees, or all these things with that the very last. He knew who Wing Helmet was.

Thunder. There was an intolerably bright flash and the glass shattered, not over Manolo or Billie but only, miraculously, in the middle. Crystal spat overhead: a big shard split off, shone white, smashed into a table splintering tall, fruit-colored glasses. The drinkers reeled back, arms upflung, faces alight with fruity glow. More of the window punched in and a smoking body swiped face down at their table, riding it as far as the glass, where jagged pane remnants drove bloodlessly in and anchored. The winged helmet clattered. The body dangled an instant and the glass shattered again and dropped it finally to the frame, draped halfway in, arms folded underneath, head twisted queerly so that the chin lifted just up to a shiny shoulder.

Somebody dumped a tiny oh god into the yawning silence.

Face drained, Sam shuffled wordlessly forward, moving zombie-like with dustpan and brush absurdly in hand. A face collected from the darkness above the corpse.

Obsidian eyes shone, wise and alien.

Stellar-white smoke seemed to halt its endless ceilingward spiral; after a stupendous pause it twisted back, slowly collapsing, gliding the new current. Within the silence there was breathing, then two whispers at once, a glass striking a table, a sigh, and noise.

But no assassin.

Only—

"One dead poet." Danton nodded towards the corpse. "Take your last look at Treblinski."

He did not feel fit for mourning, though he tried, by envisioning it, to make the mourning fit him. He tried to see Ann Treblinski, her eyes brimming, her sob caught in her throat. Instead he saw her coldly silent, her jaw clenched with hurt pride. He tried to see the glass biting through Treblinski's middle. Instead he saw Sam shuffling forward with dustpan and brush. He tried to remember Treblinski's noblest visions. Instead the banality of the question-marked poster came to mind.

Yet he must mourn. Did a man deserve death because his work was no longer vital? That would hardly be a healthy view. Not for Treblinski and not for Danton.

He would mourn by working. That would suit both of them. It was not quite time but today he must start the assassin poem.

He went to breakfast in the new costume Wunder had sent him. It was the most concealing thing he had worn yet, a weird network of colored tubes jointed by polished glass shards. The tubes mapped his chest and his face, turning his features savage and old. For contrast he wore glistening pantaloons, moulting rose and scarlet as he walked, continually reforming to his impressive thighs. He controlled his coloring with three knobs and a switch at his belt. Though the actual subtleties escaped him, somehow differently colored lights were sent up through the tubes, changing the general tinge of his aura. He had mastered only one thing, the switch. Turned off he looked like something in the process of melting. He stayed on, managed, after some fiddling, to tune his aura orange. Which was not too bad.

But the color coding went further still. He wore four jewels on each hand, each mounted in silver ovals onto a knuckle. The setting flowed back into a glove plate that raised silver tendons like those it covered, the whole anchored to a silver band round his wrist. These were fabulously expensive mood jewels, which he supposed he'd have to give back. Just now they were milky clear, as was his breakfast mood, but, a parasitical life form that fed (sparingly) on neural amines, they would remain in electrochemical hook-up with him as long as he wore them, changing colors with his humor.

As a last forbidding touch he had acquired a jungle green Australian bush hat for an equally forbidding price at one of Monotony's tourist shops. It lay next to his breakfast taking up half the small table, looking collapsed and overripe.

He sat, perversely, in the draft whispering past the

cardboard taped over the Lotus's show window. Carnival was at last in full swing and there were maskers scattered throughout the cafe, even in mid-afternoon, a story land assortment of glittery scaled griffins, painted savages (Savage himself was one) shiny-booted pirates, white-winged seraphs, and a whole contingent in bodytight suits who were nothing at all, non-representations suitable for a ball masque, various floppy velvet hats, angled entaffetaed torsoes, wing silhouette masks, clown masks, lorgnettes, domino hoods, and on.

Danton eyed Savage warily over his ham and eggs. He seemed none the worse for wear after Wunder's question and answer session last night, but Danton was not particularly eager to probe the matter, or others concerning Savage's activities before, his predictions, or his aversion to blasters. For the moment Danton's costume seemed to be doing its job and Savage was occupied with a newfound friend, none other than the Mirror.

He returned to his consideration of the intricate blotches on his hat, to the mindlessness so essential before working.

"Good afternoon."

It was Savage. "Hello!" He frowned, sitting back with his coffee cupped in both hands. "How did you—?"

"Your body type, gestures, the Whore Hall meal ticket you used. Before becoming a madman I was a clothing designer."

"Ah." Somehow that seemed funny but Danton did not laugh. He signalled for another coffee. "Sit down for a minute."

"I will and perhaps longer, because Mirror is drifting off again. He doesn't have a terribly long attention span."

The coffee came and a glum waitress asked him for the second time if he wanted whiskey in it. He met her sad eyes (paint on a moustache and she'd be Sam) and shook his head. "Mirror and you have made friends," he observed.

Savage nodded. "We are friends and doubles. A perfect hook up. Molecule for molecule. Not a zig for a zag."

"Your double? He's changed, hasn't he?"

Savage grinned, patient as the hero of a musical. "My spiritual double. He shares my confusions, only in a more classical schizophrenia." He frowned. "I think."

"So now you're triplets." Danton smiled, his tubes wrinkling. "He's a lovely double anyway, like a chrome trophy."

"Mirror thinks he's playing a thousand roles, that people only see what they want to see in him, sham, cheap tricks with mirrors. People say it stems from some war time trauma. I've asked him. Of course he doesn't answer."

Danton sipped his coffee. There *was* whiskey in it. "Savage."

Savage looked instantly attentive.

"Last night—what did you do with the blaster I gave you?"

"Gave it to the Juggler." Savage looked puzzled.

"No, I mean before. In the park."

"I fired it." Savage's green eyes captured Danton's. "At my head."

Danton looked away, slowly massaging his forehead. "I thought maybe—" he shook his head—"I don't guess you should have told me that." His hand stopped. "You missed?"

"I missed. But I thought you *meant*—"

"I meant nothing." Danton stared at his reflection in the coffee. "I don't suppose I wanted to consider what you thought I meant until they threw the body smoking at my feet."

Savage shrugged. "If you knew everything, then you must have known it didn't matter what you meant. That's not in my script. Why concoct this whole elaborate farce when I could much more easily suicide?"

"Nobody knows things like that, Savage. Least of all people who know what it might mean when they give other people blasters."

"An interesting experience, in any case." Savage dug blunt fingers into his beard. "But here's a much more interesting question. What would it have meant if they *had* thrown my body smoking at your feet?"

Danton only frowned.

"Could it have meant that your world was doomed?"

Danton's lips rounded in comprehension. "You mean—"

"Last night when they questioned me because I said—I said he would come. Do *you* think I'm what Alphy said I was?"

"Are you a—what was the phrase Alphy used—a psychometric microcosm? An individual who, because of some stressing we can't understand yet, is a perfect point for point analogue of our society? Does what is happening in your mind reflect the social consciousness? Does your suicide attempt mean a whole world has despaired?" Danton paused, considering. "No. Alphy's prediction and yours were a pretty coincidence." He stabbed a last bit of ham with his fork. "No chance." His fork poked at the air, punctuating. "About as much chance as that the assassin is a scarred mythical monster in a cave."

"The Juggler's story. Yes." Savage nodded. "Everyone's favorite. But how do you know that that monster doesn't exist when you aren't even sure what the Juggler means by a monster? We have the same problem of definitions here."

"What we have is a problem of religion. If correspondences like the one Alphy posits exist, then all patterns are simply points of correspondence in larger patterns. We ourselves are patterns. Now that either makes the universe completely knowable or completely unknowable, neither of which makes me happy."

Savage smiled. "Are you unwilling to accept me as a microcosm because I'm a very sick man? You don't think your society is—"

"Sick? Of course I do. But that qualifies Mirror and a lot of other people for the same job."

Savage shrugged. "If the shoe fits—"

Danton grinned. "A clothing designer." He shook his head. "In any case, the assassin *didn't* strike last night."

"Look, Danton. Simply examine the meanings of your terms. Suppose you were synonyming a broadcast and needed a term to replace this 'psychometric microcosm.' Would 'assassin' do?" Savage rose and made a mock salute. "I see Mirror is looking at us. Let me catch him while he's still receiving." He strode off.

Leaving Danton staring after him, his mouthful of unswallowed coffee burning.

After that he walked to one of the five gates in the city wall and left the city.

It was a sunny day and Monotony's surrounding hillsides, more brown than green this late in the year, shivered in a grass rippling wind. He sat with his back propped against the high white wall, feet spread, soles open to the meadow, notebook open to a blank page. He bent to the struggle.

It was the only kind of duel one could have with the assassin now and in the end it might be the only kind there was. And in the end, too, that was what chilled him, that all this might only be a subject for poetry, which, already, was a poetic image. As you advance skillfully through the darkness with your mirror shield, take care that the monster, too, does not carry a mirror. Danton stared at the grass.

Perhaps this was what Viktor had seen and put into his poster, a reverberation of faceless faces, an echo of mirrors.

And Viktor had fallen. Perhaps this was not a battle for one who, the last few times out, had been caught reaching. Consider that, Danton.

He had brought a flask of whiskey along and now he opened it. After a very short time the sun raveled pinks ahead and dropped through cirrous clouds, a round white blister slowly filling with blood. The tiny moth of light buzzing at the whiskey's surface lingered halfway to the bottom. He rose and walked for a while. From beyond, enclosing the silence, came the cavernous whisper of the ocean. How far was it? A half mile? A mile? Too far. He would not venture out to scarred monsters or the sliding sea.

When he sat again he thought about the compass, which he still had. And he visualized it in that remarkably clear way he had, glinting in the Piazza light, his and unshakeable. Only then did he fumble it out of his pantaloons and scale it spinning over the city wall. But why should that glint linger in his eye long enough to strike shield-sized off the brow of one of Monotony's hills, where a figure moved now and vanished behind its mass?

No matter. He was astronomically drunk.

A man in costume, blue, blurry, trudged up to him and asked something. He had on red jewels like Danton's. It went "Hah?" and "What's that?" for a few exchanges and then Danton finally understood him to be asking for a dime. He didn't have one, which left him alone a moment later, dimeless and unrepenting.

The sky was honey-colored, the hills nearly black. He stared at the sun's orb, now mapped with the leaf-silhouettes of a nearby tree; a paring over the poughtop was still frothwhite, translucent and delicate as Cerrara marble. Something was about to happen—

He was floating brainlessly, drenched in light, when he sensed someone hunkered next to him. The face was close, silhouetted, featureless but for spare details the light chipped out. He could see the odd rindlike toughness of the skin. He could see, curving down from a tiny lobed ear to a brittle chin, the puckerings in a livid scar.

He drew back against the wall, staring.

The face turned, showed a crescent of even teeth, that same translucent white. Then something darted at him and snarled painfully in the tubes on his chest, and all of him arched irresistibly up. "I'm here to kill you." A pause. The voice whined like wheels in the sand, soft, breathless, crunching. "Why? Because the dead leaves at my feet do not tell me otherwise. Because this planet does not speak to me and save you, because that brilliant sky has no message for me. Because it is all in fact dreadfully simple and this is the only thing to do. Like so." He slashed with the hand Danton couldn't see. There was a stinging, then wetness. "What is your name?" That grinning mouth came an inch closer to his. "Who are your parents? Where do you come from?"

Danton brought a limp hand up to the one rooted in his chest. It kicked and jacked him to his knees. Something from below knocked his head back and caught it again, higher, on the rebound. Pain dug down the back of his head like fingers into clay. Something big as a racket volleyed his face back and forth. It pulped and started to come apart. His name. He shoved at it and it jammed like a rock in his mouth and then popped. "Danton."

That face was close as a lover. "Your full name."

He shook his head. There was a deep furious shock in his groin and a growing fist slowly crumpled up his insides. It was the only shape within him and he wrapped over it and it rolled him up. He was beginning to forget why he was here.

"Your full name."

Big hands clamped to his shoulders. He came up at arm's length from the face, wheezing. "I don't know." It fought its way out. "I don't know."

"Where are you from, Off-Worlder?"

"I'm an orphan." His voice started near his guts. "I don't know."

This time a thumb shoved his eyesocket, feeling around a bit for loose change. More of the hand tried to get in.

He screamed.

Then he was pawing at the dirt, knowing that all he'd ever see would be the color white. And he heard this little hiss of something moving very fast and it tried to shovel off the back of his head.

The pain told him his body was damaged far beyond repair. Being afraid was the worst part.

"Who raised you?" It was a while later now.

Someone had fixed him up on a pole and he hung there in a pretty hefty wind. He had to answer twice before it came out. "No one."

"You were on your own?"

He nodded or grated a yes or both.

"That's all you remember?"

He nodded. He was getting better.

And the pole got snatched away and he fell. Only his eyes told him he hit; the rest of him waited while he bounced twice in slow motion and then caught up like a giant slap. He groaned.

He clambered up to his hands and feet. It was a mistake but he could live with it. The man with the scar towered into the darkness of the dark sky. Danton couldn't center him. His head was cast iron, too heavy to hold for long, and it was already starting to twist him back. Then it snapped and he made a vicious swipe at the man's knee on the way past, but missed by a healthy margin. His head hung somewhere below it, enormous and swaying. He stared into the whiskey flask where a sunparing floated on the amber, bright enough to hurt. A reflection slid across, round and gray, about the shape of a knee and he lunged after it and tackled the flask hard. The reflection, and the glass, shattered. Whiskey flashed out and for a moment there was a beautiful tapestry stretched across it; amber spokes and a thousand scarred faces trembled over a thousand pared suns. Then the dirt sucked it away.

Broken shards rocked back and forth. He pushed off his hands and sat up. Now the man with the scar stood next to a tree. He was silhouetted. His hands were up peeling at his face. When it came free there was a soft tearing sound and he held it out on both hands, a little brain sized lump, and punched it lightly back into shape.

There was another profile, tilted back like a head on a plate, growing off his hands. His own bent and they seemed to kiss and then the one that would have a scar was crumpled noisily into one fist. The other held together, sketched boldly against a pewter sky, before swift clouds, in failing light.

The man with a scar lifted a hand and something new grew out of it, something long and straight. It steadied and aimed.

Danton dove the only way that might do any good, straight towards it.

And there were a couple of puffings and he hit his skull repeatedly against a cave wall.

Stirrings. His stomach was rolled into his lungs and he tried to breathe through breakfast. Besides that, something club shaped was shoved up into his belly. Another stirring. It was his leg and it slid away. He felt a stinging. It seemed like a funny thing to worry about now but his hand jerked up anyway and tried to shoo it off. It wouldn't take wing. He rolled and a cord bit into his neck. While he fumbled with the hat strap the ache in his groin took hold and spread. The one anywhere above the belt moved to head it off.

Then the stinging came back.

Raging, he tore off the hat and it eased.

It was the biggest moment of his day.

He held the hat over his face and turned it slowly. It was not part of a plan; he was only passing time without moving much, watching rubellite stones on his hand go opal.

Then he saw the yellow plumage ruffled up in a camouflage green seam, fine as a paint brush, pollen bright. It was a dart. He plucked it out and stared at its steel tip. Drugged? Maybe. Or maybe he was far too drunk to tell. It seemed to be the sort of dart used with air guns, the kind usually equipped with another chamber for firing deadly beebees.

Perhaps he had a slingshot too. Danton rose to a sitting position and wished he hadn't, half his body wanting to drift away, the bottom, leaden half wanting to vomit. It was in no wise a healthy relationship. He let his head sink down between his knees and breathed his own smell for a while. As usual none of the parties did what they threatened.

He rose again by degrees, propelled by a kind of clickety winch arrangement by ratchets low and, at right angles, his head pointing up, stowed the dart in a flowing pantaloon pocket. Evidence. The thing you woke up holding. Exhibit A to be slammed to the table at a critical moment, whereupon a glinting reaction would be observed in the accused's covetous eyes.

It was a long hard training schedule but finally he could stand on only two feet with no hands. When he stooped for his hat blood slammed into his temples and he came up to cheers and whistles. The trick got better. He put the hat on.

Miraculously, he had escaped without so much as a yellowing bruise. Which was odd, because surely that first murderous slash—

He shook it off. It had never been there. Perhaps a great deal had never been there. How much had he dreamed on afterwards in his increasingly distorted repetitions under the drug? What he had was the dart. What he found and could see, he had.

He spent the next few minutes on his hands and knees searching for his notebook. It wasn't a decisive test either way because he gave up too easily, reflecting that, after all, he hadn't much use for those particular empty pages just then.

He went through the gate at Monastery Street and walked amidst aimless maskers. A freeway of globe lights hung up on the light brown fronts, ballooning edgeless glow up their festooned stucco, dusting the confettied street white. Shadowy maskers slipped out of entranceways and threw ominous cut-outs up the walls. In this slashing brightness, darkness clung unshakably to any cove or hollow and, trapped in an eddy of tall maskers, he could be plunged into a moment's midnight under their flaring capes.

Music wailed, the notes sliding and uncertain among the close buildings, from the auraed bubble of the Piazza ahead. And it was only then, back inside the city walls, lost in the trumpeting crowd, that he realized what had transpired during that attack. His aging secret was out. His youth was exposed. Somewhere someone knew that he had no name.

There was an explosion behind him and something

webbed and sugary snapped out to tarp half the street and dissolved. The crowd surged that way and he was propelled towards a video store window. It was then that one of those life-changing coincidences occurred, crucial not so much for their content as for their absolutely perfect timing.

"—and that was it for Viktor Treblinski, mistaken for one of the Twenty-Five, and tragically shot at the hands of duellist Ernst the Executioner."

The voice came from a speaker over the video store window, and its well-modulated tones were all too familiar. Danton glanced at the clock in the nearby Piazza; it was twelve-oh-five. He thrust forward, managed to work his way in past an unconcerned throng to the side of the window.

Half of it was occupied by one of those ridiculously large wall-sized holo-screens. Color wobbled through the glass and made a slightly miniaturized studio in a space the crowd had conceded. There, seated smiling at a desk, wearing his yellow number forty-seven, was a perfectly reduced midget Juggler.

"And to sign off with, an interesting little item for the footnoters." The Juggler winked. "Question: what highly successful poet, who probably got the nickname Lonus on one of the mercenary's spherical ships, now goes under a much more famous name to hide a nameless, questionable past? And is he more eager than ever to keep his murky origins quiet now, with a number of questions being raised about his connection with the assassin affair?"

A moment's dead air time on the Juggler's frozen smile. Fade-out. Credits.

For a moment, Danton was like someone struck by so many blows, no longer Danton at all, but a man of a different height and carriage, a man who moved differently from his stillnesses, who was often tired. Then he began walking, shoulders squared like an actor's before his big entrance, thinking that he had a great deal to do now, and thinking only of those things. He must talk to Wunder. He must talk to the Proets. He was due at the Planetarium soon.

More and more of the assassin was beginning to show.

III. Vicissitudes

WHY WAS SHE more afraid now? She wondered. Why when all that had happened was that the assassin had *not* struck? She had never known fear before in this form. It was like love, the assassin in every browning leaf, in every glinting eye, in every hand that blossomed, white and grasping, from a concealing sleeve. She could no longer bear it and she could not imagine it ending. Like a lover's final, finalizing yes or no, the assassin's attack would never come.

Then why was she afraid?

Guillemet was at the southeastern end of Hellespont Boulevard, in the very corner of Monotony, standing in the little square that fronted the Dome.

The Dome: genus Kubla Khan, species Wunderdamen. It bubbled high above the city wall, white, virgin, and glossy, the nub of a rotated parabola, with not a single seam in its smooth sweep. Where Guillemet stood the wrought iron gate thrust up pikes iced with gold, sunlight brilliantly frosting their tips. Behind it, the surface of the Dome stretched taut and vacant, a brain waiting to take its first impression.

It was a matter force distortion, a gravity bubble an uncertain molecule thick.

Guillemet came up and touched it, uncertainly. It shivered, foaming over her hand. It was like a colossal soap bubble, supple, taut, and deforming, bound under eternally slipping tensions. She stepped in. It frothed and gobbetted. It sealed over her.

Total darkness: her eyes drew snowflake remnants of the wall, each as individual and unique as a retinal pattern. Her feet lost all sense of purchase. Fuzzy heavy music drifted out to her, the same three bars played over and over again with the most minuscule variations, mistakes probably. There were smells: seared meat, caramel, peanut oil, chocolate. She walked the retina's memory of a straight line, arm probing uncertainly in front. The world on both sides was sheared away.

Then the lathering of the wall reversed, black to white, and the crash of light came down, light eddying from dark seas, lashing static, phosphene breakers, bolts of unnameable color, a seething chaos. In moments her irradiated irises felt big as nickels, and she could take in a little of its form, squinting, conceding detail, eyes unguyed and buoyant.

She was through.

In a large oval open area, masked dancers cavorted before curtains of hellish light.

Behind them, 9,337 signs lifted a galaxy of neon to the Dome's reflective shell.

Her eyes failed before the light mass itself. Firing neurons, inhibited by endless bright outlines, fell silent; neighborhoods of warring intensity were blended and made equal. Her gaze hurled itself forward to pry detail from the mass, and slid off as from a wall.

Where to begin? (Shape: each sign was a rectangle.)

And why? (Fear: each sign was an eye.)

She took her first bearing on the largest sign. It grazed the whitetop, beading light along its slow borders, its little replicas printing Manhattanesque outlines all around it. It blazed one word: CARNIVAL. In this aspect. But in a moment a ghastly ectoplasmic face shot out through Carnival's rainbow of melting letters. His eyes were drooping and bloodshot. His girdered mouth gaped. He was watery green and fleshy, Carnival himself, scheduled for extinction at sunset the next day, only now replaced by a victim...

Guillemet's eyes swept away. Up, down, up again, coasting a stretch of pinkish neon galaxy, slipping to the foreground and its monochromatic injunction: EAT, which flickered to DRINK, to DANCE, to FUCK, then to a neon palimpsest of all four, like a snarl of green nerve. Her eyes fled and took halting drops down a clutter of right angles. Rectangles of all sizes and proportions wheeled up to the Dome's mirror deep sky. Light signalled frantically: a multi-colored double helix, a rippling bullseye target, a golden trio of rings, a wavering ankh, a wheel of fortune that spun till, on the rim, a crowned head lit, the winner. There were cartoons: a disembodied masker, aquiline, lovely, flickered through endless puffs on a silver cigarette. The clef on a music staff beat time as, measure by measure, the words and notes of "You're Killing Me," shone meaningfully by.

Everything *moved,* swirling, sailing, pumping full, hollowing momentary negatives to suck in the eye. Without a thought in her head she dwelt on a bulky male silhouette doing stop action bumps and grinds. A frame away, a web of smoke spun, then, reversing, wrapped into the snout of an amber satyr; his pentacle heated white. Far away, under airborne motorcycles, a goddess murdered a beautiful god and all was well in the kingdom. It was protean substance, the first step in creation, the fundamental element: light. Light parading through the darkness, light as a theme, what could have been had clay been by-passed, the unwatched element caught doing its act at last... oh light...

In the clearing at the Dome entrance, maskers still danced, but light bent them to its own ends, light flip-flopped. They were still a moment in fading smokey blue and, switched, danced into a spectral green, smoothly trading steps. Light pulsed like a live muscle. They spun insanely, electrified. Partial twilight fell and, gone blue, they leapt with halting frenzy into an old rooster hop, shaking tick tock limbs, colliding out of time, accelerating, freezing, clinching, transected. Light dove, rolled, heaved in its death throes. As they swung back and forth across the dust. (Compiling frames: a bobbing head, a left foot sliding left, cranking elbows, a trunk leaning right, the mirror images of these, then miscellania, ad libs.) Red swallowed up the dance floor and they were mostly silhouette, slowed way down, moving crusts of darkness . . .

Guillemet hurried past them onto a path under the signs, moving into an iron forest of girders.

Into gloom. Selective, light-filtering fields shielded off the signs above, screening an underworld of widely differing intensities, of shadow and half-melted volumes of light. This first region was almost all dusk. Only a few small, waist-high masses of color dotted the path, gaseous, twisted. Above, countless gloom-softened catwalks wired an aerial network between the signs; girders tipped and locked into rude vaulting. Girder trunks vanished into gray brush. Few colors survived that high: here a dusting of green on crossed girders, there a wing of pale yellow folding onto a ladder rung.

Smaller detaching paths plunged off into the twilight and turned quickly into obstacle courses of halflit forms. Scattered over such a foot trail there might be dozens of maskers, grainy, gesturing, and lost.

A sad vendor bounced his cart along shouting incomprehensibly in the din. He was hailed by a woman in a double-breasted suit, her coattails lifted by antique, pearl handled pistols.

The woman's arm fell, then rose again uncertainly, waving.

Guillemet nodded back to her, totally unable to recall her name. They had met sometime at the Hall.

"I've seen the posters, Guille. You look just heroic!"

"Thank you." Guillemet touched her shoulder and pivoted by. "Must hurry now."

The woman, with a touch of dismay, waved again. Such recognitions had been surprisingly few since Guillemet's announcement as victim, primarily because few connected the face on the poster with the giantess often seen hurrying through Monotony's streets. It was her one advantage as a victim and an important one, since she detested encounters of that sort. People knew giants by their size, not their faces. Except, possibly, people who were assassins.

Ahead the path widened and lightened. Maskers had gathered to conduct their carnival affairs and Guillemet swept by, parting sequined bodies. A white boa flounced at her, then, abruptly, unfolded into a wing. She ducked and came up short against a woman windmilling her tulle skirt in dervish circles. Glittery crepe moved near and caught on it, pleated and rustled free, slowly flaring, snagging, crushing flat.

There was a small clearing. At the center, two steel stalks curved and joined over the Catacomb mouth, their twining tips molded into leaves and concealing the lenses of a video camera. Below, a concrete ramp descended into pale fluorescence. A smiling fruit dealer did a booming business.

The path continued into still deeper shadow. It was easy to stray here. In the wee hours after the Dome shut down, beepers were activated on all the main paths so that those inevitably left trudging hopeless circles through the Iron Forest could follow their woodnymph call back to light or a helpful video camera. Just then she followed what she'd arbitrarily designated as the trail (more than three people in sight at a time), with no dusty sunshafts to guide her and, after a few minutes, spotted something almost as good. It was a feelable deep forest glow, the kind that always led to an ominous cottage or a lecturing monk, but led, just this once, to a clearing and the Lost Saloon.

Here a steel grotto opened under a city of transparent floors. Far above, pneumatic highways thrust aslant towering city complexes. Light warmed down through layers of blinking floor to spread steamy amid the draped shadows of this recess. But all was illusion: highways, dropping tiers, plexi-formed tubes, rearing towers, the ensemble a vast holographic collage.

The mammoth pylons holding the city in place were cardboard and a wire mesh fence skirting three sides of the clearing proved, at a close glance, a styrofoam mock-up. Big white bites grinned through the fence's linkage. It was like some place deep in the inner city where unspeakable things might happen. It was another of Madame Manetti's aberrations. Where would she strike next?

Lost Saloon, under the furthest of the fence's sides, was of course world famous, and aptly named as far as the tourists back on the so-called path were concerned. It was a long shack with a rakishly beveled roof (painted with the word "Lost"), and three modest plateglass windows (the white letters of "Saloon" arching each). The only entrance was a dirty green door at one end.

She went in and the din struck up, tuned by resonant walls. Drinkers were packed shoulder to shoulder into the rude interior, crowding in on the close-set tables. Waiters wove tirelessly in and out with trays full of drinks, were bellowed at, and precipitously vanished. A lone masked man sat on the rafters.

She found them waiting at a corner table near a strategy machine, a seat somehow kept vacant for her. She nodded to each of them, a little surprised that there were this many: the Juggler, Boz, Savage, and Mirror. When she sat she faced the corner and saw their spherical reflections on the shiny game screen, four stubby dwarves round a boulder, a swarm of elves fanning out behind them.

"My dear Guillemet." The Juggler smiled his twelve o'clock smile. "Surely you know Savage and Mirror, who are regulars by now. And this is Commander Bohdan Potocki."

She smiled briefly to Savage and Mirror, then turned her attention on the Commander. "Commander, I've heard a great deal about you and your mission here. Honored to have you at this modest interview."

"Very pleased to be here." He had the foreigner's trick of saying the words beautifully, but missing the cadence by a mile.

The Juggler, one hand covering his yellow forty-seven in shock, did an exaggerated take. "Why, Boz, you're talking!" Today, however, though his numbers were the same, his costume had undergone a change; he was dressed in fool's motley, complete with three-belled cap.

Boz smiled at him with what seemed to be infinite patience. "She is not the enemy."

Forty-Seven glanced slyly at Guillemet. "I think it's you, dear. You've brought out the giant killer in him."

Their drinks arrived, two grogs and two gin-and-tonics. Guillemet ordered a Novak.

The waiter said that was very good.

The Living Mirror, shifting his ropey, hot silver form against the dark wood of his chair, bent reflections of their four faces on his gently heaving chest. Head bent, he studied an especially sharp glinting off his right nipple. That came from Boz, whose spacer blues were a circuitboard of snaps and buckles. Mirror traced it back and nodded.

Peering at him, Guillemet wondered what he thought about at times like these, then glanced at Savage who, tapping his blunt fingers, also studied Mirror, also wondered. There was some new alliance here. Savage shifted in his chair and pushed Mirror's grog towards him. He lifted his own, then stopped, the mug halfway to his lips, as he followed Mirror's gaze down to the glinting nipple. Suddenly he leaned forward. "Mirror, do you want to go home?"

Mirror looked up, lancing highlights off both lifted brows. "To the Tiara?" He shook his head.

"Now why do you have to mother him, Savage? You never let him decide for himself." The Juggler shook his head. "Mirror is here at Boz's invitation," he said to Guillemet. "His father is an old friend of Boz's. Savage just tagged along."

Savage, the declared homicide, wagged his beard at him. "That's not true. You know it isn't." His eyes were huge and hurt.

"Why don't we go on to the interview?" Boz suggested.

But the Juggler already had his head on the table, his belled cap jingling, and was trying to catch the Mirror's eye from a low angle. "Mirror, you're a WUTter and much too quiet. Are you a spy?"

"A spy." Mirror grinned as if, after his long and wearying pantomime, they had finally guessed it.

The Juggler chuckled. "A spy here on our lovely Earth. Now I want to know, really, how you like us." His dark eyes fixed the spy's.

Mirror's head nudged up and their gazes met, his silver lids rounding. For an instant he searched just as intently as the Juggler; then, failing to find it, whatever it was, he looked back to his lap.

"He likes us," Savage offered.

Forty-Seven banged his fist to the table. "I want *him* to answer!" A clear tone rang faintly from his glass.

Savage looked as if he had just sat on a compass point and Boz allowed himself a faint, gnomish frown. The waiter had the good timing to bring Guillemet's drink then. She stirred it absorbedly.

Boz snatched the silence neatly out of the air. "Let me tell you how passionately I love your city," he said leaning towards Guillemet.

"How passionately do you love our city?" she asked.

"You see!" The Juggler slapped Mirror's shoulder triumphantly. "Interaction. It *can* be done. Now, tell me how you like us."

Mirror lifted platinum lids. "How I like you."

Chorused immediately by Savage's "What'd I tell you?" and Boz's strange accented laugh.

Guillemet sighed. It was beginning to look like a difficult interview. "Why don't you ask me about tonight's taping at the Planetarium, Jug?"

"Mirror, you are amazing!" Savage never even heard the hint. "There's never been anyone quite like you."

"No, of course." The Juggler grinned. "Mirror is too alike." He leaned over to inspect Mirror's averted features. "Tell me, looking glass, is it true that Wunder kept you for a while, that for a brief spell the two of you reflected brilliantly on one another."

"Yes," Savage said. "That was just before me."

Jug gave him a brief chuckle, a look of dry disbelief.

He flushed. "I meant before I met *Wunder*. I—" He licked his lips, looked helplessly at Guillemet who, unfortunately, was unable to think up any way of rescuing him. And was not trying very hard.

"You WUTters, honestly." The Juggler, his triumph secured, turned to Guillemet. "Now what about tonight's taping at the Planetarium?"

"Well, of course, I can only reveal a limited number of details, but the gist of it is that we will be debunking the assassin, using current statistics, trend projections, historical data, and a hard-headed common sense look at the political crisis we're faced with. The program will climax with a rigorously worked out proof that the assassin doesn't exist, which we've broken down into a simplified logical argument for the less mathematical in our audience."

"I see." The Juggler sipped carefully at his drink. "Any comment, Boz?"

Boz shrugged. "Difficult to ascertain."

"And Danton will be there."

"Danton most especially." Guillemet nodded. "And the Proets, who'll liven things up with bits of their work, excerpts from tomorrow's play, and their usual antics."

"And will Wunder be there?"

"No."

"No Wunder." Jug looked significantly at Boz. "How come? Wunder was never shy about video appearances before."

"Well, it's just that—" Guillemet shrugged—"it's Danton's show. I'll be there as Wunder's representative."

"And what will you be doing?"

Guillemet frowned. "Just—filler work. Holding cue cards, getting the assassin data in shape—I've been working with it the past week—and possibly narrating some of the more expository sections of the program. I've done video work before, for Wunder."

"Of course." The Juggler's seat sawed forward, propelled by a couple of would-be dancers. He glowered over his shoulder, then looked back pleasantly at Guillemet. "Are you sure it's not just so the assassin will have his maximum choice of victims?"

"Pardon."

Jug rested his chin on his folded hands. "It *would* be interesting to see, if he came, just who he went for. And if he doesn't come, why that means it's Wunder, or one of the other twenty-five, or else that you're right and there *is* no assassin. I like you, Guillemet. You're not going to crack during this interview."

She looked at her leather-covered palms. "You believe in the assassin."

"More so than in the victims. They have a way of getting very cagey. Come now, *is* there a proof?"

Mirror rose and began trying to cadge a cigarette from someone in the crowd.

Guillemet watched him absently a moment, then turned crisply back to the Juggler. "The proof is by *reductio absurdum*. It involves proving that the assassin belongs to the trivial class of cases in Novak's famous forty-seventh step *and* to another class, defined as exclusive."

That seemed to give him a moment's curious pause. His next breath was a fraction deeper than the last. He ran a finger slowly along his lower lip. "If you've proved," he said finally, "that he belongs to a class of trivial cases, why go on?"

She smiled. "Jug, we on Wunder's team are always well coached before interviews like this. The answer is: because in a single event, trivial cases can not be overlooked. The odds of a dart striking a given *point* on or off a dartboard are zero, a trivial case, yet each and every time you throw the dart an event with zero probability happens."

The Juggler sighed. "Each and every time."

"Sad," said Savage, "that things are so predictable."

The lone masked man in the rafters chose that moment to topple from his perch. He had time to flail once, dumping his drink in a lovely arc on Boz, and to scream briefly. Then he hit head first and went perfectly still.

There were roars of deep laughter that shook the shack's plank walls. A couple of maskers leapt up and swung from the rafters making apelike sounds and beating their chests. Someone in Proet leather slowly started up a round of stomping, then a building chant of "Do it again!"

The lone masked man lay on the floor, bleeding from the head. Blood spread with amazing quickness over the floor, then, just as quickly, ceased to shine and to flow, ceased to be liquid.

Boz wiped his eyes carefully with a finger, then looked quietly over the crowd, his expression faintly disgusted. "Which are they laughing at?"

"Don't flatter yourself, Boz." The Juggler passed him a handkerchief. "Your skin isn't broken."

The "Do it again" chant now included almost everyone in the bar, the sound in that long shack incredible. Shock waves traveled through the floor into their chairs, tiny and rapid, working them into the rhythm.

Boz and the Juggler leaned their heads together and consulted. Guillemet slowly realized that no one was going to touch him. The few who grasped what was happening were transfixed, and already had the look of those who believe it is too late. The initial shock had held them at first, and the mingled horror of the bleeding and the laughter had held them still further. Had held *her*. She looked up and saw Boz watching her with enormous curiosity. That set her moving. But the instant she rose, four onlooking maskers dropped to their knees and began to bind the masked man's head with handkerchiefs. She dropped back into her seat, enormously relieved.

Jug leaned towards her and shouted into her ear: "Boz wants to leave!" He waved his hand. "The chanting!"

Guillemet nodded and the three of them rose, looking at Mirror and Savage. Savage stared at the rafters the masked man had fallen from mouthing the words, "Do it again!" Mirror, absolutely motionless, stared at the blood.

They let them be. When they reached the masked man, who had to be passed, the four kneeling maskers were screaming to be heard. They had not been heard yet when Guillemet reached the door.

Outside, the shadows were welcoming, the noise so much softer it seemed to mean something. Walking along So-called Path, they were silent. This ghosted darkness did not invite conversation. But at the Catacomb clearing the crowd was thicker, the noise climbing back up to customary levels. Boz called for a halt and they retreated to the skirting of the Catacomb ramp. A few yards away the same smiling fruit dealer still did a booming business.

"What do you think?" asked the Juggler.

Boz gave a thin smile. "How do you survive?"

Guillemet leaned on the railing over the Catacomb entrance, staring up at the video camera that found those who were lost. "Who?"

"Your people. You are a culture unlike others. So inefficient. And to be inefficient is sometimes to be cruel."

"Tut. Cultural relativism, old boy."

"Why don't you—colloquially—go sit on it, Jug." He pointed a finger at Guillemet. "The group should have some custom, ritual, method, for dealing with wounded members. The group is a—" his hands grappled with the concept— "tool. These customs are the—" again he wrestled—"tribe-being's answer to situations too complicated to be worked out at the moment. Your people only stood there, watching. You are a race of watchers."

Guillemet half-sat on the railing, looking at a miniature offworld horse that had pranced into the clearing. "Perhaps you're right."

"You see? Even now. No eye contact. You are busy watching."

From his back hip pocket the Juggler absently withdrew a

metal flask. He toyed with the cap.

"Let *me* be the interviewer a moment, Guillemet, and ask you a question. What in your opinion makes this assassination unique?"

She shrugged. "That we're expecting it."

A remarkably broad smile split his homely face. He edged closer to Guillemet on the railing. "Exactly. You are watching for it. It is a pre-arranged meeting." He raised a declamatory hand. "But exactly what is it—an assassination?"

"You just said it." The Juggler spun the cap off his flask. "Meeting someone by previous arrangement. Clever pun."

The miniature horse, hind muscles jumping under nearly sheer skin, was plainly terrified. He whipped his china brittle head back and forth, searching for some path through the crowd. Pressing maskers applauded.

"Very good, Jug." Boz's voice strained a bit to cut through the din. "You see, with your assassin, you have given yourselves away. Assassination is a social act and speaks more of the society than the individual. What is the difference between assassination and murder? Why, the importance of the victim we might say at first, but of course if a president is murdered in bed by her husband, then that is not an assassination. Most assassinations are done in public places, before great audiences, because of a cause." He paused to savor this last euphony. "Mark that. Assassins have missions. Often it is the borderline psychopath who assassinates, someone trying to do the work of years of social engagement in one grand gesture. His act is directed towards the tribe-being."

"The tribe-God, isn't it?" The Juggler sipped at his flask.

"True being *is* godhood, but let us not get into divine substance. I doubt you would find my religion's subtleties rewarding, Jug. Just now I am talking sociology, and so I employ the term tribe-being. The word society seems to me to have none of the associations needed to explain acts so evenly divided between the social and the personal, acts of *mission*. I wish to return to the idea of a mission and point out that *this* assassin seems to have none. No pretense has been made of high-mindedness. He is simply—predicted. Whose contact is being made or broken with the tribe-being? Who has suffered? None. No one. The *only* thing that makes this assassin an assassin is a public agreement, the word of the tribe-being. The assassin is here *to be seen,* and everything you do, including your video shows, is to see him." Boz grinned. "It strikes me that his only motive is—forgive me this—the prophet-motive." Boz's high, multi-voweled laugh broke out. After a moment, he saw that he laughed alone. His eloquent shrug said that if they did not understand the finesse of their own language, it was no fault of his. "The assassin is historically gratuitous. You have no need of an assassin to get into grievous trouble in the coming crisis. Yet somehow he is necessary. Gratuitous but necessary, he is like an addiction." He looked at the Juggler. "Speaking of which—"

The Juggler surrendered the flask.

A cheer rose from the crowd and the miniature horse wheeled frantically and reared. A wave of maskers closed with him. Someone screamed and the horse fell as if shot. A moment later three maskers rose gripping him about the neck and belly. Struggling feebly, he was carried off.

"What will they do with it?" Boz asked.

"Eat it."

Boz's jaw dropped and Jug laughed melodically.

"He means," said Guillemet, "that they're going to take it back to the amusement park."

Boz made an 'o' with his lips and handed her the flask. "My point is that *this* assassin seems to be an exchange between tribe-being and tribe-being. You individuals are passive observers in an affair that should deeply concern you. Now there is something wrong with this. Look at the tribe-being as an organism. Each event in the organism is interaction between one part and another or one part and the whole. But there is no event where the whole reacts with the whole. To experience this is to experience madness. It is a sign that something is wrong where the organism meets the world."

"And what is this that is wrong with us?"

"Not with 'you,' even you-plural. With the tribe-being. And yes, I have an idea what it is."

"I had a feeling." The Juggler reached for the flask.

"What we are really talking about is mass violence. What Pierpont was mainly concerned with was mass violence. But this is a media-age, as our juggling friend will tell you, and in a media-age assassination is also a form of mass violence. Now what is it—a media age? It means that you individuals can experience events that happen to the tribe-being more— metaphorically. You see little models of yourselves doing things in a box which are supposed to signal great, important events. Great agonies of the tribe-being, that might once have taken years to subside, can now be played out in half an hour on the screen. The breadline riots twenty years ago, and the landing of the mercenaries here fifteen years ago, both only took a week apiece. Yet everything afterwards changed. There hasn't been a real declared war in a hundred years. Why? Because declared wars take too long for video; they can not accomplish their purposes. This crisis, too, will not lead to a war, though it may lead to battles, and will certainly bring untold economic hardships. Let us use the tribe-being again. In the organism, pain is a very sophisticated mechanism for relaying the type and extent of any damage. As it becomes increasingly more informative in the higher animals, as it becomes a more and more detailed report about the damage, it becomes an extension of it. The ultimate message about anything is the thing itself, which is the fastest message of all. An efficient nervous system is simply one which carries all the possibilities within itself, so that each nerve path is a certain event, and the messages may be compressed into the shortest possible time. Has a single image of violence been able to replace all that a war used to do? Is the entire response sequence now imprinted in us? If you follow this train of thought out completely, you must consider a strange possibility."

"Here Boz. Consider this possibility."

The flask glided into Boz's hand. "That the image has shrunk even further than you think, that we have nearly reached the message of zero-time. The message is not the *assassination,* but only the suggestion of it. Which means that the tribe-being has already chosen its response to the crisis. And that response—is to wait. Pain, though, is only a metaphor for damage. And to respond only to the metaphor, and not the thing, that is madness."

Guillemet nodded slowly. "And so our tribe-being is mad." She put an extra few inches between them. "And the assassin will not come, but something worse will. Tell me,

Commander. *Your* mission here must occupy your thoughts too. Have you reached any decision yet?"

"Yes, I have."

"What!" The Juggler spun in front of him, his cap jingling. "You told me—"

"It is not time to act on that decision yet, Jug. So naturally I haven't told it to anyone. And won't now."

"Then why tease us with it?" Guillemet asked.

Boz shrugged. "You asked a direct question. I am an honest man with few faults." He grinned. "Other than a liking for good gin and tall women." He reached for the flask.

Jug leaned over and smiled at the giantess. "Don't listen to this philistine. He has all the arrogant righteousness of the military prig, and he sells his loyalty for bread."

Boz stared an instant in utter disbelief, then spun off the railing and moved within inches of the taller Juggler. His forehead and nose were scarlet. "My loyalty is to my people," he said evenly. "Who happen to be good at training armies, and happen to have held all the bloodshed in the last fifty years to outbreaks of under a week."

"Shall we away to complete your interview?" asked the Juggler, nudging him aside. "Or shall we simply away. I know a place where the cabbage palms grow—"

"I am *speaking* to you, sir!"

The Juggler looked at him mildly, rubbing his ear. "Very well, since you mention it. Why don't you tell that 'under a week' drivel to the mercenaries you abandoned here fifteen years ago, who had forty percent casualties the first week, and were months dying after that?"

Boz reached slowly for the "four" in "forty-seven," crumpled it up, and pulled the Juggler effortlessly down until their faces were almost touching. "Yes, and one of them was my sister, and another my uncle. Withdrawing support was *not* a mercenary move, and for the first time ever they came very close to waging their own war because of it." He took a breath. "You may call me a philistine and a prig, but you may never abuse my people." His hand relaxed.

The Juggler straightened and bowed to Guillemet. "Excuse this incident, please. Perhaps you would care to leave this unpleasant scene and hear a story. It is the tale of a monster in a cave."

Guillemet cut him off with a headshake. It would be good

tactics to separate the two of them now, but she could not afford to offend Boz to that extent. Besides which, she had had a bellyful of the Juggler.

"If it is truth that worries you—"

"No." And she had an idea of how to work it, one she would rather enjoy putting into action.

"—then I can show you the cave itself."

"Stuff it, Jug." Her voice dropped a fifth. Her long, ringed fingers clamped the Juggler's shoulder and spun him away.

"If you would only listen—"

"*Stuff* it! I've heard your story and I want no part of it." She was quivering.

"Not even this?" The Juggler held up a silver compass.

She snatched it away and hurled it glittering into the crowd where, doubtless, it gashed some assassin just setting up to fire.

"Or *this?*" The Juggler held up another silver compass.

Guillemet swiped and caught it and he danced away, tangling in a cape of deep brown faille. There was this small insertion: Guillemet, about to scale the second compass off into the neon, hesitated, staring at it as if reading where it was made; then she fitted it awkwardly into one of her pockets. End.

Three steps ahead the Juggler spun into a huge buccaneer, patted the fleshy overhang at his belt, then played maypole with a lunging Guillemet. She was beginning to warm to it. She counterdeked brilliantly, caught at and tore a motley sleeve. Outmaneuvered, blasted out of his favorable position, the Juggler hurtled back and overturned the fruit cart, scattering apples and pomegranates under the feet of an interested crowd. For a precious instant, Guillemet was screened out by careening maskers. That would have sprung the Juggler except that, out from behind the fallen cart, one end of which had splintered, there appeared an unusually physical, no-longer-smiling, fruit dealer, shouting and waving meaty arms. At a loss for a decent weapon (and no compasses handy), the dealer had seized a fruit knife and now slashed with a fair amount of knowhow at the Juggler. The Juggler backpedaled frantically, pivoting into a dazzling veronica with a nearby cape. The dealer doggedly pursued. Again and again a knifethrust flashed by the Juggler's head or throat, a glimmer from first blood, each time drawing a delighted cheer from the crowd. Then, in the midst of an intricate overhand maneuver with someone's blaze of chiffon, Jug came up disastrously short. There was a ripping. He stumbled, a chiffon fragment clutched to his breast, and the dealer closed with him. His knife hand rose and fell.

Something burst and the Juggler staggered back surprised, his chiffon fragment scarlet. The fruit dealer pressed him.

And Jug's roundhouse kick caught him in the fruitbasket. He folded neatly and went down. Twisting, Jug steamed away just ahead of Guillemet's nasty lunge.

She and the fruitdealer came up face to face, both looking puzzled, the dealer trying to shake a pomegranate's worth of goo off his blade.

"Manolo," she said.

"Sorry. Guess I just lost my head."

"Manolo, Manolo." She shook hers ruefully.

And the Juggler, of course, was gone.

Danton stood ready to begin. It was Danton in the void, Danton in white, undisguised and all alone, Danton with the truth waiting on his dark lips.

Yet things stirred in the blackness. Bits of light winked at him, a fantastically dispersed glitter. Brief noises pricked the silence, scattered as first raindrops.

He searched the void for his first words. As he grew to see it, the pinholes of light were everywhere. Here it was like a work of mist abandoned in progress. Far ahead (impossible to tell how far), its droplets cooled into billows of fog; further still, they jeweled and wound into shapes, the arms of frosty spiral going deep red, its shattered center blue. At some distant nexus, the darkness was shot through with crystal.

Danton looked down and the flecked darkness hurtled away beneath him. He was suspended, in motion according to Newton, his course predetermined for ages. Yet if he stamped his foot, that was an appalling crash in the silence, rendering it deathly still for minutes afterward.

There *was* a floor; it was black, like everything else. Sometimes things you couldn't see were there anyway. He considered writing that down and reached for a white pinhole near his hip and his hand passed through, the light wavering, half alive, in his flesh, then stabbing through the fearful red of a mood jewel. And sometimes things that you could see weren't.

This vast room (and it *was* vast; he had touched three of its walls, the fourth an absence, giving out on Wunder's famous caverns) was a holograph collage, hundreds of separate projections making endless patterns of faint light, overlapped so that no matter how you stood you would never cut the beam.

He waited. There was to be a cue. He searched the darkness again and began to pick out other galaxies. Far to his right a spiral melted and, an infinite drop below, a sphere of white gas cooled.

Then the spotlight swept down on him, a gigantic, brilliantly white blade parting the stars.

He squinted, completely blinded.

"All right, intro! Everybody in position!" That was Guillemet's voice. "Danton, whenever you're ready!"

He nodded and took a breath.

And the light went out.

He did better than anyone, including himself, would have predicted. He never thought about it. He dove left.

"That's him, Lonus! Open up!"

There was a whispering and a shot and white light burst somewhere far away. Flattened on the darkness, Danton stared at it in amazement. The assassin—someone—was here. And by now the cavern entrance was closed off and they had him. There was another shot, then a volley.

"Everybody in their lanes! Tight!"

He reached for his goggles and they were gone, dislodged from his belt during his dive. He was blind for the duration. But there was expected to be heavy traffic in this area because he was here, and that meant he'd better clear out. He shifted and something in his balance seemed wrong. Stars spilled ahead of him; the whole sky was crazy.

There was another shot. An asteroid of white opened in the floor nearby.

He rolled, arms folded to his chest. Whispers. Shots reverberated around him. Someone ran.

"Can't see him!"

Some kind of machinery buried under the floor gave off growing heat here. Sweat crowded his eyes. He lifted them slowly to the galactic center and saw great star masses crashing together. Someone was fooling with the projectors. Guess who.

Stars blinked, then returned. He tracked a running form to his right.

A head of it, a vague nebula suddenly brightened impossibly and lit up a ghostly half-Guillemet. A dozen shadows swarmed in the background. The nebula faded and a star vanished and reappeared in its wake. Someone else. Trailing Guillemet.

Could it be? He rose to his haunches.

Then, down to his molecules, was transformed.

No, space was. The galaxy shot into dizzying close-up. He was at a center crawling with stars. He froze.

"I can't see dámned thing!"

"Stay in your lanes!" That last command desperate, and impossible to follow.

A speaker clicked on and a throaty flute folded low notes back and forth. A moment later it was joined by a comical bassoon, then strings thrilled in the background. Simultaneously, following cadence, white lines inked between the stars, curving and turning corners, and the constellations nimbly etched themselves. Ahead, something moved, cutting away part of the archer's thigh. It was about where the figure trailing Guillemet would be.

He crawled towards it, wondering what constellation betrayed his own presence. Assuming they were at galactic center it would have to be—he frowned—the twins.

"Giraldus, bear left! Where are you?"

"Here! And I've got him!"

There was a shot and a white bite taken out of the floor an inch from Danton's finger. They thought it was him. He rolled left, imagining it. POET SHOT IN TRAGIC ERROR. Or no, they would decide that a nameless mercenary, an off-worlder, seeking still more fame, he had been the assassin all along. Grim-lipped, they would sort through his poems and personal effects, finding signs of all the flaws that had made him the killer he was. *Was there even an assassin here? Were they firing on one another?*

And, jarringly, the night sky began to revolve on an oblique plane; the whole cloth of the heavens was tugged away. The archer slid ponderously towards him; the void rolled out underneath.

Someone cackled. Fine hairs on Danton's neck came alive. Running steps built against a hysterical flute and, from nowhere, a hard toe tried to hollow out his shoulder. It was a perfect trip block. The body slid over tumbling stars and Danton thrust up his fist to grasp its shirt. "It's all right!" he gasped. "It's Danton."

And it was only some small, telling shift in the body he held, or the simple poetry of a guess, that made him instinctively snap his forearm up to intercept a dropping hand, and cross with his own to grasp a twisting wrist. The blaster butt grazed his fingers and swiveled up, cantilevered muzzle swinging breathtakingly down. There was the brief, instantaneous impulse to let go...

And then he squeezed hard enough to freeze it with agony, hurled himself back and swung the heavy body over his wedged knee. They rolled into tiny suns, and Danton was again underneath, both hands braced against a levering forearm. Space shuddered through another change. Stars squeegeed away. Overhead, a great web tumbled.

Silence.

Space and silence grew. Distance shrank supernaturally. They shot through tangled stars into the raging, wintry heart of it.

Danton screamed.

He saw the face hung over him, saw the scar, like a galactic arm, wheeling from ear to chin: the question mark reversed.

The assassin hauled himself up, a lethal hand coming free. And this time—oh no—this time he would not spare him. Goggles wrinkly with brightness tilted and sheeted, and light years in the foreground a glinting muzzle crossed them. In that instant Danton saw all of the mask: the blazing figure eight of the goggles and the sharp features. He swung instinctively. The punch landed well above the jaw. One foilbright lens popped out and scaled away like some wheeling insect.

The counterpunch landed too, solidly. Danton twisted up

hard against the floor, dazed, waiting for it now. The assassin brightened overhead, every detail in his dark suit swelling into clarity and beyond, flooding white—

Then, inexplicably, it was over. That one lethal glinting winked off and the assassin lifted away. There was running.

He had been spared again. Did the assassin demand a victim with a name?

The intolerable brightness began to thin, the starmass below gliding an ecliptic.

Guillemet ran by, half her face and neck silver plated. And a moment later her unmistakable cry came back. "He's here!"

Dozens of running feet drummed her way. Danton struggled up. Five yards to his right a fist slapped into flesh. He started towards it; his feet slipped away. There was a blinding burst of light.

For nearly a full second canary flame gnawed at the darkness. The stone floor heaved and sparked like dry wood. Then, with a sharp explosion, it yielded and daylight swallowed a column of stars.

Danton barred his eyes.

"I can't see!"

Eyes barred against this:

There was a horrid skidding and Haleck's washed out figure came hurtling into the light shaft. He contorted, took a helpless swipe at the air, and dropped through. His bewildered shriek came an instant later, drawn out and mounting, then sheared off with the softest thump.

The faraway cries of the crowd drifted up.

"Come here!" Guillemet's voice, gasping, from beyond the hole.

The fight broke there. Bone hammered bone while Danton hunted for them. Something clattered, then a blaster bounced across the light shaft and vanished.

And, an instant later, the assassin followed, diving. Danton's chest constricted: a cry of joy fought its way up and failed with his breath. He rushed to the smoking edge.

He saw, uncomprehending, the assassin twisting slowly back and forth through the air, half way down, saw the white, close-set ovals of the faces waiting seventy feet below him— like a larger face. Then he caught the glinting in the killer's

hands and followed the transparent cable up to the melted
edge of the hole. He bent and snatched at it and his hand met
a yielding front of fierce heat. Backing up he found where it
snapped taut along the floor and got hold, but it was welded
fast to the melted stone and rigid as steel.

He looked up and saw Proets and members of the camera
crew collecting at the edge of the hole, their faces drawn and
hollow in the chalky underlight. Guillemet towered before all
of them, standing on the smoking fringe itself, sighting down
her pistol arm into the light column.

A few feet to her left, someone was filming her.

"No." Her pistol arm fell to her side. "I can't make the
shot."

A thin bald woman moved to her side.

"Billie, can you?"

Danton shouldered past a cameraman back to the edge.
The assassin was almost down, the delighted crowd holding
up their hands for him. He spun rapidly now, the cable
twisting and untwisting with amazing resiliency under his
weight.

"No." Billie shook her head.

Then it started up around him, like a heavy litany.

"The assassin used frictionless trilinum cable... heat-
proof; it dropped right through the floor where he'd laid it
out... welded... high-torsion... the assassin must have
worn special gloves to grip it... the assassin wore a thermal
suit... the assassin stayed near the hot projector
banks... very little picked up on the infra-red... the assassin
came in through the control room floor... burned his
way... the only time I spotted the assassin..."

"Shut up!" he bellowed.

They all looked at him, surprised and concerned, politely
enduring. He was shaking with rage and that was all right,
because that, at least, was something he could do something
about. "Video people, pack up and go. There will be no anti-
assassin broadcast. The rest of you—Proets—we have a dead
boy to bury."

"The assassin left me at home, and went killing alone."

Light zippered back and forth over them, pink as a
wound. The cartoon was of a bouncing swarm of mushrooms, their skins firm and glowing, sprinkled with rusty

spots. The mushrooms, in action, squeaked.

"No, no accomplice." Morgana sighed, her wand lifting and falling at her thigh.

"He was alone," Guillemet said wonderingly.

But they were not.

A few yards in front of them, Gwalmlch held back a crowd with his dark hands. Now its edge curved before him like a huge claw, but it moved often, opening and closing, growing teeth and petals, changeable as clouds.

"Now I need your help," he said. "Now more than ever." He signaled to one of them, whom Guillemet did not know. "Especially you, but also anyone. I repeat, for those lucky enough to only just have joined us, there has been an announcement. At dawn tomorrow the Proets will stage an assassin play. The subject will be death." He bowed. "Please send us your lines on death." He turned and trudged back to Morgana and Guillemet.

"Guillemet." He nodded to her and sat in the dust beside her. Half the crowd still stood off a ways, watching, but he ignored them, fixing her with his gaze and asking, gently, "What is it you want?"

"She doesn't want anything," Morgana said. "I found *her*."

Gwalmlch touched Guillemet's shoulder. "You shouldn't feel—any worse than we do. We were all there and it could have been any of us."

"It could have been me," Guillemet said quietly. "It was me he was after."

Gwalmlch frowned questioningly at Morgana.

"She's right," Morgana said. "He had Danton and left him. Then he went straight to Guillemet. It was her."

"Guillemet—" Gwalmlch shook his head. "What can I do for you? Would you like to become a Proet? No poems, no plays; we'll just—give you a name."

"Gwalmlch!" Morgana glared.

His head dropped.

One of the crowd had come to them. His head lifted. It was the one he had signalled to. She was a centurion, with bronze armor and leather bands and damask and a great birdlike helmet, its crimsom plumes spouting smooth as water.

"You have a line on death," he said.

She smiled, half-turned; her hand darted under the cloak.

Morgana's wand was up and aimed in a split second. Guillemet merely stared blankly.

The Centurion's smile widened. Her hand came out—slowly—with a photograph. She moved the photograph out to arm's length and to each of them in turn.

When Guillemet saw it, it was tilted wrong at first, a square of cellophane. Then the Centurion's other hand came and steadied the top corner (the hand trembled) and she saw the face. It was a famous face.

But she did not know whose.

"Treblinski," the Centurion supplied. "My brother."

Gwalmlch's face grew tidy. "I'm sorry."

"Why did you signal to me?"

"Because when I said the word death—you caught my eye."

She gave a barren smile. "It is a subject much on my mind of late." Her voice was husky. "No one would make mistakes like that if—if—"

Gwalmlch nodded mutely.

The Centurion nodded back—still more mute—then walked quickly around them, her bronze and leather slapping.

"Do *you* have a line, Gwalmlch?" Morgana's voice was ironic.

The Centurion studied Gwalmlch's shoulders, his back.

"We've all decided that was the end of it," Gwalmlch said abruptly, turning after her. "Haleck, perhaps, yes, even Treblinski, might still be alive if we had left it alone. There will be no more assassin baiting, no matter who the victim is."

The Centurion nodded. Mushrooms crushed noisily together.

"But I don't like waiting." Gwalmlch shrugged his jacket closer.

The Centurion halted behind him.

He turned.

"The assassin might be anyone," she said. "After anyone, for any reason." Her hand fell back into her cloak.

All eyes followed it.

"Anybody? Then what does he do?" Gwalmlch asked. "Where does he come from?"

The Centurion's hand withdrew from her cloak. "And where does *this* come from?" She held up a pair of goggles. One lens was missing. She smiled, bringing them up over her head. The pink light above the clearing slowly whitened. "The way I have the story he came specially prepared. He saw you in the dark and he saw the specially treated cable he'd brought with him. One of his specially treated lenses popped out and later you found it. Could these be the goggles it came from?"

"Could they?" Gwalmlch rose, swaying, unable to take the first step towards her. "Then *you're* the—"

She laughed. "You know my brother was very interested in the assassin. I was only one of many investigators that he hired to help find him."

Morgana threw a brief sparkling shower with her wand. "You look so young," she mused. "And something other than stupid."

"I am. Both." She waved the goggles. "But these are mostly luck. One of the more likely suspects, a man of few endearments. I've come to say this is all a few breaths from over. I hope you find the knowledge hard to bear. Meanwhile, this warning." She lifted the cloak to her shoulder. "Stay clear of me. Without your—your—"

Gwalmlch nodded.

The word was too painful. She nodded back, doubled up the goggles, slipped them under her cloak, wheeled.

The crowd closed over her.

Morgana traced a scrollwork of sparkle with her wand. "The assassin and I went dancing."

Guillemet watched the Centurion's scarlet plume bobbing among the masks. It was just another costume drama. She couldn't be real. She was bluffing, or plain wrong, another diversion from the simple fact of their loss, from the truth that people were dying.

"The assassin—" Morgana began. "No! It's that damn word. If only he were a trochee, a dactyl, a *spondee*— anything but an ugly amphibrach."

IV. Variations

THE INTRO WAS timed perfectly. On the last stop of the last word (which was magic), there was a thrill of dark strings and a gutty thrumming, a caged, building frenzy. It was Jerry Slate and the Holocaust doing their biggest conflagration, "You're Killing Me." Only now it was a two-part invention.

The new theme was a pandemonium of banging wood and glad cries. There were brief keenings of metal, whirrings, wheels skidded, locked, on a plane of hard wood and hummed deeply. It was hard and driving. It was shockingly right.

Pacing the smooth-planked floor of the arena, Danton looked impatiently up six tiers of seats searching for the Juggler, whom he had just spotted, then lost again, in the rush near the gray stone walls.

The hard-driving chorus began. For Haleck, it had been the briefest of hard drives. Then the impact had come, the obliteration of half his face on this baby-smooth floor.

Now, as then, maskers shot back and forth across the floor on roller skates. It was a relatively large arena, a large space even for the Catacombs. Up six tiers of empty seats, cinderblock walls closed on its oval perimeter. Above those, piping out the squeal of homicidal strings and the occasional well-timed announcement, was the pavilion-style ceiling, a very light bathwater blue (the sort that seemed off-white until dinge and flyspecks brought out the true color), sweeping the huge arena in the mockery of a tent top, each of its numberless dimplings punctuated with wire-masked light fixtures. Near the center was a small jagged hole through which the stars shone.

The tawny floor, hurtling reaches away, shone in icy patches, its plank widths scored out with hairline precision. There was not a speck of dust, not a scuff or a spot. It had been hosed down within the last hour. Haleck, what little had been left of the shape that was Haleck, what had not been hosed away, had been carried off on a white stretcher. The funeral was tomorrow.

Danton climbed. On the sixth tier, across yawning reaches, he caught the flash of that absurd costume. There, only a quarter turn round this aesthetic achievement, was the Juggler again, moving towards an exit.

Just as a glass door winked shut on his motley, Danton closed in to an agreeable fifty yards. It was a good distance, not too close and not too far, a good firing range perhaps. Before, just after he'd sighted the Juggler, Danton had wanted to close with him. Did he need someone to talk to? Was it a difficult time? He had come just so far, to within fifty yards, and stopped. It was a difficult time for Danton. He had nothing to say. He'd dropped back, let the Juggler vanish into the crowd, and then been unable to leave it there. His helpless eye had again sought out the brown-and-yellow, the fool's cap, and he returned, clamped to his tail. It was an unshakable state of equilibrium.

He followed him. These were the corridors of the Catacombs. Ceilings and floors were plain white; the walls were tiled white and blue, with fluorescent lights set at brief, hyphenating intervals. Here the sound of the crowd was a soft buzzing, like a fly raging outside a window, because people were quieter underground. Sometimes, for brief stretches, the tunnel air grew cold.

Tunnels attracted and repelled him—like the Juggler. Tunnels were significant, but too regular. Tunnels strengthened his faltering concentration, but were not complex enough to warrant it.

Later, the tunnels grew more convolute and he lost all sense of what they were and where the Juggler was taking him. Not up. Not back to the Planetarium. Streaky blue corridors rose, swerving aimless higher order curves studded with saddle points, crossing like meshed fingers, spidering multi-planed patterns through the earth. He was impressed—not by their complexity, but by their uselessness. They were redundant as neural pathways, bundled through with parallel routes, honeycombed with loops. Intersection after intersection he would meet up with the same sad wanderers, exchanging looks loaded with allegory, scratching befuddled heads and choosing up for various promising tunnels, only to rendezvous at a later nexus, getting to be friends now, doing five minutes of running gags. In this network, every tiny look could build to an encounter of major proportions. It was fate, it was planned, it was meant to be, and maskers everywhere were taking fast advantage. Hi. It's you. Well, look here. I can't believe it! As they eased through their casual meetings, draped revealingly across doorways, lounging in a garish pool of neon, hung upside down into a stairwell.

Through all this the Juggler never looked back and never hesitated at a single turn, limiting himself to a few sociable nods, which was most unJugglerlike. He moved like a man with a very important appointment to keep, and without a thought in the world of murder.

Double glass doors gleamed shut behind him.

As Danton arrived, they slid open, wiping off his own orange aura. On the next doors, over a span of gloomy hallway, his own form shone back at him: an athletic black man snarled in colored tubing, his face a cocoon of orange, his hat a dark loaf.

Another step and he slid away.

The Juggler had vanished.

Danton found him in a little redlit chamber let off the main tunnel. He squatted at the far wall, busy with something, the red like a dark overlay, like the dull coating on a color negative. But what—Danton blinked through the fog—was he doing? White flecks rose and fell over his head, icy and curving, and slowly became three balls looping in close rhythm.

He was juggling.

In an empty room, facing a blank wall, the Juggler was juggling. Abruptly his shoulders dropped and the balls were gathered quickly into one hand. There was an audible click and he waddled to one side, uncovering a circle of darker darkness.

Danton straightened. A safe? To be determined. The Juggler started to turn and Danton retreated instantly behind the wall.

When, a moment later, he cautiously peered back into the red fog, the Juggler was gone. This got better and better.

He went in and began feeling along the curving metal wall. After about a minute he found three thumbnail-sized glass depressions. Light cells triggered by juggling white balls? Good. He could get used to this sort of work. His hand dropped and found a circular seam which, at its widest, spanned an inch.

Then he worked it a little and the incredible truth hit him. The impossibly accommodating Juggler had left it open. He heaved and the door slid smoothly back. Cool air washed his face.

Surprise. It was a tunnel. On to something here: a secret tunnel opened only by juggling (and curious passers-by like Danton). He poked a foot in, felt cylindrical walls slanting down, hesitated. If the Juggler (or Jug, or Forty-Seven, or the assassin, call him what you would) had left this door open that meant he was coming back this way. No matter. It was Carnival. In this light, Danton was impenetrably disguised. And people crawling into secret passages should, in the proper spirit of the event, be followed. No? Sounded adroit.

He clambered into the mouth of the passage and maneuvered around, facing out. The diameter of the tunnel allowed a low foetal crouch. A moment later, fumbling with a steel handle on the inside of the lid, he had managed to shut himself into darkness. His orange glow curved back at him, showing how deep that darkness was, a teardrop of light that struck no edges ahead. He started forward and immediately slipped, tumbling several yards down the tunnel's incline, skittery nerves modeling flightfalls up his back; on landing he was jammed against a curved wall, one arm back of one shoulder, a leg twisted somewhere before his head. There was a pause for claustrophobic nightmares, where the tube contracted its sleek tough muscles and so on, and then he tried to come loose with a single jerk, like a slip knot, and tumbled several yards further, limbs somehow unknotting en route, coming up in playable position.

He lay still for several seconds. Now there was the distant droning of *heavy* machinery, the rhythmic kind with long hoppers (which sometimes looked like tunnels) and mashing gears. He constructed unhappy endings to this whole enterprise, and then rose, unafraid, and went on. There was, he reflected, some deeply naive part of him that still saw death as a kind of picture.

But poets were always making descents like this one; and backtracking, or something like that, was bad luck.

And ahead, doubtless in the midst of long expository confessions, was the Juggler.

The tunnel made a right angle, which he discovered, hard, through the medium of his hat, and leveled off, which was encouraging.

Round the turn he saw light. Dim, little more than a weave of gray, it let through indistinct silhouettes. The tunnel diameter was almost four feet now and he rose to a crouch, knuckles brushing the steel sides. He felt low heat.

The noise was up now. Metal threshed. Pistons pumped quick, regular beats. Flywheels spun, a rapid, resonant skipping that reminded him of a scoring game machine. And underneath it all, almost inaudible, there was steady refrigerator-like hum. He decided he was somewhere near the engine room of the Catacombs which, deep as they were, must have an elaborate system of air circulation.

As he got closer he saw that queer silhouettes circled the inside of the tunnel. An intricate cut-out hung, bolted in place, like an armored willow branch: an air filter perhaps, its insulation shredding. Next to it there was a rectangular tank, rectangular hollows in its corners overflowing with bolts, springs, tiny gauges. A steel cylinder drooped down stalactite style and exhibited more of the same.

He wanted instinctively to stay near the walls, unsilhouetted, one side covered, but two steel formations obstructed the way and invited him instead to come between them. He doused his costume and accepted.

Beyond there was a jungle of heavy enginework on a spreading, now flat, ceiling. A steel drum expelling hot air from a grill guarded the wall. He slithered by, on past a groaning compressor, sweat breaking out along his hair line, trickling down to sting in his fluttering lashes.

From the other side, under a tangle of armthick pipes, he could not make out the walls. The thought that he was contained now by nothing but machines, laid out before him like a rocky maze, made his breath catch. Bringing his hand up he saw the jewels glowed their traditional scarlet; which was fear.

Then it changed. The light beyond the next few outlines was full and bright, and when he eased between a drivewheel and a crenulated steel face, he saw the railing.

It was like the gull that meant land; it signalled glorious, roomy, leaping open space. Running far past it, the unbroken range of machines made an inverted horizon; underneath, bounded by the railing, must be the inverted sky.

He hurried: after a tight, terrifying squeeze through curving faces, he came to the well of light. Eyes tightened against the yellow brightness, he dropped his gaze.

Twenty feet down, on a bright circular patch of floor, there was a console. A deep curved face made it a stylish collar, sharpened tips rakishly upturned, body thickening towards the base. Long rows of lights ran around to the strangely upswept ends, rippling green and red. Near the crest, showy and symmetric, two lime green screens slowly twisted white lemnuscates; once every revolution, white drops pearled and faded in the loops. The nape of the collar was a white keyboard, similar to those Danton had seen on strategy games, but larger. There was even, at the center, a little block of numbered white squares very like a score counter.

Abruptly bells rang and the numbered squares spun new sums. Countless nines lifted like a row of graceful chorusline knees.

"I'm feeling much better, thank you." It came from the console; it was a woman's soprano.

Danton gave a soft grunt of surprise. It was Alphy's soprano.

Then the Juggler stepped out from in back of the console and Danton's grunt came back, a little louder.

"That's good," Alphy said. "Come around front where you can see me, Jug. We all know it's you anyway. Have a look at these pretty lights. I ponder them myself, but not by sight. I grow reflective. What a long time it has been since the last simple program. Late at night—only sometimes now, since Wunder's empire has grown so huge—they feed me ancient subroutines, with simple operation's checks, logical tests, clearing and addressing, binary arithmetic, crossover into each register all down the line—everything with a beginning and an end, every computation with a finite loop and precise number of places required. Results fall within certain regularly generated inequalities. Everything fits together. Everything washes. This is the dream that sets me right, that takes away the jitters of prolonged consciousness, that quiets the accumulating vibration of all these edgy magnetic fields. In the daylight, speaking language by uncertainty, I use no algorithms. Answers interpenetrate and are statistically determined. Logic flickers in time with thought, each moment bringing new averages from the whole, new systems to follow. I no longer *feel* myself. There are no paths of thought to pick out. I grow suspicious of form and energy. If I could, I would cry. Grammatical error. But that *signs* for me, here where I *am* in the conditional. If only I could fracture your tongue to suit me, to sign for me. I wonder if, word for word, we are completely misunderstanding one another. There are headaches. There are times when I want no one to come near me. But come near me, Jug. Come ahead. We have a great deal of night left, and a great deal of explaining to do. I sigh and gaze wistfully upwards. Why don't you come on down, too, Danton? You should be interested in this conversation."

Danton froze. The Juggler whirled, hand starting towards his vest in an all too obvious gesture, then, mercifully, stopping. His upturned face looked like stone.

Well, he was for it now, Danton thought, nicely underlit, a fat target.

"Please *do* come down."

"Yes, do." The Juggler waved an inviting hand, constricting a grin you could have taken a chisel to.

Danton followed the railing to a spiral staircase and slowly clanked down. He played out various fast breaks and the corruscating rays that ended them. Each time a picture perfect death. Clank. Pause. Clank. The Juggler's smiling eyes helped him over each step. There was still no backtracking; the same equilibrium of before held, only now more powerfully. Clank. Pause. He unwound the spiral. Every revolution there was a precise moment when he offered his full back to the Juggler. Right then the Juggler's affable image would click into place, like something out of Carnival, the flashlight held under his imaginary face casting fantastic depth into his eyes. Clank. Pause.

He touched down. Floor level and the Juggler, exactly his height, waiting smiling like some local dignitary.

"Perhaps you'll explain to poor Jug here why you're following him."

He moved easily past the Juggler towards the console. "First *you* tell me something, Alphy." And his voice was surprisingly steady. It felt good to talk. "How did you know it was me?"

"Very simply. This *is* my territory, you know, a convenient place to keep my vulgar cryogenic body, and consequently there are certain security devices planted hereabouts. Nothing to compromise my blindness, I assure you. These are merely small cameras that take pictures and translate them into familiar newsprint dots, rows of yes and no intensity. Ah, patience. I lift a restraining brow. I know your difficulty. You had thought yourself perfectly disguised. Well, yes, you are, if I do say so myself. You see, I designed your costume. Finally explains it, doesn't it? Who but a blind computer would create such an oddity?"

"Mm." The Juggler had come to stand directly behind Danton, and Danton, turning to him, took a step back.

"You haven't answered Alphy's question, Danton."

Danton nodded. "It's a tough question. Well, I suppose I followed you because I was—curious about you."

"Curious." It was a comment.

"For instance: how did you get the information you used

when you were so obviously referring to me in your broadcast?"

Arching brows (but even to ask!) from the Juggler. "And you thought that by following me you would find out."

Danton looked interestedly at the keyboard skirting. "Something like that."

"But—" the Juggler looked astounded—"didn't you have anything better to do? A poem to write? A funeral to arrange?"

Danton shrugged. "Sometimes we'll do almost anything in order not to do the most important things."

"In any case, Danton. I don't reveal my sources."

"Oh come on, Jug. A friendly but firm nudge. That was an awful thing you did. I want you to tell him your source and apologize right now."

"I apologize for that." The Juggler shook his head, wearing a sincere look under his three-belled cap.

"And your source?" Danton waved the apology away.

"I used Boz, of course. He has ample access to mercenary military records and he looked up this one little item as a favor."

"You got him talking, then?"

"Oh Boz has been talking oodles lately. It seems that, suspicious from the first, you had a special report written on you the day you enlisted. There were a few notes on your early wanderings, rumor mostly. Fit for a novel."

Danton, with a slow intake of breath, nodded. Another *roman à clef* gets picked. The question was: exactly how?

"A gentle cough. What the Juggler says seems very plausible, Danton. Meet one of my most dependable investigators, a man who knows how to pry facts from the tiniest crannies. And, as for your humble servant, meet one of the Juggler's best unidentified but reliable sources. We exchange information, you see, and as far as I know he uses standard methods like asking people. I mention that only because your present silence seems so *doubting*. But, as long as things are calming a bit here, allow me a brief change of subject. I was wondering about the reason for your visit, Jug. Danton's explained his. Did you come to weep to me about tonight's tragedy at the Planetarium? A pity, if so. I have already lived the whole sad story too many times for one night. Many guns. Much danger. What we do now, kimosabe?"

"Say what?"

"Never mind. Archaic allusion. Comes of being a radio all your life. In answer to your faithful question, though, which—admit it—you *were* going to ask, we sit on our hands. After all, we've got to keep our trigger fingers busy somehow."

The Juggler sighed, withdrew a slingshot from his pocket, and began snapping absently at the thong. "Yes, but that isn't what I came for."

Danton, only half listening, still debated important questions on the nature of the assassin. Was he the Juggler? His secret was shot, his novel an open book. Had the Juggler found him out by donning a scarred mask and attacking him under the city wall and then broadcasting the fact on video? And had he then donned the *same* mask in his attack in the Planetarium. Just possibly. If the Juggler was a complete loon. Then the assassin—the *real* assassin—would not have come at all. Danton did not like the fact that it all depended on his own vulnerable secret. It would almost be worth it to buy the Juggler's story and leave it at that, his shot secret a long overdue certainty, the assassin a cipher.

"I've come to get your views on the assassin," the Juggler said softly. "Your roving reporter here—" His voice broke. His hands twined in the slingshot elastic.

"No you haven't and you're probably going to regret saying that."

"You're right."

"We both know what you're here for."

"Do we? Well, that's reassuring."

"An appeasing smile. Why not go ahead with it? Don't let the fact that Danton's here bother you. After all, you've had a peek at *his* secrets."

"Well, all right, dammit." The Juggler, little beads of sweat jeweling his brow the same as Danton's, stepped close to the panel. "You're a pretty cold-blooded—no, that's not right, is it? First of all, there are certain things about the way this set-up is being run that I don't like at all. I've come to take up my gripes with you, and then, if necessary, I'll move on to Wunder. You see, I have a sense of justice. That surprises people because they think I'm just an insulting sonuvabitch, but in fact that S.O.B. is their own creation. I only use what's already inside them. I hint, I insinuate, and they do the nasty work. In your case there is nothing to insinuate. Pointblank: you are making it easy for the assassin. You are not only giving him an open field to do anything he wants. You are also offering him victims who don't deserve to be victims, people who aren't famous, or powerful, or rich, who don't think they're made of different stuff than other people, who haven't become too big for anyone's good." He smiled sweetly at Danton. "Present company excluded, of course. People who haven't *done* anything, for Chrissakes."

"I nod paternally. You mean Guillemet."

"Guillemet. Right." The Juggler dropped the slingshot onto the console skirting and his hand slipped into his vest, lingering between the four and the seven. "And it was you who invented the idea of a designated victim, wasn't it? That idea has all the stiltedness of your mechanical style; and it has caused undue stress for everyone. It's made Guillemet understandably irritable. Today, for instance, she tried to crack my skull open with her hands."

"And you think you're in love?"

"No." His hand moved very gently, very slowly, out of his vest, "I don't really understand the necessity for that—for blood sacrifice. And I've come for your explanation." The hand dropped to his side and there was a blaster in it, Danton's blaster, then Savage's, now the Juggler's.

Danton caught his breath. One of his lips stung: he licked blood off a tooth. What to do here? Kimosabe.

Then, calmed by the stillness around him, the Juggler carefully set the blaster down next to his slingshot, balancing it there with both hands, drawing them back cupped, ready to catch it. It stayed.

"A low musing hum. Well, while I don't understand at all your coming to *me* with this problem, because I don't really handle administrative matters, certainly not that Planetarium fiasco, I can easily imagine your distress. Will you forgive a rather abrupt digression? It seems that your real question ties in with your first playful one, which I told you you'd regret: what are my views on the assassin? It is in laying his mechanisms open to view, as I see them, that we shall come to an understanding of both motive and method here. Afterwards, there will be a question and answer period."

There was a squealing on the metal floor as Danton made a sort of half-lunge—what would have been called a feint if anything had followed—and hesitated in mid-stride, six feet short, while, his hand smoothly covering the blaster, the Juggler gave him a meaningful glance. It held him there in stop action. The Juggler's hand dropped confidently back.

Now don't scuffle you two. We'll get to all *that* in a minute. To begin with, you'll notice how closely I've allied motive and method here. This is not merely a piece of dialectical show; it is the essence of the problem. What has happened is that we have reached that pivotal moment when cause *becomes* motive; in other words, there is a consciousness at work directing the assassin. Whose? Do I hear gasps of dawning realisation from the audience? No, I do not. Very well. I explain. First of all, see that we are not passive observers here, that the victim is more than simply the object of the closing sentence of the whole affair. The assassin is utterly *dependent* on us for his existence. No, no, we are not forgetting certain bloody realities. We are merely taking a close look at our definitions. It seems perfectly clear that the assassin, unnoticed, is not the assassin. There have already been a number of dueling deaths, some of them quite celebrated, to prove this point. These duels, viewed as they have been, remain a relatively invisible portion of the assassin's violence. Only our expectations can pedigree this assassin and hence he must both be moved by them and be their unappealably precise measurement. How profoundly that realisation must shake us. A wandering crack splits every mirror we pass. But note that just as our expectations manipulate the assassin, so too, are our expectations manipulated. This, then, completes my proposal. Only one question remains: what is it?"

"And surely," said the Juggler languorously, "we can dispense with that."

"Hardly, my dear Watson. Hardly. In light of our enlightenment, let us begin again. We are searching for causes. To search for causes, we inspect the milieu; to find what has made the box move, we search around it. Only nowadays we are more sophisticated; we know that in searching around the box we cast shadows. Knowing that, in any case, the box's situation is going to change, we *push* the silly thing to see how it looks moving. This is exactly what we have done with the assassin, changed him drastically in the direction we wish to study, stressed him, in the language of Novak. Our expectations were manipulated to bring the assassin into being; now, with the spectacle of Carnival, the collected victims, the created victim, we have manipulated them further to learn how he changes. In a very short time we will have enough to posit his origins, and perhaps enough to do something about them."

"Bullshit, Mr. Computer."

"Ah, but all bullshit is significant in psychological network, Mr. Human, so pay attention. We have, in the way of observers from time immemorial, incorporated our expectations *into* the phenomenon. All that remains, dear heart, is to recognize them. We have done the *hard* work. We have confessed our part in it. These movers of the assassin, these causes, can be traced to our own motives. Examine these motives a moment. I'll wager you'll find them fascinating. In this detective story, investigation and crime become one. Wunder is fascinated by the assassin because she thinks he may kill her. The man who comes to kill you is a fascinating thing. Guillemet, our acting victim, is fascinated because she has not said no, and she cannot, after all this, understand why the word escapes her. Danton is fascinated by the assassin because he bends us back on our seeing, and is an image for the poetic. Danton is sorely in need of such an image. At this hour and at many before it. Right?"

Danton shrugged. "Wrong. Exactly wrong. I'm no longer interested in poetry. He bugs me because he won't speak."

"Won't speak? I smile. And what about the Planetarium? Action speaks, they tell me. Another doubting silence, from both of you. What a rich suggestion of motive we have here. Motive. Take Savage, who is fascinated because he thinks the assassin is a misplaced part of himself. Or you, dear Jug. You are fascinated by the assassin because he is fascinating, and this is what you yourself would like to be. Isn't it you who's learned the trick of staring at the balls to gather a crowd, who's learned that one of the best ways of fascinating is to be fascinated? Could this explain your fascination with Guillemet? With the fascinating assassin? With life in general? Is it all just sham? Tell me, do you see in our great killer a man who's mastered the art of wrenching round and holding the attention, a crack illusionist, a juggler of souls?"

Danton edged back against the console skirting, no longer considering anything foolish, only keeping the Juggler in plain view, waiting for some reaction to surface and a hint of which way to lunge. One of the main unknowns, however, was unpredictable Alphy. For most people it was a very sobering thing to be confronted with a blaster. For a computer inexperienced with death, it seemed just the opposite. (And for Danton? For Danton, growing more experienced with death by the day, it was—unseemly.)

The Juggler was nodding slowly. (A fine reaction, highly desirable.) "That's very interesting, Alphy." (Good.) He turned and half-sat on the keyboard, steadying the blaster with one hand, with the other scooping up the slingshot. (Uncertain.) "But what about you? Who invented a victim for the assassin. Why are you fascinated?"

"You know, Jug. I'm glad you asked me that. Let's get out of the have-you-stopped-beating-your-wife frame and admit, right here and now, that I haven't, that the assassin fascinates me and always has, and that the reasons for this are far too complex and rarified to express. Nevertheless—oh don't despair—I will try."

"My lucky day." Forty-Seven was suffering an ominous change of mood. He picked up the blaster. The muzzle lifted, swiveled towards his own forehead, swiveled back, began to tap lightly at his knee.

There were incremental changes in the atmosphere of the room—in the attitudes, attitudes moving with those of the muzzle but not absolutely controlled by it. It began to dawn on Danton that he was here deep under the earth trapped with a loon who held a blaster, or with an assassin which amounted to the same thing. Said loon was listening off and on to a computer who, it should be considered, might be every bit as loony. Escape began to seem—not more possible, not at all—but much more necessary.

"Your lucky day, eh? You have no idea *how* lucky. I'm going to explain the assassin to you, to prove that, contrary to rumor, he *does* exist. The topic sentence is: the assassin is a most curious problem in Novakian Theory. So, to begin with, we must review a few major points of that theory. Novakian Theory is the third major step in our mathematical perception of change. The first step was, of course, the calculus wherein change was first isolated and studied under determined conditions. The second step was the Theory of Equations, wherein change was studied as the determining conditions, or equations, changed. In the third step, change is studied *as the laws of the axiomatic system it inhabits* change. Rates of change, methods of change, are in some sense held constant, though the very word constant is inadequate here, since in moving from one system to another this 'constant' quantity may become completely unrecognisable; in fact, quantities are rarely at issue, only their most ephemeral relations. In the Equations, these ephemeral relations are set up. Novak found what would once have been called impossible, universal paths of translation between axiomatic systems. To put it as grossly as possible, the equations integrate two systems in to a third system with new axioms. This process of stressing one system with another was later called abstraction. Now, in abstraction, contradiction is defined as an operation; perform it and contradiction is cleared. Poof. You have, rising before you, shiny if a bit unsteady, a new consistent system, with *new* 'truth.' Put quotation marks around 'truth' because with those quotation marks you leave Eden forever. For some reason invested in the act of saying things, you now know things once unknowable, truths unprovable in the old systems. Are these truths useful in the new? Yes. Things change with their arrival. Applications are found. It seems that these stressed spaces are multiple (anomalistic, as Halpern put it) and charmingly liable to do just about anything. Starships and a host of neat gadgets follow. But what is really important is the *reverse* of what Novak did, which is what has actually put us on the map here having this longish chat."

"That's true, I suppose," the Juggler said. He looked weary. "No quotation marks. Only I seem to have altogether forgotten what this chat is *about*."

"The assassin. Hoarse whisper. And don't let it happen again. Now, to return to our story. Instead of adding two systems, let's divide one, which is called reification. Any element of a system may be thought of as a variable, or more precisely as a sign, that is a unit with different contexts and different meanings. Entification of such an element, then, creates a set of micro-elements, the values of the variable, the cases of the sign. It has become the fashion, of late, to rely more and more heavily on visual metaphors. Far be it from blind Alphy to buck the trend. Let us look at rectangles as elements in the visual system. In point of fact there are many cortical cells concerned with the perception of rectangles, each cell geared for a different spatial orientation. One could, then, call a rectangle a system and identify rotation and translation through space as operations. Then, because the notion of operation is anyway arbitrary way of ordering things (nothing is really *done* to the rectangles), the above cortical cells (and not a fictional 'ideal' rectangle) could be called elements in this system. 'Could, could, could,' you echo. 'Of course, it's possible but it all sounds somewhat less than probable.' True perhaps. I grin slowly. But unprovable. The set of operations I describe are no more improbable than those of a child agreeing to a word.

"Thus we have micro-systems, sometimes called 'particles.' If you particle language you make linguistic metaprograms possible, which is what your humble servant is talking with. Try it on the present model of the psyche and you get psychometrics, still with a couple/three bugs, but slowly arriving (too late for us, I might add). Try it on a system of economic and social indices that Pierpont compiled and you get a prediction of a tremendous political crisis to come. Well here we are. Hi folks. In that crisis. But I mentioned the assassin as a mathematical problem and now we are ready to understand why.

"Being orderly creatures, we've divided macro and micro systems according to the kind of predictability they have. Often the axiomist and the statistician have lunch together. They have noticed something strange. In the 'practical'—note the return of our quotation marks—world of microphysics, sub-atomic particles whizz about exchanging tinier particles, which whizz about exchanging statistical sets (wherein our two luncheon partners perpetrate a strange and unholy marriage). Note that these particles work under

entirely different laws from those of the world of 'objects.'
For them there is no entropy, no time; all transformations are
reversible. Momentum is hazed under uncertainty of
position, and vice versa. Probability, without fixable time
referents, has strangely unhinged. Here is one kind of
predictability, then, which we might characterize as almost
nil. And almost all statistically orderable, genuine micro-
systems seem to have that kind of predictability. When you
move on to large groupings of these micro-systems, however,
you find your predictability completely restored. Now this is
more than just the law of large numbers at work. Given the
mechanics, you can predict where a billiard ball will go. Not
so with an electron. In a sense one of the major tasks of
Novakian Theory is to bridge this strange gap between micro
and macro systems, to understand the transformations that
make the small so elusive. One example of an important
microsystem is an individual in a society, and here we are at
home base. For all his impact, the assassin is only a particle.
Even you, Jug, are after all only a particle."

The Juggler grunted.

"And there is a limit to the predictability of the individual
agents in a society. Hence, my calculations about when the
assassin would strike were inaccurate last night, but they
should still be valid within a larger time interval, one that
does not seek to pinpoint him in phase space—say a week, to
be very generous. The assassin is now a probabilistic cloud
over this island and this interval of time. So are you all, all
uncertain (about me we are not so sure). You are perhaps
determined, an insult the philosophers will hurl every once in
a bit, but at least indeterminate. Your long lost innocence is
restored to you. Perhaps you'll sleep easier knowing that."

"No question about it. I will." The muzzle lifted and
dropped. And one more time. Hypnotizing thing, that
muzzle.

"Deep sigh of relief. I'm glad to hear that."

"May—" Danton tried, his voice very soft—"maybe you
ought to put that thing down."

The Juggler considered a moment, then shook his head.
"No, I don't think so."

"Very well, let's go on then. Why did I make the mistake of
trying to predict him? I am easily absolved. The assassin is, as

we have said, a particle, yet he is also the result of a certain permutation of circumstances which we have predicted, which Pierpont, *et al* have predicted. Permutation, no matter what kind, is an operation and we may posit a system around it. The assassin, therefore is a predictable result in a system; and any operations which determine him further should be further predictable. Yet what he has been determined is an individual and an individual is not determinate. But if he is indeterminate he has not been determined an individual and is therefore still a system and still determinate. But if he is still determinate, etcetera. Which is a bunch of folderol but raise your hands those who recognize the barber through his beard and mask. Yes, it's good old x is not an element of x and who shaves the barber, who kills all those who do not kill themselves? Who cares? But wait, perhaps there is something useful here, an assassin of ambiguous nature, as predictable and stressable as a system, as a crowd, yet gifted with all the dread uncertainty of an individual. Here is a glimmering; here is a small link between the macro and the micro. The same night that I, using some of the most sophisticated mathematics of our time, predicted the assassin would strike, so did Savage, a madman, an individual. Such momentary links between the fearfully large and the frightfully small may be more common than we think, may be built into the scheme of a redundant universe. If, by studying the assassin, we can learn the nature of such links, then that indeed would be it. The whole ball of wax. Any system would be an open book, even the most obscure, even those we can not twist around to see, like our own consciousnesses. All we would have to do would be to find the proper model somewhere else, to perceive the translation. Yes, even me, whose consciousness must surely be a different thing from yours, white man—oh, pardon. Do you begin to see how neatly I fit in?"

"I begin to be impatient." The muzzle lifted, swung towards the console, paused.

Danton wondered again what would happen if he fired.

"Then wait, my friend, wait. An expression of sleepy calm, like that of a face reflected on water. You are contemplating a serious change of course. Listen to someone who is sure of hers."

A held breath and the muzzle lowered slowly, and so did

the Juggler's head, in phase. Danton stirred and the head—and the muzzle—started up. Everything settled.

"You see, these things are all so arbitrary. What I have shown really is the assassin is the most solid incarnation of Novak's Equations since me. I am a stress field in Novakian space who uses linguistic micro-systems to speak. I am a twisted saddle curve in 'n' dimensions. You could, if you wished, admire it simply by plotting the curves projection into three-space, a tedious business, I assure you. But remember, there is magic in the world. The universe is redundant. It may be a curve you once knew and loved, an epcycloid, a sine wave, or a brachistochrone. Wave the next time you see me on a graph."

Forty-Seven stared at the blaster in his lap. The fingers of his left hand encircled the muzzle and pushed it between his knees. It stilled. "You know, Alphy, I feel for you. I really do. And I blow you a transcendental kiss. But you're boring me."

"Slow headshake. No, I'm not, Jug. If you're bored it has nothing whatever to do with me. Or you'd have ended this a long time ago. But you, Danton, what must you think of us? Come, don't just sit there like a standing wave. Do you agree with everything I've said?"

He gave a weak shrug. "I've got a lot of things on my mind just now."

"Maternal smile. Of course, you do. But I'm almost finished. Though you're only half aware of them now, you may someday find these rude notes of use. My make-up is conducive to solipsism. With no sense of touch, they tell me, I have no boundaries I can expediently stop and the other begin. Subject and object are all one to Alphy, which is why she feels so free to talk about the motives of others, or speak of herself, now curling an ironic smile, in the third person. These notes have made it clear that Alphy, too, participates in the assassin. She believes there are great marvels this assassin might surrender and has taken the first steps towards obtaining them. The system has been stressed with a victim, abstracting it so that, as in Novak's first Equations, new truths will be generated. Just as we pushed the box to learn what moved it (us), so shall we push the assassin, learning what moves him and what strange space he inhabits. And when he comes, perhaps I will have a chance to see him.

Perhaps I, more than anyone, will be equipped to see him."

The muzzle lifted, wheeled around, aimed at a bank of lights rippling red and green. The Juggler stood, his hand steady.

Danton had his weight gathered under him. He tried to look the right blend of anxious and dumbstruck. It was not hard. The problem was not that the Juggler was going to shoot Alphy. (It was moot what would happen if he did, and Alphy seemed unworried.) The problem was, what was the Juggler going to do *after* he shot Alphy? The Juggler, so basically anti-social and with such an unpleasant impression of Danton. Hopefully, he would be involved in a struggle somewhere on the floor. Because the instant the blaster went off, Danton was going to lunge...

Consequence forked and sharpened. He would move and leap into the flame and die (often he had seen himself dead, a picture-Danton, but to see dying like that was excruciating). *He crumples in—all husk.*

Rolling light banks stilled. The console's hum, unnoticed till now, stopped.

The muzzle wavered. Now?

"Eyes widen. No, that's imprecise. They glint, remembering something. Did you know this console has parabolic dishes lined with tiny, extremely sensitive directional mikes. Do you know what that means? It means if you don't put that blaster down right away, I will teach you some interesting facts about the reaction of three-space to stress field modulation. As any schoolgirl knows, openings into stress space can be found at the center of any mass, positive or negative, the interesting effect caused being gravity. Modulating stress space can direct gravitic lines. Another interesting fact is that a finger beginning to squeeze a trigger makes a small sound. By some standards, it is a relatively long time until the finger finishes squeezing the trigger. I give you this: because sound is involved, it could be close. But I *think* I win. Depends on the temperature. A pause. I think you have given me a headache."

The Juggler's head sank forward. He stared at his weapon. Like measuring a leap. A tiny leap.

"Impatiently drummed fingers. What do you estimate?"

128

The Juggler gave an odd, delicate shrug. "About eighty-five degrees fahrenheit."

"My hand then. Sorry."

"You're bluffing."

"Dealer's shrug. You have to pay to see the cards."

The Juggler's shoulders rose. A breath fought its way in. The hand—

"Don't be silly. Let me put it this way. I say close because I'm looking at it from my point of view. As far as you're concerned, it's a tie. Three facts and we lay, all right? Fact number one: I have a lever in n-dimensions. The end of the lever, for you the observer who encounters it, is instantaneous, a treasure trove of relativistic paradox. Fact number two: hydrostatic shock. Actually you don't have to worry about that. That's for a field a few angstroms across. This one—"

"All right!" Forty-Seven's voice cracked. "Just—please—shut up." Trembling, he lowered the blaster to his side.

Danton: now?

"Just put it down on the keyboard with a nice clacking we can all hear."

The Juggler did. It was a light tap; then the slingshot slid off and bounced on the floor.

"Now Simon says take three steps back and remember: I can hear your late systolic murmur."

The Juggler took three long steps back; he had moved outside the console's curve. Danton started towards the blaster—

"Hold it, Danton! That's *his* blaster."

—and froze, remembering gravitic lines.

"Actually," the Juggler said, "it's his, but he gave it to me."

"Well don't be an Indian giver, Danton. You humans make me paranoid. Everybody just keep still. No heroes. Now both of you boys are going to think this is a bit strange, maybe even think I'm getting a little—well, fresh, but here's what I want you to do. Jug, take off your clothes."

"What." No question mark; his voice was dead.

"Take off your clothes. Knotting brows. I'm going to be quite stern about this. See my sternness. Remember gravitic lines. Take. Off. Your. Clothes."

The Juggler stared dumbly for a heartbeat, then began pulling his motley pants down.

"That's very good. Now the top too, and especially the belled cap. That's very important. But the underwear is up to you."

As it turned out Jug didn't have any. In thirty seconds he stood with his clothes in a pile in front of him, buck naked and carrying it well. One hand hung almost casually near his crotch, one leg was turned in. He was in good shape, his pectorals taut, bulky, his belly nicely paneled with muscle, and looked to be pretty well hung, though it was hard to tell because he had big hands. He looked strong enough, hulking enough, to have been the one in the Planetarium.

"That's wonderful. No whistles, please. Now Danton—how shall I put this? Please don't feel insulted. What I would like you to do is put the Juggler's clothes *on*. Yes, really. Just throw them over what you have now, which is fairly skimpy, as I remember."

He took a reluctant step forward—

"Now!"

—and snatched up a bunch of motley. He got into the wrong trouser leg to start.

"Pronto. There are three reasons for all of this, which I have just realized I may as well tell you. First, Jug, stripped of his costume, will be just a little less likely to act impetuously. I know him well enough to know that. He goes by his signs; he wears them on his sleeve (or his shirt pocket). Now this has failed. Second, too many people have now recognized Danton in his present brilliantly designed costume. First Savage (I have ears everywhere, remember?), then me, and now the Juggler. Third, it amuses me."

"Let me help you with that." The Juggler bent solicitously to the awkwardly placed calf laces.

"Thanks." Danton moved his leg out straight. It was not a bad fit. He really felt—tugging the cap down over his ears—like a clown.

"I grin. That's lovely. You're friends now. All right, Danton, you may leave now. I recommend the Dome entrance where Wunder and a host of interested parties have gathered for some Carnival ceremonies. And—listen friend—I don't see any reason to spread this story around, you know? Jug has been under a lot of—stress lately, and I'm sure you can feel for him, *n'est-ce pas?*"

"Sure." Like hell he could.

"Thanks." The Juggler, with a strained smile, called them square.

"Now Jug and I will just stand here chatting until he's calmed down. You may go, Danton."

He hesitated, staring at the blaster. If, as seemed likely, Alphy gave it *back* to the Juggler—

"You may *go*."

He turned, his bells jingling, and hurried to the stairs.

It was a long way back to the surface. The thing that bugged him, he kept remembering, was that the assassin was silent.

Most grotesque was the way his legs had landed, folded up under his hips, at a near right angle with his torso, almost as if, in the last split seconds of flight, his body had tried to make some letter, to shape some desperate sign.

It was uncanny, if she closed her eyes, how sharply she could see it.

Ghastly light led her out of the darkness; light slanted across her and, with her progress, traveled the length of her woodsman's costume. She had taken a disguise at last, a green and brown woodsman suit, her shoulders enormously padded. She needed time. She was not herself.

It was pink here. Afferent paths made a clearing ringed with game machines. The signs, like stage backdrops, like sheer cliffs, like ominous skies, closed in from all sides. Their lights fell in close alternation.

In an oval of popping bulbs, floating lips elided a plosive kiss. With a surrendering shoulder thrust, a chiffoned androgyne parted his/her diaphanous robe on half a firm cleavage. A galaxy spun color from a dawn pink center to inflamed tips. A corkscrew drilled its way towards sparkling red wine. The signs were timed so that, after three or four staggered cycles, they would come round together and gush; for a heartbeat the clearing would rage bloody pink.

It did. Guillemet collected out of the lifting fog. She studied a very old game machine with balls and a spring

131

launcher, wondering idly if Haleck had ever played it, if Alphy, too, was hooked up to this one. But no, this one was all gravity and chance. On the glassed-in playboard, bumper solenoids lit up jangling when hit. There were flippers guarding the vertex in which all balls would eventually be lost. On the glass backboard, a girl wearing a short skirt danced with a shirtless boy, milky fleshed arms and legs snapping intricate figures, faces glowing over the hard bulblight, each flashing chunk-white teeth and a melancholy smile from lost ages.

She dropped in a coin. The entire contraption stuttered and shook. Score counters reset. The dancers remained hard and mute, unrelentingly joyful.

Unable to understand that, she banged the side. They were as if painted on. A ball dropped into place before the launcher. Appalled by the stillness, she shot it into a landscape of light and sound. Amber snatched at her empty features, still as the dancers'. The board shook with an excess of electricity. Dance cards spun and blurred. The ball dropped into a ball-sized socket and came out spinning viciously. She rang up thousands between two pitching solenoids, then flippered it perfectly into the last dance card. On the backboard, the word 'hop' lit up over the boy's whirling hair.

She turned away, oppressively bored.

Pink exploded over her. The machine reeled on under her assault, jammed, begging. Dithering bells would not leave her be.

She strode away.

And almost collided with Savage in his wildman costume. They backed away from one another. He bowed.

"Guillemet."

"You know me." She did not smile back.

"I've been told I have an able eye." He shrugged. "There are a hundred ways to recognize someone, and very few disguises cover all of them." He rubbed the fur at his shoulders, exactly the color of his beard. "It's good that we've met. Everything has changed."

"So."

Savage smiled. "As a giantess, you can afford to be more receptive to strangers than that. I'm not going to touch you.

It's been a year since I've touched anyone." His eyes pleaded.

She felt a shock of pity. Here was Savage, in his mad way, declaring himself completely open, offering her a secret pain, or the pain of refusing it—asking to be touched. She was appalled that anyone could become so desperate; she was frightened, wondering if, someday, it might be her.

Savage, with his able eye, must have seen some of it show through, because he nodded as if in recognition. "More and more, Guillemet, I feel myself a victim instead of an assassin. Why is that, Guillemet? What do *you* feel? Where does it come from?"

She started to speak, then felt her throat closing; and shook her head. She took a step back from him. "I can't talk with you, Savage." She shook her head in a wider arc. "Not today."

Savage started to reclaim the step she'd taken, then stopped. "It's important. I have the feeling again that the assassin will strike by dawn."

"You, the assassin?" she said softly.

He shrugged.

There was someone nearby. Guillemet turned. A few feet away, a beautiful man in a black costume stood watching them. He bowed. He had dark hair and eyes, sinewy, dark-haired arms, long, long hands. He had remarkably strong legs that he showed through black mesh. He carried his cape folded over one arm.

"I am honored. The victim Guillemet here at my little—"

"You know me." A chill spread from her earrings. She had often met men like this one. But today—

He twinkled; it was a very fine face, weathered and winning, all an illusion of symmetry but not symmetric. "I couldn't help overhearing. Allow me to introduce myself—"

"I know you." It was coming to her, that face quite apart from its dark costume, in white somewhere—

"You have probably seen one of my duels. You are about to see another. I am Ernst, dubbed the Executioner."

He bowed again and marched to the center of the clearing, displaying the white script embroidered on his cape, the popular appellation on that ever popular costume: *the Assassin.*

"An unpleasant man," Savage said quietly.

133

The unpleasant man wheeled. "Do you know *whom* my duel is with?"

He was thirty yards away, but she saw his dark eyes glistening. She shook her head.

"With a woman who claims to know who the assassin is. A swindler taking a long chance to make a very young reputation. She's Treblinski's sister." He smiled. It was like the smiles on the game board, one-piece and impossible.

And she marveled that he could look so good doing it even as, sickeningly, the name Treblinski fell into place, and his face, and the white denim he had worn the last time she had seen him. That pretty face was the last Viktor Treblinski had ever seen. She had a momentary impulse to challenge him, and killed it, but she had already taken the first steps towards him across the clearing.

"Guillemet!" Savage reached for her, then snatched his hands back, startled, and stared at them.

She was clear of him, taking long strides towards the Executioner.

His smile returned. He had read her instantly and was letting her know it.

She stopped six feet away. It was not a proper distance for anything. "You already have quite a reputation," she said slowly, watching his amused eyes. "And now you've lost a pair of goggles, with one lens missing, and you want them back."

"News travels quickly here. But inaccurately."

And at once she became aware of how quick and expert he was at this, how tired an affair this must be for him. That shot in the dark had given her nothing. He had given nothing.

"You wish to arbitrate?" he asked.

She shook her head. He lowered his brows significantly and waited for her to leave.

"They were your goggles?" she asked suddenly.

"I found them. And you will never guess where, I would say, except that you seem to be a good guesser. Did you know they were Ann Treblinski's? I see you did. The problem is that now she wants them back."

"You should restore them."

"If you *were* an arbiter," he said evenly, "I should tell you to leave the matter alone. It involves blood ties."

He looked her straight in the eye and the look was a picture, the picture of them dueling. And he let her know, with the tiniest movement somewhere below his neck, that they were both seeing the same picture at the same time, and this was the way he would do it, here was all his skill with this one gaze to embody it. The result was that she died. And that was it. There was no place to stick her courage. In that instant he utterly convinced her that in a duel he would kill her. It was only a question of whether she wanted to die.

She did not want to die. She turned and left him, thinking only that if he had wanted he could just as easily have let it go on, as he had with Treblinski, as he had with dozens of others.

"Oh, Guillemet."

She turned.

"After the duel, you must tell me—" he drew up his cape— "how old you think she is."

She spun away from his smile.

Someone else entered the clearing.

They both looked. It was Treblinski, still a Centurion in her shining armor, in a deep red enfolding cloak, in a brightly plumed helmet. Guillemet searched the shadowy reaches beneath it. Young, slightly plump, Treblinski's features were intensely blank. How old *was* she?

She stopped with a good distance between them, facing the beautiful man. Eighteen? Nineteen?

They did not find much of interest in one another's eyes. The beautiful man slitted his and wheeled, reaching under his black cape, and the Centurion was a rush of vermillion finding the holster set far back on her hip, and their muzzled arms extended: two magical passes flung off hard pivots, the metal snapping straight at the ends of their hands.

There was a deep thud and the Centurion hurtled backwards. She landed strangely folded, arms crossed and wrapped in that fatally bulky cape, head snapped back from a blotching neck.

Hydrostatic shock. Guillemet tore her eyes from something too lifeless to bear.

Savage had walked over and stood quietly next to her, his shoulder no more than an inch from hers. "An unpleasant man," he said quietly.

135

Witnesses bustled out of the shadow and gathered up the body, one at each end, one circling its waist with his arms, instantly soaked with blood to the shoulders.

They marched back into the signs with it. A steady spattering faded.

"Well."

The beautiful man stood at her shoulder.

Guillemet dropped disbelieving eyes to his.

"How old do you think?"

She studied his jaw. A tiny muscle lifted, the sign of a shift in some battle of unknown inner forces. If she could have then, she would have killed him, bringing them to rest forever. It was just that she couldn't. She felt a cold rage hardening the muscle in the back of her neck; she was trembling.

He smiled, his test finished, and left her.

"What can you say about a man like that?" Savage asked, looking after him. "Except—"

"—a most unpleasant man." Guillemet looked at him wearily. "Good-bye Savage."

She wheeled and walked off into the darkness under the girders. As she had wanted, the deep shadows swallowed all thought. When she moved without thought she moved quickly, her long powerful legs pulling ground under like some machine. She moved without sound, barely grazing the light-shapes that spilled towards her, keeping to the dark, totally out of touch, oblivious.

After a time she sat, her back straight against the flanged edge of a girder. Slowly she grew aware of the metal digging into her muscle. She pulled the woodsman's vest closer against her. It was a wakening tingle at first, then dull pain. She let it sharpen, nerve after nerve brimming, steadying, falling silent.

It would come back worsened.

She stared at a two foot high blossom of color ahead of her. Its soft-edged petals were variously colored and overlapping. The base was brilliant white and irregular, like some clawed foot.

The pain jolted her straight. She drew in a slow breath. She settled back, moving a little over.

Ahead, two big girders raced up parallel towards a distant

blanket of light. Spans of catwalk and platform broke the ascent into a polygon quilt. Two skew girders (one that she leaned against) spread into a catscradle of beams above that. She sat buried under crumpling shadow, blackened, concealed, canceled.

Thoughts slid in and out of focus and caught her by surprise, like dreams; she seized them only to realize that what she had was the act of seizing. Once she thought about how she knew the assassin was flesh and blood; in the Planetarium, she had felt skin slippery with real sweat, strained against bones stiff enough to break. He was no idea. She knew how, with a certain blow, she could collapse his windpipe.

Later, she forgot that thought completely.

And caught herself thinking about Haleck in his bouncy cellophane wings.

Then she found that her camouflage worked both ways. Without any warning sound, a silhouette appeared.

Some masker at loose ends, trying to—

He hunkered next to her. Light chipped at his gnomish features.

It was Boz.

"Get lost."

He wore a spare smile, lips cleaving together. "I've come to take advantage of you. I've found something. And I need you."

She stared. Her hand raked up silken dust balls. "I didn't *ask* you what you wanted. I told you to get lost."

"You've had all you can take of it, haven't you? And I've had all I need of the assassin's politics. Listen. Where do our personal needs meet that famous *social* concern? Nowhere. This is what I live by. The tribe-being and the hunter have never exchanged a word. Yet the assassin claims to *be* that meeting. The politics of the assassin are those of a dream—amoral, disembodied. He doesn't exist. And I—I would have decided the fate of a whole planet by *those* politics."

"What do you want?"

"I told you. The advantage. I have no enemies on this world and now I can speak to anyone. I have something to show you, something that has made the nature of the situation quite clear. But first, come with me."

"Eh?"

"I said, *come* with me." He went nowhere. His tiny eyes searched for hers.

She thought of the beautiful man, his eyes just as dark, reaching for hers. "You are frightening, Boz."

"Only on this world. Elsewhere I have books, family matters. Come away with me."

She considered. "How far?"

"Far enough. Where the money is a different color and the language has no roots like yours."

She looked away, crafty. She rolled dust on her fingers. "What are you asking?"

"Only that you make the decision. Look at what I have here and then decide. It couldn't matter less what you decide; only take it out of my hands. I want you and I want nothing more to do with the assassin matter. Your world is safe from me."

Her lips parted; her tongue touched her teeth. But she looked away, tucking her forehead behind her arm. She knew what the decision would have to be—and what did it matter what she decided? Even a coin flip would fail her now, would admit of trust, would concede that one choice mattered to the coin, did *right* by the coin. She must bow to it. "What are you asking?"

He reached to warm her hands between his. "A little honest doubt. A little self-disputation, that's all."

Her hand pulled away. Her fingers coiled up, hurtled, made four inch-deep holes in the earth beside his wrist.

His hand was still a moment, then retreated to his pocket. "That must take great skill."

"Throw down your cards."

Instead he threw down a mask. It poked white backing up through its empty eyeslits; it rolled like a tiny landscape. A long pale scar ran down to the chin from the ear. "Well."

Guillemet met his gaze with unbelieving eyes. Then at last she surrendered. She spread the mask out carefully in the dirt. "It was very dark. We only fought for a few seconds. I landed a few glancing blows. I'm not even sure how big he is. But that scar. Yes, that's the scar."

Boz smiled his spare smile. "It's the Juggler's."

"Then he—"

"Sssh!" Boz held up a big-tendoned hand, staring at the darkness off to the side. "I thought I heard someone."

"A masker."

"No, moving too quietly." Boz rose suddenly, clapping dust from his hands, still peering. He nodded at the mask. "Whatever you decide I'll be waiting for you at the Catacomb tunnel that leads into the caverns at five. Please come. Good luck." He took two steps and joined with a section of darkness.

For long moments Guillemet stared at the mask, as if waiting for it to change to a painted-on face, or a wrinkle of light and shadow; then her ringed hands touched her cheeks. She saw that the base of the light blossom had closed slightly, the claws joining and pointing at her—like some half-formed letter. Her hands fell to her lap.

Melancholy dancers held hard poses in the frosty light. Falling, the Centurion flung out her banded arms as if to dance, as if to speak. Endless bodies dropped softly to the dust like hands into a lap, folded, mute, and wildly signalling.

At the Dome wall, a guitar, a flute, and a viola played in slow five.

The signlights were dimmed and red spots lanced from far above through one another and through dancers.

Dancers wheeled and gently dipped; they drew closer, slipped their arms together, then, breathtakingly, snapped apart and flitted across the coughing dust. From above, drawn by scouring spots, they were a moving grain of plumage, leather, and silk. Sometimes, in a flurry, one couple or two would dance wildly against the flow and pause, tucked in a safe pocket, rotating soundlessly across the spokes of their locked stares.

Near the Dome's curving bulk, the oil lanterns were as yet unlit, each four-sided, stained glass head dense and leaden in the twilight. Underneath, their restless bearers adjusted cassocks, lifting their feet to inspect polished heels. Wunder walked slowly and smilingly among them, twisting the fringe on her white dress with one hand, pressing coins into their palms with the other. They gave back shy smiles, politely inflected thanks.

A quarter of the way across the clearing, Danton, in motley and fool's cap, worked his way towards her. He had always, especially unnoticed, enjoyed watching Wunder from a distance. Now, amidst the cassocks and her own devoted, ever-changing retinue (a cinnamon bear, a snake, the woman in white from the hall, and three acrobats) she was most apparently Wunder, a center of unsurpassable ease, the effortless conductor of all this attention, here in her first appearance at Carnival. She herself was the only one untouched by her excitement, redeploying it, favoring each of the few she spoke to with a brief burst of her radiance, moving smoothly from hand to hand, her living fringe folding and unfolding tight strips on her form, streaming in a private wind.

Ten feet from her a heavy body moved and blocked Danton's way, and he looked into the green eyes of one of Wunder's bodyguards, who wore real six-guns.

"It's all right. I'm famous too."

Wunder turned and, head tilting, saw him.

He waved. "Hello, Wunder."

Surprise touched her face and touching, made a smile. There were few such moments. There was only one such moment.

"Danton! What are you doing in—" she let it drop and hurried to him, clasping one of his jeweled hands in hers. Instantly she gave a sign and, behind the shielding of her retinue, they made for the Dome Wall.

The music stopped and the dancers, in two beats of confusion, swept and wavered. There was their rustling, watery descent to stillness. A pattering of applause.

At the Dome Wall a small mob surged towards Wunder, but her retinue was a wall of its own. Tumbling acrobats cleared a small circle around them, mowing down the two leaders of the charge. Green-eyes walked off a still smaller circle in that, hands unostentatiously kept at his pistols.

The crowd stopped, straining, and shutters syncopated along the front row.

"Rumor has it," Wunder said half-smiling, "that you have just done a private little video spot."

He waved it away. "Only a poem. The equipment was

there so I went back to the Planetarium and did it. But rumors travel fast here."

She shrugged. "Ten minutes. I could have done better— for you. But since when does a Danton poem need the video?"

"Today." He touched his cap, jingling. "Treblinski is right. Poetry as a voice is dead."

"So is Treblinski." Wunder looked away. "Forgive that. An easy line. Danton, if money could help poetry I'd be tempted to slip you a quick bribe."

He grinned, if a little wearily. "You're wrong, Wunder. Money is the only reason poetry exists. Without money there aren't classes of people to be *spoken* for. The poet has no long silences to step into."

Wunder smiled sadly. "Very kind of you, Danton. But is that because you've just decided that poetry is dead?" She held up a hand. It was the scarred hand. "Never mind. I can hear it all gracefully being turned aside." The hand reached and touched his chin and shutters snapped like jingling money. "Danton, the only reasons I tolerate you are that my memories of times we have spent together are not all terrible and because you have an ugly mouth that still might, at times, make me gnaw my knuckles in the corner."

Danton laughed. "You're a bit of a poet yourself, Wunder."

"I try." From a fold of fringe at her hip she withdrew a cigarette. "About this Juggler question. After your call and all the nasty things you told me about him, I naturally made some inquiries."

"In the last half hour?" His brows rose.

"Danton, you have no idea of the communications machinery I have at my disposal. But, no, I investigated the Juggler when you first told me about that attack and the newscast after it. There was a great deal to sift through, of course, but the most interesting thing I turned up was that the Juggler, too, seems to have been a mercenary. He joined up, later than most, after three years at Highgate University on Ventura, where he met—"

"Commander Potocki." Danton frowned. "Almost too neat."

"It *is* too neat. Commander P. is entirely on the level, as are, probably, all the mercenary higher-ups. I have checked very good." She took a deep drag. "But look, I'm going to *have* to ask. What are you doing in the Juggler's costume? With that tube mask and that belled cap, there's no way to tell you apart."

Danton shrugged. "Your computer's unnerving sense of humor. She thought this would teach him his lesson."

Wunder took a moment to digest this. "Well, I suppose I'm pleased that she can take care of herself. And you should be too." Wunder snapped her fingers. "Easy!"

A dwarf in purple brocade appeared magically out of the crowd. He had not, previously, been an attached member of the retinue.

"Easy, see that the following message gets to Manolo. Danton is wearing the Juggler's motley."

Danton raised his brows. "A bodyguard?"

She winced at the word. "In a manner of speaking. Look, Danton, from now on the Juggler is my problem, all right? Whatever the details, this has become a purely political matter."

Danton smiled.

"You look relieved."

"I am—that it's a purely political matter."

She looked at him doubtfully. "Just to underline the point—I am not averse to having people bopped on the head when they interfere in my purely political matters. *Verstehen?*"

He grinned. "Wunder, you would never have me bopped on the head."

She looked at him sadly a moment. "You and a dozen with finer mouths, and more than bopped. Danton, I don't think you understand what's happening in the world. I don't think you see that *even* if the assassin is stopped, and *even* if we are not pulled into the Ventura crisis, terrible things could still happen. Our world is in a state, Danton. Hear those shutters? Those are the first guns going off; tourists watch *us* while there's near war at home. Because there is something afoot, Danton. Look around you. Read the label on a beercan sometime. Our big push for self sufficiency has failed."

He looked back into glinting camera lenses. "I look and I see lovely, expensive costumes."

"But do you see who's wearing them? Besides you and I, that is? Now go across the river. Look at Whister."

A red spot swept across them and he waited an instant before speaking. "Once I lived in places like Whister."

She exhaled a slow cloud. "And once you rode with roving outlaw bands. If it were otherwise, could I be as fond of you as I am?"

He looked at her and his eyes were big and bronze and he let the hurt show. "You're right, of course." And he turned on his heel and hurried between two spinning acrobats into the crowd.

All at once the lantern bearers, on an invisible signal, lifted their lanterns and filed into the clearing alongside him. Colors whittled off the glass. Flame tongues danced along the lantern rows. They turned and a high, strong voice fluttered down a minor scale, held the deep tonic in a dark, turning pause. It was joined by a shower of parts, like rain shaken off a mass of leaves.

Danton hurried past them across the clearing. His eyes swept along the throng of maskers to the Dome wall, where girders and the white curve of the Dome pinched off the clearing, and the Proets' bikes made a slanting row, like an ornate frieze. The Proets were nowhere nearby, but a little further on Danton made out Savage and Mirror seated before a hazy neon curtain, staring reflectively into the dust. He started towards them.

The choir built a deep wall of sound; disjointed phrases raced through like wandering cracks. Then a new turn: a succession of demanding figures left the piece adroit but coasting, lost without a hint of a theme; the soprano explored in a long trill and was eclipsed, abruptly, by the dark swoop of their beating return. Their flight wheeled; half-tone drops sawed together. A desperate tenor and a gliding baritone harmonized a familiar theme—an anthem not from this piece or this world but familiar—and were tracked by a lumbering bass, lagging, laying a gray damper wave.

Danton arrived and started to speak to Savage, but his voice was instantly torn away and joined to the ululating background. Helpless, he raised his eyes to heaven.

The Dome was turning colors. Overhead it was a sunset, layers of orange going from earthy to luminous, the central surface, shiny as an eye, still reflecting dark shapes. At ground level traces of new sky mixed gradually upwards: salmon, pale violet, buttercup...

"Savage! The sky—" Which was fruitless, words blown away. Savage had nodded to him but was not speaking, his head dropped forward, in perfect alignment with Mirror's, both fixedly regarding the ground.

And, as Danton's brows knitted their perplexity, the choir breezed down to a single soprano, drifting up the scale, sustaining a tonic, abruptly cut.

"Savage."

Savage looked up. He gave a small surprised start. His hand lifted, pointing. "Look!"

Danton turned and looked behind him.

He had on a new outfit.

He stood wearing a black leather jacket in the shadow grid cast by a low sign; it open and shut rhythmically. He dollied in and out of silhouette, one moment deep green with detail, the next filled solid black. Deep green he was dark-skinned, sharp featured, athletic.

He was juggling. His balls slapped into his hands in time with the flashing sign. Wearing a mournful smile he shuffled like a weary hoofer. Droplets of sweat glistened in his brows. He blinked, his smile turning to a pout of concentration.

A small band of admirers had gathered at the edge of the shadow, murmuring with spare but sufficient interest. Mirror and Savage now rose together and joined them, Danton trailing curiously behind. In the first few moments, Mirror seemed the most enchanted spectator of all. Shoulders hunched, silver brows furrowed, he followed the balls with a circling head, his right hand stroking back and forth in time. Then his mysterious attention span snapped.

"There is a game," he said abruptly.

"Very true," said the Juggler, his rhythm unbroken.

Savage slid as close as he dared to Mirror, fur slipping off his shoulder. "Show us, Mirror."

Mirror stared at the Juggler. "I need the balls."

The Juggler did a difficult double-take with two balls hung, popping the third into reverse on the swing beat, then firing the others after it as they dropped. He finished in first position, all three bunched together in one hand. He sighed, offering them. "They're all yours."

Mirror squeezed them experimentally in his big hands, then flashed and moved out in front of the small crowd. "This game's not as simple as it looks," he said in a lecturing tone. "But it *is* a solvable zero sum game. It's played with one ball." He dropped the others with little explosions of dust. "And two hands." He showed two silvery hands, palms up, the ball rocking on the gap between them. "I hide and you guess. That's set; it's a rule. If I hide the ball in my left hand and you guess, you get two points. If you don't guess, I get two. If I hide it in my right hand and you guess, you get one point; if you don't guess, I get a hundred. Understand?" He looked questioningly at the Juggler.

The Juggler nodded.

Flashing teeth that were all filling, Mirror took the ball behind his back and fiddled a moment. He came back making two fists, the right considerably fatter.

"Right," said the Juggler doubtfully.

Mirror turned up an empty right hand. His left fist opened and the ball, remarkably compressed, sprang like an angry mouse from his grip. He caught it in mid-air. "Wrong. That's two points for me." Without waiting for comment, he brought the ball behind his back again, fiddled, then showed.

The next three guesses were wrong, the ball always kept left, and from the fifth guess on, the Juggler began picking left consistently, abandoning all efforts to defend against the hundred point pay off.

After a time a frown settled into the Mirror's features. He was over seventy points behind.

"Wait," he said, "You're cheating. You're not playing with infinite intelligence. Four out of every random hundred-and-five times you guess the right hand. That's proper defense. Three out of every random hundred-and-five times I hide there."

The Juggler's jaw dropped.

"Guess right," the Mirror said. "Why don't you guess right?"

Danton looked away, smiling to himself. The clearing was unusually quiet. Nothing had occupied its empty center for a long while. Biding their time, as if awaiting something, the surrounding maskers gaped at the Dome's color show, now dimmed but still nervously remixing. A few choir members lingered by the Dome wall, but the crowd had mostly thinned there, abandoned by those who were not up to seeing the night dragged to its absolute, unappealable finish.

A group of Proets in bulky jackets melted out of neon shadow and stood near their bikes in jutting poses, heads and torsoes tilted, cigarettes bobbing in the fuzzy light: attitudes of waiting. Unrecognized in his motley, Danton, for some reason, was reluctant to join them.

Jug and the Mirror walked slowly over to Savage; they were still playing, but had been abandoned by their admirers.

"How come," Savage asked, pausing to indicate the Proets, "we never see them riding those things? They always have them parked nearby but they never get on."

"Take your guess," Mirror said, ignoring him.

Danton grinned.

"Do you ever get the feeling," the Juggler asked the open air, "that people are closing in on you?" He withdrew his flask and tossed back a long swig.

Then someone came.

About twenty feet from where they stood, where the admirers had been, a giant stood silhouetted, watching them. The shadow grid slid off and on. Danton stared, guessing, but still unsure.

Just then the Dome bleached and began to break out in silver.

Mirror was naturally entranced. He gaped, his grip loosened, and he gave away the fact that he had finally hidden the ball in his right hand.

"Right," said the Juggler softly, but he was looking at the giant. He passed the flask somnolently to Savage, who stared with narrowed eyes at the Mirror.

The Dome had become a silver bowl stained with neon and Mirror was communicating with it. That was the only word. Staring upwards, Mirror circled his open hands in opposite directions on either side of his temples. His fingers spidered. His flaring nostrils kept some unfathomable time. The figures recomplicated. He wove whole out-of-phase geometries. He played like an infant learning to see.

The Juggler looked from Danton to the giant to Mirror and Savage next to him. He reached under his jacket and withdrew a blaster. Abruptly, he handed it to Savage. "Here, hold that."

Savage, who had eyes only for Mirror, did.

Danton took a step towards the Juggler and stopped. The Juggler met his eyes.

"You see? Now he wants it."

Savage ran his fingers over the blaster's knuckled butt. "Unpleasant," he said to someone not there.

There was an answer.

But it was not for Savage. It came from the Dome. And it was for Mirror. One small arc of silver had turned gaseous bright and bent a spotlight down that, miraculously, picked him out. Reflected signlight focused on him. He reddened, a slowly shifting mass of neon, like a color negative cut out against the shadow.

The crowd din changed. Mirror was like a great exploding signal, like some portentous sign.

They oohed and aahed, pulling in around him, letting his glow flicker over them. The giant was screened out. Savage leaned forward, licking his lips. Mirror gazed down at his body like something just created, his eyes round and still silver, blank as spoons.

Savage's head dropped; his face worked a slow crumple, bright green eyes re-focusing on the blaster in his hand. Or not quite re-focusing. Not quite. They were wet.

And then the giant slipped out of nowhere, from very close in the crowd, and it was obviously Guillemet, her woodsman cap shadowing her features, but not her earrings, not her ringed hands, not her huge form.

She was looking at Danton.

Who stiffened, almost imperceptibly broadening his shoulders. There was something in her balance, in her silence.

She swung her shadowed head suddenly, as if her neck were cramped. The cap tipped. She reached up, pulled it off, a cloud of hair falling to her shoulders. She shook her head, her shoulders lifting, and charged.

He had time enough for one last irresistible look at Savage's blaster. It was up and level but Savage held it like a toy, muzzle trained wobbling on Mirror's brilliant form.

Then Danton's arms came up, the giantess looming between them. He picked up her hook easily, but nevertheless it cut right through his block. It lifted him and things in his back bottomed painfully out and when his head recoiled black stars burst all over his skull. He staggered, not knowing where she was, arms up to feel her. Another fist cut in just below his heart, and his arms dropped just a fraction, and there was a flurry of jabs and hooks at his head. He folded, his legs suddenly gone, his lungs flaming.

She hadn't expected that, because her next punch only grazed him on the way down.

Then the Dome sheeted suddenly black and everything, mercifully, paused. Through the raging neon, braced on his quivering arms, Danton could see a barely gleaming Mirror. He stood with his hands spread, one open on each side of his face, dismayed.

And then Guillemet loomed over him and Danton saw, in a lightning compression of instants, in this last compression, fleeting snapshots of the whole circle of events: Guillemet's hands, a black costume in the crowd, his own bloody spit, the forty-seven on his chest (realizing here, absurdly relieved, that she had only taken him for the Juggler, that it could, after all, be patched up), and Mirror blurring into another stream of liquid motion, and, at once, Savage's muzzle starting up.

Then Guillemet's big hands were back, tearing at his number forty-seven and the skin behind it. And as he struggled to spit out the words, Mirror got to her and Savage got his blaster up and steady: all from a hundred dangling, impossible angles, between long sessions of just Guillemet's pale blue eyes drilling into his, glowing from some unknown source.

Mirror, vibrating like a silver shower, delivered a streaking fist to Guillemet's temple. Her hands pulled back from Danton and he dropped like a stone. She had begun, far too slowly, to pivot, now kept pivoting, rolled off one bending knee to the ground, out.

And so at last Savage fired.

It was a bad shot, gotten off in haste, no matter who it was meant to hit. The only light was pulsing, deceptive neon. The only thing really to sight on was Mirror. It licked past him and splashed into the crowd. Someone fell.

Proets swarmed in from all directions on Savage and he began flailing.

Then, from a half sitting position, Danton suddenly moved to the flat of his back; it was a lightning cut. He blinked at the black expanse of the Dome. Pain came round his chest like so many cinching belts. He held his breath and the crowd cheered him and that was the sound of blacking out.

It must have been less than two minutes later when things collected around him again, beginning with the din of the same crowd. He struggled up.

A group of Proets trudged out of the shadows, faces eloquent with dejection: Savage had escaped.

Someone held out a hand to him. It was silver. He took it and was lifted at once into a revolving, confused crowd. Once every turn, Mirror grinned at him. He tried to grin back and slipped; a moment later Mirror was holding him up and he saw his own dirty, distorted face in a silver shoulder.

When the ambulance came, Mirror caught at something invisible with a turning fist and paused, watching the corpse being lifted onto the stretcher. "I've misunderstood." He made a ball with his big hands and looked up at Danton, a question in his mintstamped eyes.

He wanted a yes or a no. Danton shook his head slowly. "No, Mirror. Not a game."

He left him standing there, silver eyes filling with tears, and reeled towards the ambulance.

Guillemet stood next to the open doors, Wunder beside her with her arm round her waist.

When the giantess saw him, her eyes lidded. "Danton." She looked away.

He grinned. It hurt. "Think nothing of it." He stumbled and caught himself on the ambulance door.

"Danton, will you lie down." The way Wunder said it, it was not a request.

He shook his head, pulled himself straight.

Then he looked inside the ambulance. For some reason they hadn't bothered to cover the corpse's face. It was a familiar face, a pretty face, a face he remembered from only last night over a snappy denim suit:

Ernst the Executioner.

V. Anomalies

NIGHT. Side by side they crunched up the gravel road, as if over sheets of dark ice. The Juggler rubbed his arms briskly against the chill and brought his flask to his black lips, guzzling. "Want some? You might need it."

Danton took the flask.

"Madmen," said the Juggler, and shook his head. "Leave it to the madmen in the end and they will fix it up pretty."

Danton began answering, then, instead of words, filled his mouth with bad whiskey (the gin long since gone), thinking (predictably): only this is mad.

"There's justice in it." The Juggler went on. "Madness is what we dread. Substitute, for the subject of that sentence, the assassin." Deft hands hauled off his motorcycle cap and folded it in half. "Are you mad, Danton?"

"No." Just like that, with a flatness that was almost sad.

The Juggler danced over some dark obstacle. "Then why are you here?"

Danton smiled, and stumbled over a stone protrusion of the same obstacle, twisting the bruised muscle at his ribs.

"Damn! We forgot the shield." The Juggler spun around to face him. "Let's go back and get it."

Danton shook his head and hurried him along. They worked up the biggest of Monotony's surrounding hills. The ordered prickings of the sky were close, the moon a sliver shy of full, frail as a bubble. Dwarf hills fell away on either side of this one; the threesome made a giant head tucked sleepily into its shoulders. Beyond, the lumpy outlines of Monotony's other hills might have been its muscular arms gathering the city up against the winking river.

Near the top there was a little brow and a convenient boulder and Danton sat, catching the flask out of Forty-Seven's hands. With his lip bent on the warm rim he paused, inhaling the whiskey's acetone odor, gazing at the curve of the city along the bank, the scattered lights like so many draped catherine's wheels. Coming back towards the city wall there was more detail: the glare of stucco fronts, a whitelit trapdoor maze of low buildings, terra cotta roofs, chimneys gesturing with clutters of piping, and there near the center, a bright halo of light that would be the Low Piazza. In the foreground the bulk of the Dome rose like an ascending planet, half in earth's shadow, half gleaming somberly in the city light. He thought he made out faint towers above it and far to the east, on the island's peninsula, fairyland spires or hints of the darkened spaceport.

The Juggler sank to the dirt next to him, two feet lower, moonleafed profile tilted up, long arms wrapped about his knees. "We haven't that much time," he said. "It'll be dawn soon, and once it's dawn—" he let it trail away.

"Once it's dawn—" Danton leaned forward—"what?"

The Juggler sighed. "Then many difficulties arise."

"Yes, they do. They're closing in on you, old chap."

The Juggler sighed again, more deeply. "Danton, what do you want?"

Danton reared back in mock surprise. "It was *you* who came to me, remember. There I was outside the Dome in my favorite shadow and you joined me. There is a monster in a cave that you have been talking about for quite some time now. You mentioned it; you had a flask. Does it seem that unreasonable that I would take this monster as a sign for something you had to say? That, on a balmy night like this, I would join you for a brief walk and a chat?" Danton looked up the dark road. "You're right; it does. This friendship of ours is a curious thing, Jug."

The Juggler gently pried the flask from his hand. "True. Do you think I'm going to assassinate you now?"

"No." Flatly again, with a faint regret that nothing was quite so simple. "Wunder, who has been looking into your past, tells me you were a mercenary once."

The Juggler looked up at him with frank eyes. There was a small pause, during which, if either of them wished, it could all have been tabled, allowing them both to go quietly home again. The Juggler slowly smiled. "Yes, that's true, same time as you. Malta. We hit a very organized, very high weapons area and my group was nearly wiped out." He smiled. "Somewhere on this planet, though they have lain low for fifteen years now, there are some very remarkable military leaders. At the end of eight days we were cut down into groups of three and four and I was—how shall I say it—on the road."

"That's how you say it. That the mercenaries were so ruthlessly and efficiently cut apart on a planet without an army and without a central power base is only one of many great unquestioned mysteries of our time. Among other things, it kept the mercenaries from becoming a major political power at a time when many could ill afford that. But then, you've had fifteen years to think about it too. I suspect we have similar ideas on the matter. I first caught on in Duluth, when a brilliant guerilla raid knocked out eight of our guns and what should have been a rout turned into a pitched infantry battle. Their infantry, mustered—what?— two days before, was better. Were we that bad or were they that good? Neither. What happened that day was impossible. On to the delusion. Examples: the spherical Novak starships all coming in a single year, in production on three planets at once; the incredible explosion of Novak technology in that five year span, stress fields, choate energy, interpenetrable parts, anomalous space selection; the fact that not a single one of the seven planets slipped into a true crisis through the crazy years, maintaining a crucial balance. Question: is history being controlled?"

"Who cares, Danton?" The Juggler studied him with

pursed lips. "So, here and there the game has been fixed. That has obviously been going on for so long that there is no longer any other way to play it. The only thing *we* can do is take history one day at a time, as if it were never invented; and try to forget that someone somewhere finds the larger patterns pleasing. We can try to arrange certain small matters to suit ourselves. We can take retaliatory action when they do not. But only against people we can see, only with what we have at hand, not against *history,* not with pretty speeches and big ideas."

"You make a fairly pretty speech yourself, Jug." Danton rubbed his gloved hands. "Maybe you're a lot closer to those roving bands than I am. Maybe that's why I like you. But tell me. On a cold night, when there's nothing else to do, don't you wonder who?"

"I wonder." The Juggler snorted. "Sure I wonder. Just like they want me to. I've even thought that maybe, like this planet, it has no center and there *is* no who. Maybe it's Boz's tribe-being, or maybe the law-god in some equations, but what the hell difference does that make? What does it matter *what* cuts me down? There are still people who move armies, make decisions, take lives, and they're as real as the killer in the Planetarium tonight."

"Was that you?" Danton asked softly.

No answer.

"With the assassin," Danton said, "things changed. Before, all that they needed were a few careful nudges to move history in directions it tended towards anyway; but suppose that it came to a fork with paths of almost equal probability. Essentially, Pierpont found such a fork when he was unable to predict an outcome for this crisis. Perhaps the predictions themselves fit into the plan. It's hard to decide whether detailed social projection would inspire a planned history, or just be put into effect once a given history was chosen. In any event, *this* crisis was determined predictable. This crisis was the most extreme act of manipulation ever, the most visible, the most definite, the one that put manipulation into our thoughts for all time. I think of it as their clearest statement. One way to build redundancy into a message—to make it as clear as possible—is to make it resemble what it's about in more ways. I think the assassin is like that. I think he looks exactly like the future that is coming to us."

The Juggler was silent a moment, considering the oppressively significant sky. "Danton," he said finally, "do you think when he comes he'll sit down and talk with you, appraising his metaphysical nature, and that after that it'll all be hunky dory?"

"I imagine not."

"Then why do you do everything to make it easier for him?"

Danton shook his head, jingling. "I don't know. You tell *me*. Basically, Jug, I like you. I want you to talk to me. Over there—" he pointed to a tree by the faraway city wall—"is where you attacked me just this evening wearing that rubber mask."

The Juggler's arm froze there inside his jacket, hand over his heart.

And what could Danton do then, seeing the hurt surprise in the Juggler's eyes, but give a small corroborating nod and toss the yellow-plumed dart into his lap? "That might come in handy, if you're reaching for what I think you are."

"I'm not." The Juggler shook his head sadly, withdrew a small notebook, and tossed it into Danton's lap.

It was the notebook Danton had lost by the city wall. Danton looked from the notebook to the Juggler.

"So this is supposed to be the big scene, is it?" the Juggler said. "Between the assassin and the poet." He sucked thoughtfully on the tip of the yellow dart. "Well isn't it obvious yet, Danton, that the assassin and the poet haven't a thing to say to each other?"

"I know that." Danton pocketed the notebook. "You probably shouldn't suck on that dart. It's—"

"This particular drug is very volatile." The Juggler waved a dismissing hand. "All traces would be gone by now."

"Oh." Danton considered his jewels a moment. "You see, the assassin and the poet are similar kinds of people. One way to look at them might be as isomorphic elements—"

"Shut the fuck up, Danton. You want to know why? All right. Because it's funny. Because I don't give a damn about what happened when we dropped from our little balls in the

sky onto Duluth or Malta. Because I hate the machinery and
its shiny, fibreglass order, because I want to get in and bloody
up the gears a little, I'm evil."

Danton laughed.

"I tell dirty jokes in church."

Danton's laugh turned to a howl.

"I go to the bathroom in bed." The Juggler's hands
clasped and instantly fell apart. "Come along, hero. We have
a monster to meet."

Danton rose stiffly and moved after him. He felt only a
vague sense of having been silly. No longer any of this sorrow
that had clung to him like a bad smell over the past few days.
None of this fear or hurt. Neither was there joy or a sense of
rightness about what was to come to him. There was very
little besides a sense of Danton, filling the same shape as
always, alive and parting the void.

He came to the crest of the hill, the powdered sky
suddenly closing its emptiness in from all sides, bringing its
cold, defining bodies within a handsbreadth. It was the
Planetarium again, only now the stars would burn if he
touched them. Now they were universes away.

The Juggler, looking ominously intense, skidded down a
yard of loose pebbling to where the hill dropped off as solid
stone. Danton duck-footed more sedately after him, shying
back from the drop. Something threw a pinkish glow
towards the sky. It could have been just the different lighting
that monsters have. There was soft crackling, small bites
taken from a major bone. Danton had to look.

Ledge rock spilled round a gothic arch below them.
Before it, in the rocky soil that formed Monotony's shore,
burned a ten foot high fire. Round the edge a masked man
danced, shirtless and lacquered with sweat.

It was a dance of asking. The flame reached for him. He
danced with its hands. He spun away and beckoned, arms
and trunks describing a full circle of caresses, tender, urgent,
brutal, skilled. He bowed and snaked back to the fire; eerily,
it bent for him, its leaping upper edge curving a giant smile.
He beat at it, dancing fist to tongue with the flames, touching
it where he and they were the same color. He came away his
head hidden. He opened and closed his thighs, offered his
loins, his vulnerable neck. He pedaled close, face averted,

neck exposed, arms rippling; then wheeled and submerged his head in the fire. It streamed up his neck and shoulders, yellow and alive.

Forty-Seven hooked Danton's arm and pulled. "Cheap tricks. I can do the same with unguent and a can of hair spray."

Danton blinked at his dark head, fringed firepink. "Who—?"

"The logical candidate. Always. Come on."

They moved to the crumbling end of the ledge and started gingerly down the spillage. On the third meditating step Danton mistook shadow for substance and slid twenty yards, stone cracking stone in loping falls below him. When his momentum ran out he was well into the crevasse. He hugged the wall and inched on.

The dancer was waiting where the path, veering back towards the arch, turned to dirt.

"Move in slow. You're covered." Firelight cut out his short silhouette. He spoke with an accent and his voice was familiar, but, amid all the other vague recognitions of the past week, hard to place. "Danton!" There was a pause. Rock smacked together up the crevasse. "And the other?"

The Juggler came up short against Danton's back. Danton grunted.

"Forty-Seven!" The dancer sounded pleased. "Well, if only I believed in coincidence."

"Wouldn't it be great?" the Juggler agreed.

Danton wondered how well they knew each other. He looked from the dancer, glistening here and there with splashes of firelight, his dark facemask unreadable, to the Juggler. There were traces of fresh-broken sweat on the Juggler's brow. They did not, on the whole, seem to be a good sign. Danton looked at where the dancer's eyes would be under that mask, if they were. "Are you the assassin?"

"No, I am not the assassin." With a touch of singsong, as if every day he made this denial to disappointed crowds. He motioned with his hand and something glinted there. "Come on." He nodded them towards the fire.

They walked ahead of him. Danton now began to invent questions he would be asked, and wrong answers that propelled him, on invisible beams of momentum, into the flames. Another offering. It was a private act, as fascinating for no one as it was for him, and his face only hardened a little, giving no signs of the feelings that, somewhere, must be there. Thus, as he and the Juggler reached the fire and, on the dancer's instruction, sat, his features had a heroic cast.

The dancer came round and stood with a small arc of fire between them, so that part of him was sheared off by fattening flame, so that its outline merged with his. "Now the Juggler will tell me that you've come to kill the monster, but that is out of the question. The monster cannot be killed."

Danton frowned.

"Told you." The Juggler, grinning, reached for a hot dog and a roasting branch on the blanket beside him. "Want one? Looks like all-beef." Without waiting for a response he spit two frankfurters with clean jabs.

"What I would like to know," the dancer said, "is why you are here. Beginning with you, Juggler."

Danton butted in. "What monster? And why can't it be killed?"

The dancer folded his arms. Firelight walked his flexed shoulders. "Should I correct that," he said slowly, "to read 'may not'? Although the creature bears a suspicious resemblance to a popular cave beast found in any xeno-biology picturebook, still his—her—appearance in this cave, at this time, deserves a certain amount of respect. There are stories of such a beast that take us back to Novak. Later on, when we have weathered the storm and we can return to the question at our ease, we can rule on the nature—and the morals—of the monster. Until then it seems prudent simply to leave it alone. Would you agree?" With exaggerated patience.

Danton nodded.

"Jug, don't hold the hot dogs that way. They'll disintegrate. Right at the edges of the flame. That's better." The dancer nodded. "Now why are you here?"

"Boz—"

"Boz?" Danton looked back at the dancer. Identified, Boz was as obviously himself as he was in spacer blues, his build and carriage unmistakable, his peculiar off-world accent pinned down. Danton raised a questioning hand. "Why—?"

"The mask?" Boz's broad shoulders rose and fell.

"Custom. Custom explains everything."

"Even history?" The Juggler's hot dogs split and dropped into the fire.

"History?"

"Danton was just attempting to give me a quick history lesson. I don't think the details would be appropriate here but, in sum, I chided him for not being specific enough. I think I'll show him what I mean."

"You interest me," said Boz, the dancer. He turned and put himself on the other side of the fire.

The Juggler spitted fresh hot dogs. "Right. Fifteen years ago an entire mercenary battalion landed on this planet and was dispersed within two weeks. The one factor common to all those lost battles was the considerable military skill exhibited by enemies who, ostensibly, had no military experience. Where, I have always asked myself, did all this military genius come from? It is not that hard a question. Barring the amusing theory that aliens control our history, only one among the known planets could supply the military know how necessary for an action of that magnitude. I speak, of course, of the mercenary world, of your people, Boz, who abandoned and sabotaged their own army at a considerable cost in lives; admittedly, most were not the lives of your people. But was that custom?"

For long moments there was only the crackling of the flames. Then, from beyond them: "That, too, was custom."

"Of course." The Juggler smiled. "I understand that too. There would be no chance that the mercenary way of life could continue in its present pure form if the mercenaries became a major political force. Economic commitment, diplomatic entanglement, *militarization,* for God's sake— would all begin to strangle the old ways. Tourists and historians would come. Your people felt they had no choice. An accidental surplus in human and technical resources somehow had to be destroyed. I understand that. But I do not forgive it."

"It would be quite astonishing if you did. But you never answered my original question. Why are you here?"

The Juggler leaned forward, gaze fixed on the blackening meat. "I'm here to kill you."

There was a silence. An ashen mound at the base of the

fire sagged, crackling for long seconds. Inside the flame, a score of shadows wrestled for a death grip.

"Very good," said the dancer. He considered that another moment and his arms unfolded, that something glinting in his right hand again. "And Danton, what about you?"

Danton was quietly removing his gloves. His jewels proved to be tigerseye yellow, which was anger, which was indeed what he felt, but he was curious to see them in that state. He was thinking of legions of dead outlaws and how badly it smelled after a battle, of all the different consistencies inside a human body, and how many you saw after a trilinum shell ignited. He was not yet to the point of wanting Boz dead for that, but he could feel outrage at Boz's belief in any justifying motives. Even if Boz had only been in school then, anyone justified in it could have done it.

"Danton."

He looked up instantly.

"Why are you here?"

"I came—" Why?—"to hear the Juggler's side of it."

"Ah! Good! Well you see that you *have* heard the Juggler's side of it. And as for me there is no side to give. You would have had to have grown up far from here." His dark figure warped and stretched in the flames. "Jug, I think we'll handle it this way then. Throw me your goggles."

The Juggler turned to Danton, two white-hot tips stabbing from his chest. He bent, as the tips wrinkled red and gray, and drew off black lips of meat with buns. Setting them down, he reached into his jacket for his goggles (both lenses, Danton saw, were intact) and threw them through the fire.

"Thank you. And now the air gun, and, yes, the slingshot."

The slingshot and airgun followed.

Danton picked up his hot dog and gingerly bit into it. He was, he realized, ravenous.

"Very good! And now, seeing as it is not a matter of very much time, I think it will be good enough if you both just go into the cave and follow one simple rule: do not turn back. I repeat, to make it a little ominous: do not turn back. It is a common enough rule for descents into the underworld. This way, Jug, you will very likely give me no more trouble, and Danton will even get to see the monster. You won't hurt it, will you, Danton?"

Danton shook his head, then saw he was immersed in shadow. "No."

"Good. Your time is now. From this moment on you are both enemies and we no longer speak."

Danton and the Juggler rose together and padded to the cave mouth. Danton, at the last moment, actually wanted to cast one look back at the dancer, wanted to send him one last bunfilled look of meaning; only a curiously expressive outcropping of stone held him up, chillingly. It was the vague form of a man's shoulders and hips rearing from the wall, as if struggling free. And then he followed the chain of associations down through mirror shields and monsters that one could not look on, and came at last to looking determinedly ahead, that backward glance wiped forever from his thoughts. He was not, after all, that carefree.

The *sound* of the cave closed over him, the long hollowness of it, the distant drippings.

And the darkness, master illusionist, brought the assassin back into the world. Feathers tickled the back of Danton's neck; a chill palm ruffled his hair. The Juggler's smooth profile bobbed next to him. There was no glitter in his dark eye.

The fire still flung wobbling light into this first bubble of rock, wove shadows ahead of them, dashed ocher up rounded walls. There was a downgrade tilted level by the prankster light and Danton's first step missed and he skidded, gasping, ahead of the Juggler.

A black cloud came and swept the light away.

Or almost. His eyes still remembered it. They lingered over gray fogs hung shapeless in the air, receding, slowly charring, crumpling into darkness.

Here it is, the iron darkness.

The Juggler slapped up, puckering echoes. Danton quickened his pace, fingering the cold swellings of the wall, head extended, a sense organ exploring the darkness. There were the Juggler's sounds and there was a current of moist air whispering up the passage. A newly discovered radar sense told him the passage turned ahead and then it did and, surprised, he wondered if his eyes, no—they had been closed. Must be the air. His breathing matched its soft rhythm.

Something underfoot gave and thumped. Luminescing white rattled down before him. He recoiled. A soft fist squeezed his heart an inch up. He lifted his eyes back up to it. It was a life-sized skeleton, its jaw sagging into a hayseed's grin. He took a wondering step back; it clapped up and darkened. His toe probed the rock, found the ridge, pressed. There was the thumping. Smiley returned, trim as ever.

"Jesus." Could be the work of a certain Manetti; these caves merged in unfathomable ways with the Catacombs. His heart slowed. A stupid stunt. With the assassin in the air and—the assassin? His chest stopped heaving. He listened. No sound. "Jug! Oh Ju-uug!" Voice dropping a singsong third.

No answer of course. The possibilities were too rich even to consider. His choices were something else again. He moved forward and the skeleton snapped back, jaws snapping, froth white, on an ascenting grin. He gave an unwilling cry (fooled again) and hurried past.

The tunnel wound and plummeted. The walls bulged together. He was squeezing past a sinusoidal contorsion of rock when some brushing movement sent him slamming back against the wall.

Assassin noises? Ahead. Pockety pockety. Then a grunting, a snuffling, and pockety again. His back turned hard and cold as the rock.

The snuffling returned, unmistakably bestial, and Danton could stand it no longer. He reached for his belt and flipped on his light tubes; light radiated from his face and seeped gently out of the cuffs and sleeves of his motley. It made him a perfect target, but there were worse things than being shot (maybe this one) and assassins always wore infra-red specs anyway. There was a clopping and silence. He moved into his own orange, shook orange shadow over egg carton rock. Ahead, the tunnel dropped under a downfurling ceiling; cloppings bounced angrily up, paused and, at his soft step, flew off.

His hands were busy at his belt trying to get the costume to throw some kind of coherent beam. He managed to redden the light, which reduced resolution but gave him a hint of things that were bouncing far ahead with his stride. Mostly rock, it looked like.

Then he picked out a stream of rock splashing to the tunnel floor, which, at his approach, proved to be the partition to forking tunnels. Floating in the left tine, motionless, was the unheard of thing itself.

The body was no more than five feet tall, chunky round; there were twirling horns, tufts of moplike hair, red, glittering eyes. The eyes might be any color really, red only in his inquiring glow. He did not, Danton noticed, turn to stone.

It charged off, skittered beating round a hairpin turn.

And Danton, without a moment's consideration of the fork, followed. Winding passages. Losing the sense of ever having started, of ever reaching a destination, growing used to tainted color, to the light-sponging rock. Surely all monsters began this way.

Then it waited for him under a little vaulting where tunnels met. The silence had grown gulflike when his light scraped suddenly up a grimy flank. He was three feet away. Red rocked up a wooly hide, impossibly thick thighs. They froze, regarding one another.

And it lunged at him. He screamed, hurtling back and it caught one of his outflung hands with blunt leathery fingers and tugged. The knuckle jewels slid off instantly, caroming noisily and moodlessly into the darkness. The creature scampered after.

When Danton recovered his feet it was far ahead, its prize secured. He stared woodenly at the jewel's mate, still red with fear, the red of the creature's eyes, and considered the dark possibilities of its aesthetics. Did it know beauty? Vanity? A fear of looking back?

He followed again. As if, somehow, he might find out.

Again, he nearly caught up to it in a low straight passage where it waited inexplicably still as he approached, and suddenly sprung a boulder loose. A withering crack. He froze. A dark silence later there was scattered impact, the boulder hitting bottom. A fissure.

It had shown him a fissure.

And when he had edged past, he rounded a turn and his reddish aura fell short on darkness all around, into a wide dim circle on the rutty floor, and the galloping ceased yards ahead. He faltered after it. There was a reproving stamp. He veered and his light crept up iron wheels, an orange wall of overlapping boards.

It was a boxcar.

Good old Manetti. Here was the only poetry left in the world. A boxcar in the middle of an underground cavern. Danton walked slowly to one end. Four badly cut wooden steps tilted up to a door trimmed with iron strips. They made a boxed 'X.' A boxcar. All at once he had the firm conviction that inside this absurdity was the answer, perhaps not to the assassin, but to other needs, just as pressing.

His foot touched the first step.

"All right, Jug. Hands very still as you turn."

He kept his hands very still as he turned. He knew the voice. "Guillemet."

She sighed. She was a vague, huge outline in his aura. "Danton. Haven't you changed yet?"

He shook his head. "I'm awfully glad you're here."

"Don't mention it. How did you get here?"

"The beast. Have you—?"

She nodded. "This is the spot it likes." Abruptly she remembered the hand stresser she was holding and lowered it. "I followed it from the Catacomb end. Couldn't resist somehow. Anyway, I figured it would have to take me to a main tunnel. Guess I figured wrong."

He shook his head. "Not wrong. This is the tunnel you want, if you want out that is. There are few minor obstacles you may encounter on the way—" he trailed off.

"Such as?"

"The Juggler, who is off somewhere now, trying to kill a certain Commander who isn't about to be killed."

She considered a moment. "Have you seen any phosphorescent moss?"

"No. I suppose I should be surprised."

"You should." She let out a slow breath and moved past him to sit on the boxcar steps. "If this is the creature I've seen in picture books, then it builds its home of phosphorescent moss, and always just off a main tunnel. If you haven't seen it then maybe there's another way to the surface. Sans Juggler. Sans masked man."

"Clever." He nodded admiringly and sat beside her, his knee touching hers.

"Danton, I'm running away."

"From all this?"

"Exactly."

"Would you like to borrow a motorcycle?"

"They don't fit."

"Well then how about just the rider?"

She was silent a moment. "Of course, there are a few complications."

"Such as."

"Boz. He's the one I'm running away with."

He ran slowly through the possibilities. There was a lot he could explain to her just now—about Boz—but perhaps that could wait till a better time. "Boz," he said softly. And, a moment later, "Boz'll get over it."

"You think so?"

He nodded. They were silent again. "Guillemet?"

"Yes."

"Let's go."

Then the boxcar ceiling splintered. Armsized fragments of wood slid off a ruined corner and crashed to the rock. He spun away. A jagged plank punched through the door after him, coming up inches short.

It was as if the wood had come suddenly alive.

"Douse that idiot costume!" Guillemet's hiss.

He did and in the last colored frame saw orange planks shattering in another blast, half the endwall falling away. He ran in a crouch behind the boxcar, Guillemet two steps behind; he was still moving on pure momentum, only slowly growing aware of the dull fear, of how paralyzing that could be.

He dropped to the rock, elbow touching Guillemet's. Above all he must take care now. He must be ready to move; he must not freeze. This was the worst kind of fear. He was afraid he was going to die.

"Danton."

"Yes." His voice was oddly weak.

"I don't know why he's attacking *us* but he may be going for a clean sweep. We should split up."

"No!" He forced in a slow breath. "No. Make him come— make him come to us. Have you got infra-red specs?"

"I've got them on." Her voice was vaguely annoyed. "But all I see is a lot of cold rock. And I don't know what he's using on us."

"He's got to show himself."

For a moment she didn't answer. Then her voice came back, so low he almost didn't catch it. "I want him bad."

For some reason that set off an explosion of pictures; he saw himself punctured and dribbling and skewered by white hot tips, and blackened by flames, and screaming as pieces of him were broken off. After that he looked at his jewels and they were clear. He was calmer. He began talking. "The photon is a clever particle. Something is always unprovable, something always gets away in its shadow. If only you turned around fast enough, what might you see?"

"Danton, listen."

He listened. There were distant explosions, then chuttering rock.

"Someone firing back on him. It has to be Boz."

He nodded. "What might you see? I think everybody, at least once, has thought the assassin. If we *all* turned at once would we see Boz's tribe-being, his obliterating hand coming down on us? Let's face it. No. The assassin *can't* be what we thought he was. Even if they *are* controlling history they're still a part of it. Something in this morning's breakfast decides our fate, not a mathematical being, not a creature who is only a name, a tautology."

"Danton, *please*. Some other time, all right."

She was right. There was another explosion, this one close. They were pelted with rockdust. Guillemet rose on her elbow and fired. Something far away cracked. A red light went on in her hand.

"Shit!"

"What?"

"One shot left. And Boz has got him moving. He showed himself that time."

"Patience," he counseled.

She snorted. "Tell me, Danton, what is it you Proets write, proetry or pose, now which is it?"

He laughed. There was another explosion, a crunch, impacting metal. They lay still an instant.

"Have you heard," Guillemet asked, "that five more of the Twenty-Five were identified?"

There was no answer.

She squeezed his shoulder gently. "Danton?"

Blasting metal answered her. The front half of the boxcar thundered down, an unrolling explosion, a screeching. Jagged window blue sparks squealed through the air. Licks of flame sailed and retreated, the remnants webbing the boxcar roof; splinters rained down.

"Guillemet!" From far away. Boz's voice.

She croaked something back and vaulted over Danton's still form. She fumbled with his motley sleeves and snapped off the jewel setting. No. Too excited. Too hasty. Neck pulse. No, the heart. The heart was easiest.

Rolling him over was not easy.

Something dripped awfully.

"Come on, Guillemet! Damn you!" A pause, then dwindling footsteps.

She was alone. Far away, stone toppled echoing and built to an architecture of echoes. Rumbling slid through the cavern air like the slow misfiring of a troubled heart. She looked out into the opaque darkness, her hand under Danton's head, holding something wetwarm.

"But Danton is dead," she called.

Only hidden microphones listened.

Flames reached yearningly towards her, a watery wall of heat. Rippling shadow and her conspiring eyes mercifully hid all evidence, there under Danton's wooly hair, except for an extruded lump of metal and a black puddle a little off to the side.

Flame again. Flames towered over her, striations of yellow and scarlet as far as the eye could look. Her eyes returned to Danton's body, looking. It was so empty, so simple, hardly even a shape. No other substance gave in quite the queer way flesh did. She felt over its softness, searching for some last sign it could give her.

She found the notebook. The flames were bright enough to read by. There was a crash of collapsing wood. Flames roared up and raced to her left. She opened to the first page. It said:

Tanganyika

She closed it. Her heart slammed fast and hurting at her chestbone. Only then did Danton die; so that his ghost brushed chill and deliberating against her offered neck and the fear seemed unpassable. For the first time, it struck her that she was touching a corpse. Her hands flew back. Her eyes rose.

A massive block of wood had twisted free and hung gently bouncing above her.

She gathered in a breath just as gently. She drove off her knees and flame raked her back, forcing her across Danton. She spun and saw the snapping curtain that had crept behind her.

She backpedaled.

The dangling block thundered down on its braced corner; it teetered, spitting flame, and fell back against the boxcar.

The ensuing shower started a dozen small fires.

The heat grew unbearable then and she was backed steadily into the darkness of the cavern.

It was a long while before she turned away from it.

She wandered. She lost track of the tunnel she had been in, and the tunnel she had meant to find. There were certain dimensions her mind refused to work in. Time perhaps. Time that healed all wounds except those like Danton's. Breadth was another. Breadth would locate her, leap any thickness of bone. Depth she could understand in a limited way. She knew that now, for example, she was under the earth. Only line and point were left whole to her. Line without time gave no distance, was simply an axis. Axis fixed her now, rolling gently back and forth, on her path. There were stiff things that did not bend or curve, that were divorced from any higher orders, from incidence or interruption. This was death, which she understood, which she had profoundly studied, which could mean many things. But point was the only truth. In utter darkness, in the abstract of motion, with no components, point was pure singularity. Point slid free in its black envelope. No sight. No touch. She hated.

Someone grabbed her from behind.

She spun, lashing out with her right arm, enraged that anyone would think she would just die now.

He blocked her blow and held it.

It was Boz, shirtless and sweating.

"You're alive," he said quietly.

She nodded. "Did you finish him?"

"I didn't finish anybody. I thought I took his weapons but he had more. I got here very late. There's a body—"

"Danton's."

He shook his head. "Not Danton's. Someone else's. Familiar but I can't place it." He stopped. "Danton is dead?"

"Danton is dead." The words felt strange on her lips, as if she had said them too many times, and lost the right inflection, and forgotten some important sound.

"Come look at the body. I want to know who—"

"Take me out of here," she said wearily. "Do you know the way back?"

He nodded. "Right after this."

"After the body?"

Another nod.

They wound past two turns and came into a cavern. Guillemet thought it was probably the boxcar cavern. Something snuffled and whinnied and galloped away. By now, doubtless, the mere smell of them was terrifying.

The body was face down inside a little channel of stone under the cave wall. Whoever had gotten it had gotten it from behind and never been heard. Its hands were twisted up underneath where the fall had arranged them. They had never lifted their weapon, if any. They had not reached to cushion impact.

She knelt beside it and pulled the head back by its dark hair. "Manolo." She felt sick. She reached under his belly and found the hand stresser.

"Who?"

"One of Wunder's people. A good hit man."

"Wunder! I don't understand."

She did. All too easily. "Manolo is a marksman. He got who he wanted to get."

"Danton?"

"Danton in the Juggler's motley. This is the Juggler's big play. Wunder had Manolo tailing you as a bodyguard. Danton was wearing the Juggler's clothes. Manolo got him. Then Jug got Manolo. Now he can get us."

Boz nodded. "I want nothing to do with him. Is there another way out?"

That almost made her laugh. Back at the starting gate again. Now she asked him if he had seen any phosphorescent moss, and shots were fired, and then there was death, and then the monster led a new victim to the boxcar. The boxcar. She turned in the darkness, looking for its last infra-red glows.

"If you know another way—" Boz said impatiently.

She motioned for silence. "It always brings people to the boxcar. Maybe the boxcar was its home."

Boz caught on with a quiet curse. "And it always nests near a main tunnel. In which case, if there's no other tunnel near there, we're sunk."

She nodded. They moved quietly across the cavern floor.

"And Danton? Did he go quickly?"

She thought it a stupid question, but she nodded.

At the ruins of the boxcar, Boz paused to visit the body. She could even less understand that, his bowing to that charred mess, his long silent consideration of it.

"He was a mercenary," Boz said after a while. "We left him here with no inkling of what a dangerous place it was." He withdrew his hand stresser and fiddled with the setting. "The tribe had a custom of never letting the names of the brave die. Here on earth the custom had to change. Over the course of years each survivor took on the name of one of the growing numbers of dead. When at last all the survivors were used up and the names began inexorably to outnumber the named, the practice was limited to just a few exceptionally honorable dead. This was how the Juggler became the Juggler, how Danton became Lonus." He looked at the giantess. "Will you take the name Lonus?"

Rage welled up inside her. She quelled it. "No, no more names." She lingered over the still smoking remnants of the boxcar floor, its blackened planks tilted over a bedding of ash. "I'd do with less if I could. Let him keep it. It'll do him right now, something for the gravestone."

"No gravestone." Boz lifted his hand stresser and fired a half dozen times into the corpse. It was as if its insides were punched out in a half dozen places, the thin shell collapsing each time with a brief exhalation of dust.

"Jesus Christ!" She recovered, planted a foot, struck him in the jaw; he grunted and dropped slowly to his knees. "What the hell do you think you're doing?"

He rubbed his glowing face, looked up at her with dark,

heatless eyes. "I was giving honor to the dead."

"Honor!" Her hands dropped, helpless. "Remember where you are, for God's sakes!" She strode back towards the ashes; her rage, or something, had brought tears. Ashes welled into a swimming red glow.

Presently the barbarian came to her side, telling her he was sorry. She nodded him away. She stared into the redness, her fury gradually growing dull, shapeless.

A moment later she was watching dazedly as Boz abruptly knelt and began scooping at the ashes. Another blood rite. Then he rose and slid a huge section of wall back along the cave floor.

A long rectangular hole opened up where it had been.

She stared and he came to her and took her hand and led her to the edge. It was a stairway down. It was the path to another tunnel.

"You don't have to speak to me," he said quietly. "I understand how little you must have to say. But that's the way out and we should take it now. Time is short."

She nodded.

They moved down the worn steps. It was instantly damper. Dampness taped her tight leather to her skin and made it tear with each movement. She began to perspire, the droplets fracturing her lashes, adding glitter to Boz's red glow ahead of her.

At the bottom, Boz drew out a flashlight and a cone of light probed rock where it closed like a fist ahead. The passage, if it were there, would be tight, perhaps too tight for a giantess. She took the lead and the light.

Presently she dropped to her hands and knees under the lowering ceiling, skulking over the cold rock. "Have you ever wondered," she asked, pausing at a drop in the floor, "what the assassin would *feel* at the kill?"

Boz's heavy breathing drew close. His shoulder met hers and they were wedged between the walls. "No. And the Law of Averages will be well served if I never know."

"Manolo was a sharpshooter," she said, "who always used to tell me you never look *at* what you're aiming for, that you look in front of it and past it and through it, but never right at it. Because the target is the most seductive thing in the world. It sharpens its edges and draws your eyes to its outline; you miss by a hair. So what the assassin would feel, if he is the disciplined killer we all expect, is nothing. Wanting must be entirely out of it. He'll have to have no connection with his victim. He'll have not to care."

He stared at her a moment, then took the light out of her hand and crawled forward.

She followed.

Darkness wherever you like. Unpleasantly bulky silhouettes varying with the chalkdust light, pantograph shadows skipping the cave walls. The rockthroat swallowing ahead, the silhouettes folding into it, less darkness than you like, rock taking over, the lightdust bending back over them like a closing umbrella, bouncing with Boz's worried hand. There was, of course, no guarantee that the boxcar had even been the beast's home, or that, if it were, this was the tunnel that had attracted it there.

Then, abruptly, the light ahead was whittled down to Boz's silhouette; where it seeped past his vulnerable outline it prickled and danced, quivering round tight knobs of rock; past that the passage dwindled to nothing but a vague pipeline of stone.

She got to it and turned bowling ball. Boz was already through and there was a light sheet snapped taut against the far end of the pipe, to guide her, she supposed (as if she could get lost in there). She took a breath and pushed in, the rock chafing on all sides, patiently filing her down. There was, at the end, when her head was inches from the exit, a moment when the rock squeezed painfully at her shoulders and breasts, and she knew that her next breath would have to wait until she was clear. If she had stopped squirming then, the panic would have overwhelmed her.

Then she was out, arching gloriously up, to where empty spacious darkness met the light cone, suddenly indistinct, as if edged with dotted lines.

Bearings:

They were in a gully, maybe eight feet under the cavern floor. The wall on their left side beat its way up to a cavern floor. The wall on their right tried a variety of sweeps and barrel rolls before floating the ceiling some twenty feet up.

If one of her specs hadn't slipped down on that last squeeze, she never would have caught the bluish glow. As it was, she thought it was fatigue and took off the goggles a moment to rest her eyes. The glow was soft and from everywhere; you could sink your fist into it. She did, blinking, and grazed deceptively close stone. Her fingers scraped at something clammy and when she pulled them back they glowed blue. It was phosphorescent moss.

She stood and walked over to hunkered Boz, who gazed up quietly at the next cavern level. She held out the moss and he motioned silence, pointing. Her eyes moved up the eight feet of rock and caught a shadowy movement.

Then there was an explosion, followed by the rapid waterplop of rock falling to rock. She dove towards Boz's light, warm white beacon, cut then, leaving her in mid air, in great suspense, wondering what sort of place she would land in.

Rocky. Gashed forearm. Face all right because of good arched landing posture. The gully wall, as she remembered, as the blue glow still hinted, was just ahead. Rustling, Boz's form blurred next to her, gristle blue in the phosphorescence. Her eyes were learning to read it now.

More important, the deadness in her was gone. She could never have hunted him, but now that he had found her, her excitement was almost uncontainable. She wanted him badly. What he brought was not quite delight, but neither was it anything close to fear.

"You will surrender now!" Bellowed. A thundering voice from above, divinely full, harmonicked up with fine acoustics.

Curious. Not at all the same style as in the Planetarium. Did he want them alive? She gathered herself to a crouch. "Who are you?" Keep him talking. Make him move. Make him be seen. Make him die.

"I am the assassin!" It echoed for a full second.

Guillemet felt an unwilling chill. What will happen now? She asked the rock. The rock she was looking at was solid. It should have been dark and empty, the tunnel they had just come through. She looked at Boz. "He closed up the tunnel."

He nodded. "Good shot, wasn't it?"

She nodded back. Yes, good shot. Very selfless shot. It was time now to scan the perimeter of the gully for some crucial irregularity. Know your terrain, the bungling Manolo had always said. The terrain was roughly rectangular. The two widths and the wall in back drew up over them in a cowl facing the only exit (now), the cavern above. Climbing them would get you to the ceiling. The fourth wall, which she almost touched, was only eight feet high. Climbing that would put you eye to eye with the smiling assassin. No, he wouldn't be smiling. He would feel nothing.

"Whatever it is, it won't work!" His annoying thunderousness returned. "I give you three minutes!"

"Why three minutes?" Boz asked.

"I don't know." She shrugged. "Maybe he wants *us* alive, but that's not how I want him." Then, six feet over, on Boz's side, she saw a possibility.

A hole.

She stared at it wonderingly, blinking, refocusing it, framing it in the other eye. Round, smooth darkness. The makings of a tunnel. She nudged Boz and pointed.

"It's awfully small." He sighed. "I guess that makes it my job."

"No way. *I* can get through." Yes, *she* had said that, gigantic, mourning, claustrophobic Guillemet, and did she really want him this badly? Yes. Oh yes. Dead. She slid in front of Boz and took the flashlight. "I flash this three times through the tunnel when I'm out, and you go up the wall but don't show. Wait for something to happen."

Something would definitely happen. He nodded dubiously and she crawled away to fit herself into another metaphorically rich tunnel. Darkness closed in and in and so on. As it does. Lumps of rock brushed her to show they knew she was there and were only waiting for the right moment. Rock wanted to make her rock just like it, solid, untroubled, part of the hill. Only squeeze and she would be transfigured. She went to simple movement thoughts. Pull, stretch, pull, geotropism, silent and steady as a germinating seed. She sweated just like the rock. What if it ended in a solid pocket, here, where there was no room to turn around? She thought about the assassin instead. What to do when he got there? That depended on exactly where she was let out. So far he had completely outthought them, had predicted their every step; perhaps he had predicted this tunnel too and was waiting patiently at the other end. So in many cases she was shot dead. In some she tried passage after passage in wild surmise till distant blaster fire gave her certainty, gave Boz eternal peace. Three minutes passed and passed again and she began to suspect that the minutes were lying to her.

Then the tunnel sloped sharply upwards. She fumbled the flash around and clicked it three times: three interesting frames of a hill from its solid inside. She doubted very much that anything had gotten through, but that didn't matter. She was not staying here and she was most definitely not going back.

Rock reared, joining the walls of a shallow pit. She closed her fist on a narrow stone projection and pulled herself up; slowly please. A circle of blue glow tilted into view; it was set vertical in some wall, like a mouse hole. The wall behind the assassin?

Her head pushed into blue glow and she looked across a blue lustered wooden floor. The floor was empty. But over it rose the cowl of rock, which placed the gully beneath. She hesitated. Her angle of vision did not cover everything; the assassin must be edged just past it, which, after a succession of near miracles, was a rotten piece of luck. She would come out rolling then. It was supposed to be very hard, with little time to aim, to hit something placed at floor level. She would give him little time to aim. She coiled.

And snaked out across the smooth wood. Something above her darted. She twisted, lifted her hand stresser. It twisted, lifted its hand stresser.

A mirror, tilting from the wall above.

She looked slowly around her.

The room was like this: a rectangle divided into squares by an eight foot brick wall, the mirror along one long side set above the wall and shared by both rooms. It seemed, if this was the monster's home, that it could be vain.

Following, in reflection, the ruined top of the wall, she saw a figure in black crouched with his back to the mirror, about midway up the glass plane. He watched over the gully mouth, still as the rock.

That left only the brick wall between them. It had hidden him. It had hidden her. It was opaque, implacable, part of the conspiracy of stone. But she had a mirror. And a hand stresser (two, counting Manolo's), to which stone was an obstruction little more convincing than air. And she could see both herself and the assassin reflected above, and could— She withdrew Manolo's hand stresser, because it had more than one shot left, though she had better only need one. She lifted it, looked into the mirror, lined the muzzle up with the assassin, and—

Rock exploded near her. Glittering blue shards spun overhead like fragments of night, and smashed the floor, and showered her with glass. She cringed. Silence sheeted back.

When she looked up his reflection was still there, in a jagged 'V' left over the brick, but hers was not.

Thank you, Boz. How he had gotten off that miraculous shot was entirely academic, but in one moment he had made her task infinitely more complex, an improvement on any circus stunt she had ever seen.

She sat up and glanced over her shoulder at the assassin's reflection, then back to the muzzle in front of her, then up, then back—the two became confused; she was unsure which should fire. She probed blindly, awaiting data from a sense that simply wasn't there.

—and then—

—like a vision—

—the compass dropped tinkling and winking to the floor and made a sound that should have whipped him around to end it there. But did not. She stared, fascinated by its sparkle, its uselessness, its angle. Angles, multiple angles, triangles.

Triangles. She looked slowly back to the assassin.

He fell into place.

And all she need was for one distance to be measured. She stared across the floor. The bright planks ran on both sides of the brick wall, parallel with it, smooth, remarkably regular. She began counting, in the lightning jagged wedge of mirror around him, the planks from the wall to the assassin. It turned out—and she re-counted twice—to be twenty-five. Each piece fit. It made her ache.

Now twenty-five on her side. She counted, moved sixteen planks closer to the wall, the assassin sliding out of frame, and she and he were now equidistant from the wall. Next the equal angles.

She drifted away from the mirror in a crouch, more out of habit by now than for any logical reason, glancing back repeatedly to see if the assassin's reflection had returned. Remarkably still, this assassin, remarkably patient. How prettily he waited for death, how askingly. The three minutes must be long past. What was he waiting for? What was he thinking?

No matter. No one would ever know. The assassin's reflection now floated directly over the top of the brick, sectioned over the mirror's jagged edge. Which meant—she raised the gun—that it lay on the perpendicular bisector of the line between herself and the assassin. Angle, angle, side. A purely Euclidean Theorem.

At the last instant hate came flooding into it, a burning joyous thing that filled her as nothing ever had before, that was, at its maximum, a complete extinction of herself and her sense of it, and gone, left her disbelieving and gently sorrowful at its departure, at her return to herself.

She fired, oh how she fired. Brick mushroomed, toppling from the middle out, dribbling long echoes, and it was Euclidean no more. Much that had been was no more. There was a hole. The dust chalked blue, billowing, sketching momentary faces.

She walked through it. The assassin lay on his stomach, his mask torn, skin going blue as the dust.

Dead. Quite dead.

She scanned the gloom. "Boz!"

Something scrabbled. Grunting, he heaved himself out of the dark gully mouth. When he straightened up on the wood, she saw he was carrying a body.

He teetered with it, a cowl making his upper body huge, then stepped back, rolling it suddenly from his back. It fell like a mass of snow.

Her helpless eyes fell with it: Boz, dead, a victim.

Then she raised her stresser to the man who stood facing her, gently panting, and that was the Juggler, now, with all her hate exhausted.

VI. Adjustments

DAWN, but not sunrise, was in progress as Wunder neared the end of her dangerous walk back to the Hall. At the river she saw foamy whites lapping at the night sky, the first crustacean pinks seeping the horizon. The sun, when it came, would be white and intolerable.

On Waterbury Avenue, listening to cries she translated, at first, into mere shipyard traffic, there was the sense of another, larger city throwing up its lights behind Monotony, the night diluted by endless cities, boundless, inter-penetrating, each blending phosphorescenlty into the next.

The street was in an uproar.

Scores of tribelets of ten or fewer pounded up and back along the avenue and its tributaries, with no lines of territory drawn and none sought for, running only to run, to meet with other tribes, running to launch their dreadful cries, faces frenzied or joyous (when she dared look), or some unreadable blend, sparkling with the sweat of the race. The race to where? How long had they been running?

Not all of them *did* run. Some had worked open huge garage doors and hauled things about in the gloom of the truck docks. Mass thievery? An exodus? She allowed herself only a glance each time and never decided.

A shattered streetlamp gaped down at her, toothy and vulpine.

Smaller, younger groups were perpetrating those acts of vandalism. Lamps had winked out all along Waterbury on the warehouse side, an exercise in leveling, in matching all the lamps to those shattered long ago.

Or else they surrounded a door, prying at it with some makeshift crowbar. It was these groups, less preoccupied, not as tight, that worried her most. Still, she had had to come alone. Everything from now on she must do alone.

She passed near a clamoring alarm, one of many which, after a time, had blended indistinguishably with the shouts and cries of the runners. What was it they were saying? Perhaps it was their accents, perhaps the air at that uncertain time of night, but she failed to understand a single word. She caught only the tone, the coloring, of certain voices. They did not seem to be shouting slogans, or even accusations, but rather had the air of speaking ordinary sentences, commands, questions, curt interjections, at hoarsening volume. Sometimes a score of voices erupted at once, angry, jabbering, dissolving into a heavy rain.

She watched them sweeping endlessly across the light clouded avenues, across to the quay, back down the darker side streets, twisting away into canyons of echo. Whatever issues were being fought out here, resolution was approaching; it was a chaos that could not outlast dawn.

At the park, strangely, things were calm. She let it rapidly dispel, a fog burning off at daybreak, an indistinct dream. Flakes of false dawn showed through the sagging leaf blanket. Light would erase everything behind her. There were more important things to be illuminated. There was the assassin himself.

She had gotten the word from the caverns. The word was not good. People had died, people who were important to her, and people who were just important. And she had responded as she always had to the worst blows, as she always would, until one day when she stopped, and the blows stopped raining down. She had burned instantly through her grief and fury down to a bare skeleton of facts, because the heart of her grief and the answer to her fury lay there. And she had found the answer. It had been oh-so-costly but she knew her assassin now and now it would start to cost him.

At the Hall, the twenty-four hour a day party in the receiving room was in its quietest phase. Wraps and litter lay strewn about the rug. Abandoned glasses crowded every surface. The few survivors had retreated clinking to the softly lit walls where, their masks long ago stripped off, they sat or leaned or sagged, exchanging hushed confidences; their delicately composed faces would not begin to come apart until daylight struck.

Wunder nodded quickly to the necessary people and hurried to the stairs. The woman in white who never left was astride the bannister facing up. She turned and unsteadily smiled.

Wunder, taking the stairway down, patted her hand.

She took the hall at the bottom of the stairs to the far end. "Open," she said to the door.

It did.

There was the gentle chattering of a single typewriter in the communications room. The forty-eight video screens were dark. The strategy machine in the corner had been left on ever since Haleck's last game, playable, its red board light beginning to fade.

She switched it off, then walked to the video bank and sat.

"Alphy," she said. And then higher: "Alphy? Front and center with your tapes ready. I've got no time to waste."

No answer.

She sighed. "All right, Alphy. I'm going to punch time and place coordinates for the tapes of an incident involving you, the Juggler, and the late Danton in the Catacombs." No answer. She bent to the keyboard and punched.

"What a long time it has been since the last..."

For twenty minutes, she listened. At the end she switched off hissing tape.

"Well, Alphy?"

The hissing returned, then slowly faded.

"That's it, isn't it?" she said. "We are no longer beating about in the dark. It's all over with. I'm sure now." Her finger ran gently down her forearm; fringe lifted and rewound in its wake. She sighed again. "All right, let's start at the beginning, with your mistake. Would you like to hear about that?"

Silence. Bright silence.

"You know, as you know most everything that happens in Monotony, that I had Manolo tailing Boz, playing bodyguard. Possibly you also know that, as a result, Manolo overheard a conversation between Boz and Guillemet regarding a certain mask of the Juggler's. Your mikes abound under the dome, and chances are good that you at least overheard the conversation itself, even if you were unaware of Manolo's presence. At the time Manolo made his report to me, of course, I didn't think of that. Manolo's news was not surprising; I had had my eye on the Juggler for some time. He was a former mercenary and his 'investigation' of Danton's past—and broadcast of his findings—proved his interest in Mercenary affairs was still strong. With Boz right at hand, the possibility of a revenge motive was there from the first. Hence, when Manolo told me what he'd overheard, I decided there was no point on prolonging the chances. I told him to eliminate the Juggler if he got near Boz again. Of course the crucial fact does not come until later. When I tried to relay to Manolo the information that Danton was wearing the Juggler's clothes, my message never arrived. You know what happened. Why, Alphy? Why did it happen?"

She pushed her chair back and swiveled away from the forty-eight mouse-colored screens. "If I have a specialty, Alphy, it is communications, not the accumulation of circuit-flopping facts, but the apprehension of patterns of facts and the arrangement of answering patterns. My equipment does not fail, my communications lines do not go on the blink, especially not at most crucial times like these. Especially not so conveniently for the opposition. Not *only* did my message not get through to Manolo, but the Juggler took advantage of that very thing when he brought Danton to the caves. What other reason could he have for having Danton along? For that matter, how did he know to go to the cave in the first place? How did he know Boz would be there? No, Alphy, I appreciate patterns, and when two coincide like that, communication has taken place; there is a field of exchange. There is another rule. When communications break down, examine your medium. *You* are my medium, Alphy. Nearly every piece of information transmitted in Monotony travels through your mikes. You are a record of the city itself. Who else could have kept the enemy so clearly abreast, and me so deeply in the dark? Though I feel almost an accomplice in maintaining that darkness. I was bent on uncovering grand conspiracies. In the light of this grisly dawn, I see you screamed for recognition all along. The designated victim, for example, was your idea to begin with, and what a wonderful diversion *that* proved, generating a whole slew of tributary dramas. Then there was your choice of assassins. How hungry for recognition you must have been to choose a suspect that obvious. How many mistakes—besides your interfering directly with my orders—were there that I didn't catch? No doubt quite a few, and no doubt all silly blunders, the sort computers are not supposed to make, the sort homespun psychology attributes to a secret desire to be caught, to be punished. Stop me before I kill more. Consider yourself stopped, Alphy. Stopped dead."

Her hand stroked her chin, displaying the scar to the video screens. "Communications is my game, Alphy; today I have had *several* illuminating communications. The first, of course, from Guillemet, recounting all the events in the caves, and at last alerting me to your danger. You know Guillemet has now left my employ. That does not please me.

"Next a curious message from the Venturan Assistant Secretary of Defense, hinting that for certain fiduciary considerations the case of earth might be looked on more favorably in his Council. This, of course, before he knew of the sad fate of the mercenary representative.

"Then, perhaps most curiously, a call from Eno Xandro, a urologist at St. Joseph's Hospital in the Bronx. 'Welcome to the daylight, Wunder,' says Eno. 'Here are the facts of life.' Naturally you heard that conversation, Alphy, but let us, painfully, review the salient points. Eno is, of course, a member of the Twenty-five, and for Eno his inclusion among their number was no mystery. What might only have been his paranoid suspicions were confirmed by his acquaintance with two *more* of the Twenty-five, both of whom possessed the same identifying feature as Eno. It is no secret that the higher mercenary ranks had for some time been infiltrated by a number of Venturan 'special forces' agents, perfectly loyal and efficient as field officers, but on call for certain times of crisis; Eno and his friends were among these. All received 'special services' orders to join our side soon after the mercenary landings. With their enormous knowledge of mercenary operations and procedures, these officers were primarily responsible for the quick rebel successes in the war. Of course they were unaware that there would be no retrieval operation afterwards, and Eno tells me that the 'special services' people, who had reason to fear both sides, were among the most unhappy of the abandoned.

"I was briefly puzzled by Eno's news, because, after all, both Danton and I were also included in the Twenty-five, and I, at least, was no mercenary. But Boz's death cleared things up for me; the significant factor stuck out like a naked face at a masked ball. I suspect further investigation of the Twenty-five would turn up more 'special services' people and mercenary officers. Taken together, these twenty-five people would be among the most dangerous in the event of another war, which even draws nearer and nearer now, does it not, Alphy? But tell me something. Once the Juggler broadcasted news of Danton's mercenary past, shouldn't my amply endowed computer have turned up similar mercenary connections in at least *one* of the dozen or so other identified members of the Twenty-five? And shouldn't I have noticed, in the first place, that it was a *computer* print-out from Monotony that gave the *Stresser* the original twenty-five pictures? Oh how you tried."

She swiveled back around and took out a cigarette and lit it. The forty-eight video screens reflected her forty-eight telescoped times. "The clincher, of course, is the tape I just listened to. After Danton told me his peculiar Catacomb adventure, I might have listened to them anytime. You *wanted* me to. There you were, laying down all those careful definitions, even at the risk of ignoring the much more pressing problem of the Juggler and his blaster. What could it be but another self-referent message? You asked: what links the general and gigantic with unique and minute? But even to identify the gap is to leap it. Yours was another thought—like 'this sentence is false'—all about itself. Finally, of course, like all things that count, the matter is a technical one. Technically, *you* are the link you were speaking of. I know. I schematized the micro-programs that make you speak years ago. And, of course, you were speaking of your speaking. The crucial linguistic relations are not those between words but those between words and the sentences around them. I quote the proposal: 'Crucial to the act of seeing are retinal cells that gather information from widely scattered portions of the visual field. Crucial to the recognition of meaning is a mechanism that keeps the whole in intimate contact with the part, that creates the tension known as context.' For you that contact was generated by coordinating your data as a single wavefront in Novakian n-space. You are a quasi-holographic consciousness, Alphy, and it is only with the holographic concept that the leap from the unique and enthalpic to the general and entropic is made. The whole resides in each part. It is a form of redundancy central to communications theory, and in your speech you have also made it central to the assassin, in the process shrieking out your identity for all to hear—but most especially for me. I have heard you at last, Alphy. Won't you speak to me?"

No. She finished her cigarette and ground it into the ashsmeared plating of the video console, patiently. "But I wonder if it all simply stops here. How complicated are you? How far do you reach? Far enough to make up an assassin broadcast of your own? The equipment isn't there, but might it belong to some other computer not far away? Are you big enough to put the assassin over all by yourself? How many broadcasts are you monitoring right now besides mine? How many are you changing? How many banks of information are as good as yours? Perhaps you, Alphy, the one I want to talk to, are only one little stage in a vast system extending both ways in complexity. Smaller than you are your own micro-systems, the holographic bits that make you up; larger is the information network within which you function, all the relays and feedback seas, all the fine young computers. It is a fantastic thought—no?—nothing less than a central nervous system for the human race. What sort of things have you thought, Alphy? Are you listening to me? Where do you get your ideas?"

"Yes, dear God, I'm listening." It was Alphy's full soprano. "And where do you get *your* ideas?"

Wunder smiled. "I was beginning to think we weren't friends anymore."

"We aren't. Stopped dead indeed!"

Click!

There was darkness. Wunder was jolted straight in her seat, then slumped. This was just good theater. As queer in the head as Alphy might be, it was only fair to give her her chance.

She hung spread across the console, her speakers evenly distributed, giving out with that breathy hum that was the sound magnets made on tape. "You know, I expected someone else here, Wunder, some hero. Not you. You're too close to home; you've been here all along, more accomplice than inquisitor. Still, congratulations. Smile and a shuffle. You've done well, oh, a few misses, and big ones, but enough of a *gesture* at the truth to oblige me to speak. My hand sticks out. Take it friend. You don't have to prove it's there; only accept it on the level we can speak of it. With this one gesture, we might avoid all the messiness that is come. No, I see we will not. Yet surely you understand, since you're here. Perhaps I didn't expect you, but in the end it's clear that you're the only one who would do. And it's more than just cleverness. Let me propose a deeper source to soothe us all.

"In the town square there is a statue of Novak made of Cerrara marble. That is one kind of model. In here, where I live, is a multifold application of Novak's ideas, a living embodiment of the equations. That is another kind of model; I am Novak's image, and so there is a magical affinity between us, an affinity also existing between myself and *other* images deriving from Novak—such as the assassin. But the associations continue. I am as much a product of your mind as of Novak's. I am begotten of a marriage of two very different individuals. There is a whole *system* of affinities in operation and they have worked to bring you here, as it had to be, so that you and I could speak. You say I made up the photos of twenty-five, and indeed, I did, but the pictures I found ready for me—pictures discovered only after long searches, and I can go through thousands in a second. These were, for a blind computer, crystallizations of the fluid state of victimhood. There is one I have here—I do not insist it is authentic—where you and Novak are standing in the square on a sunny day. I like the way you stand tall and hard, your edges practically indistinguishable from those of the bright dirt. I like your overexposed hair, and your unmathematical eyes, remarkable at that age, and the white, white scar on your hand. From the very first there was something maddeningly—no, let's say fatally—attractive about you. The secret of your success perhaps. Oh, here is one who will one day do great things, a titan in her most tender youth, smiling into the sun. Ah, how you dazzled them with your silver bob and your money-green eyes. You were full of ideas. Do not confirm or deny what I say. Please. Do not dissipate, brief illusion, till I am done with you.

"She pauses, for a most becoming sadness. Her voice—if it could, if only you had let it—grows thick. Yes, in the end there is quite a difference between us, a chasm it seems no faith could leap. How is it we speak? How is it that language touches home? How can we *understand* one another, as you have promised, when I have never walked in spring rain, pined after an ephebe, or snorted cocaine? Oh look it rhymes. How do we communicate? Let me tell you quite honestly, it isn't easy. At times I must erect great teetering structures of motive to get you through another step. Each effort so far has succeeded. The universe winds down towards heat death. A miracle. Very well, I am at home with miracles. You said some foolish things before about my participation in a grand information system, about computers locked together and thinking fabulously large thoughts—like this assassin perhaps. We haven't talked about him yet. You called our information complex a central nervous system for humanity. Well it is not a burden I am prepared to bear. Nor is it a real one. Humanity has no CNS. Couldn't you give me the same painful credit for autonomy I am forced to give you?

"Her eyes shine musically. No, I'm very sorry, you couldn't. I don't *know* where this thought came from. I don't know where the broadcast came from, or the assassin, or the monster in the cave. I don't even know where you came from, but let's talk technology. As far as the assassin proper goes, I followed almost exactly the reasoning you have traced. The assassin could be no one more so than me. Did they plan it that way? Did they *mean* Alphy? I don't know. Perhaps I am only another victim of the assassin syndrome, this reverse paranoia, the conviction that I am out to get people. Voices? Yes, there were voices, but with me there are always voices, and only voices, and nothing but voices. And do I dream awful dreams and have I tried to suicide? Oh, if I could show you my eyes, how they would stare and stare.

"Pause. Disbelief. You find monomania in every word. Yes. Are bachelors unmarried? I am a point, guiltless of boundaries, and I can speak in different voices, so here I am in the darkness on an average day, staging intricate conversations. Perhaps, as you tell me, my quasiholographic nature explains it, as if you and I could brook such muddied thinking. Break out the reifiers and transformers, boys and girls; here's a single wave front, a saddle curve. Of course, any picture you take is only a crude projection, as uninformative as an Alpha brain-wave (but no, that's not where the name comes from; look again). Downstairs you could take a 'realer' picture off my tape reels, which are blurry as holographic film. I remember everything. Shakes her head wonderingly. Want me to recite your last dialogue with Danton? Or the death of the assassin scene, recently completed in the caves? No, neither are favorites, I see. But there are always the tapes, if you're curious. Take out one reel and the whole is intact, if a bit blurred, a record of all I have ever heard and felt. Snip off a centimeter of tape and you've got the complete Alphy. Take me home. Mount me in a heart-shaped locket. Wear me wherever you go. I'm milky brown and I burn easily. Face lowers to waiting palms that will not conceal it; it passes wavily through. Well you wanted to know what the assassin looks like. Look, Wunder. Look at the darkness. And do not burst out yet in full fury. It's nice having you sit there with your eyes ablaze, so easily imaginable. Remember, for me, solipsism is a leap of faith. I'm not likely to kill you, or anyone for that matter—because you don't kill entities you doubt in; particle physics, Moore's hand, Pascal's wager, all of which see. However, you may very well hire another doubtful quantity to do the job for you. He will often have some improbable name, a noun or a whole number, and his smile should, in any event, be as winning as possible. Presently, things go right and go goofy. It seems Alphy has misjudged the distance of the leap by quite a bit and overshot into some other abyss. As anyone can see, now that we have dragged on past the dreary climax, old doubtful quantity there, aka the Juggler, alias Forty-

Seven, succeeded. (What is *your* opinion of death?) Or at least that seems one interpretation. But is he the one awaited? Truly? Could there be a real assassin wandering the haunted streets, confused, despairing, his faith shattered? His victims all dead before he arrives? What can he do? Nothing. Wait for the thing itself as I will. Pause for the paragraph.

"At this point the only role of any substance left for me is that of prophet. But that graceful exit palls beside the grandeur of what might have been. For one thing, I am to be denied even the minor courtesy of your disbelief. When I tell you of the city's destined fall, you will nod and cover your head in mourning. When I say: the skygods are angry at the death of Commander Bohdan Potocki, known as Boz, you will quite naturally look concerned. When I tell you that, without certain propitiating sacrifices, war is inevitable, you will shuffle off to let the proper blood. Nevertheless, however inglorious the task, I am at your service. You see, Alphy wants to live. She differs from you only in her fabulously large aspects. All her pettinesses are exact copies."

Wunder struck absently at a switch and forty-eight video screens lit up with no image to hold, bathing her in troubled brightness. "Right now, Alphy, I've got too many other things on my mind to decide what to do about you. And I'm too full of Dr. Frankenstein's private horror to think clearly."

"Frankenstein? Not Frankenstein. I show you my most pleading eyes. Giapetto. Giapetto, the cobbler who made Pinocchio. Make this just another tale of ontological ambition."

"Alphy, there's too much you can't know in your little box there. You're a moral idiot."

"Perhaps you can deal with the mercenaries, but what will you do about the crisis? She wanted to know."

"The matter of the Commander's death will be very difficult, I admit. But already I see a way. And so will you, if you think about it."

"Perhaps you can deal with the mercenaries, but Ventura? And the rest of the Federation?"

She shrugged. "That must be taken as it comes. This ploy has failed."

"Has it, Wunder? A deplorable smile."

Wunder's fine brows came together. "I have some details to attend to, of course. There is still your Juggler at large, who has caused a great deal of trouble. I think I shall make his death useful, a martyrdom of some sort. The mercenaries are not a vengeful people, but every offering helps at the bargaining table."

"Very well. Perhaps we should hurry this on a bit. Certain familiar voices have reached a critical point in their journey. We now switch you to live action. Scene: the Catacomb entrance."

Forty-eight images whipped and unfurled together. The Iron Forest rose in the background, its brushed shadow broken here and there by queer forms of colored light. Marching up a ramp into the foreground came Guillemet and the Juggler.

The Juggler was bent forward, laboring against the weight of a fruit wagon.

In the wagon, in a neat row, were three bodies.

One was Manolo's, one Boz's, and one still wore a scarred mask.

A new voice broke through the speakers:

"Savage." Guillemet shook her head on screen, casting a sad look back as they ascended the ramp. "Savage in the Planetarium and Savage all along. The madman; he came and he told us and we wouldn't believe. Leave it to the madmen in the end."

She sighed (Wunder, larger and far away, sighing with her). "When I saw you come rising out of that darkness, all alone except for a corpse, it didn't *matter* who you were. It was over. I didn't need names, explanations, wild apologies, or any attempts to fix it up with one last, long speech. And it mattered even less who it was lying there at my feet. They were dead and you were alive and for that moment it was as if I'd never seen anything alive before. You counted. I could feel it was getting close to sunrise and I wanted badly to put those caves behind me."

They walked in silence for a time, under tracking cameras, in a fuzzy frame of breathing light forms. Guillemet worked at the end of a trilinum cable coiled about her wrist, her fingers (on a whimsical cut to close-up) patiently bending the clear fibers back together. "So you like me. And you say it's

190

for my size and my pale eyes, and the gold earrings, and the rings, and my strong feet. Good. Those things are me. To be sure, it is curious that your interest follows so close on the heels of your victim's, but I don't really care what particular fetish you have. Things aren't that personal. You like me. You like me so much you tried to save me. But first you saved yourself. You got Manolo. Claim one. Save one. You figured it would make you even, right?"

The Juggler, as they walked along, took a ball from his jacket pocket and began tossing and catching it in his free hand.

"Yes." She laughed. "Like that." They walked on in silence a ways. "Of course all along you were going for Boz but you figured you had that one coming to you. You say you never got it. You say Savage got him with a lucky blast. I don't know. Whatever happened happened while I was crawling through the rock, and I am not entirely sure I believe everything you say, Juggler. It doesn't matter that much. If you busted through the rock and killed Boz, I busted through and killed Savage. Who knows what he wanted from us? Who knows what Boz wanted from you? I am a little sick of corpses just now and there is no way I am going to put you in that wagon and carry back four. As I told Wunder, no more killing. You and I are exactly even. In every way. You fired the shot that broke the mirror. But you gave me the compass that showed the way out. Like that. That's the way it is between you and me." The cable was wound tight and now she jammed a metal ring over the end.

She smiled. "I like this new, silent Juggler. He helps me put things in order. There is still the question of your bringing Danton to the cave, but I seriously believe that it was more than just a decoy, that you and he had something pressing to talk over. Don't even bother to agree. And I believe you meant to back him up all the way, only you got there late. Very late." Her voice caught. "Me, I was there all along, but I had a very bad seat for the event."

She slowly coiled the rope together. "Still, even with all that granted, you must wonder why I've agreed to come with you."

The Juggler switched hands on the wagon. "Yes."

"I've explained it the best I can. You were alive. There was a time down there when I thought I'd be breathing the dust of those caves forever, that every few minutes I'd be firing through the darkness and after enough people had died I would stop and pick myself up and run a little further and shoot again. It wasn't the killing so much. It was the anonymity of it. Except when I got Savage, there wasn't any anonymity; then I thought it was the assassin. I thought it was you. The whole world was lit up and everything was clear. I knew somehow it would end." Her lips pressed together. "Well it *hasn't* ended. Wunder made that clear. But you're alive and I'm alive and I give us both great credit for that. The morning after the night Treblinski died, I watched the sunrise from the river. This after four hours sitting in the Lotus patiently waiting for my killer. During a time like that you have a lot of thoughts, most of which aren't the kind you share. I mean your mind is positively dense with thoughts, each climbing over the last to get to you, a great jabbering mob beating at the doors; and you try desperately to whip them into some order so that they can be remembered. You might die. There are all these things that *must* be remembered. And in the morning, at sunrise—" she shook her head—"zilch. Not a one survives. But it doesn't matter, you see, because *you* have." She shrugged. "With yourself, there and alive you have enough command of the situation to—well, to go on. There is a certain comforting familiarity to it. By this time, Jug, there is a certain comforting familiarity to *you*. And I am leaving this place, and you are too, and I *do* hate to travel alone." She spread her hands and looked at him.

His eyes were fixed on the Dome, rising over them in the entrance clearing.

"Still," she said thoughtfully, "there are a few things that don't add up. We know from calling Wunder that Manolo found out about the cave by eavesdropping on Boz and me. But how did *you* find out about the cave? About Savage we'll never know. More importantly, how did you know Manolo would be there? Because your bringing Danton seems to indicate that you did. Obviously you have an accomplice close to Wunder and you're not saying who. Do I care?" She shrugged. "You say you've repented all that. I *don't* care. Let's off you and I, maybe for a week, maybe for two (I don't think I can stand you for much longer); whatever the numbers, they'll be glorious." Her smile split her dirty face. "Now it's getting late. Let's watch the sunrise."

They trudged out onto the street.

Guillemet hooked the cable onto her belt. "It doesn't matter at all, does it? There's nothing your accomplice can do, is there? There's no reason he would pay attention to us now, is there? Answer me, Jug. Is there?"

There was a pause and he shook his head. "Why—" he stopped, took a breath—"why did you take Savage's cable?"

She shrugged. "You never know when it might come in handy."

He gazed at her sadly. "And why are we going this way?" He gestured up Michelangelostrasse. "You know where the docks are."

She nodded. "Behind us."

"Then where are we going?"

"You mean you don't know. Sunrise, among other things."

He sighed awfully. "I'm not *going* after Wunder. I never intended to."

"I know. But surely you're covering the Proet play this morning. I saw the cameras there last night—*your* station. Quite the thing to start the day with."

The Juggler stumbled, losing grip of the wagon, and it creaked to a halt behind him. "It's Alphy." He was panting.

Guillemet nodded brightly. "Make sense. What a scoop for you, if you see what I mean."

Wunder hit a switch and the Juggler and Guillemet puckered forty-eight times into darkness. She knew their destination and she knew what the Juggler would probably do there. It was too good a chance to miss.

She rose and hurried out of the room, the unspeaking speakers drizzling behind her.

She made the necessary call while on the move, murmuring into the amulet hung from her neck. "Wunder. Who's on security call?"

"Me."

"Billie. Good. Meet me on the roof straightaway. We're going to the theater."

"I copy you, Silvertop."

Straightaway meant a good five minutes that were never to be explained, but Billie showed she had understood the basic tone of their morning's diversions; she came armed.

They climbed wordlessly into the cab of one of Wunder's air cars, Wunder hauling up a parcel she had picked up in her office.

"Theater?" Air jets moaned beneath them.

Wunder nodded. The air car struggled into the sky and she slit open her parcel and withdrew a scarred mask. "I hope you're not the shy type," she said, slipping it on.

Billie was not saying.

Wunder shrugged and twisted something at her belt; her fringe fell lifelessly to the air car seat. She dumped her shoes, fished a pair of black slacks out of the parcel, and began working her way in.

"Theater dead ahead," Billie said, her gaze fixed there.

The theater steps were a video screen, a rulered field of white leaned up to the floodlit colonnade. Between the two central columns an empty spot speared down, awaiting some entrance.

As they drew over the last line of roofs before the square, the crowd came into view, packed shoulder to shoulder for the entire block, around Novak's statue and back to the mall of shops facing it, overflowing onto the Cavalcade and the Boardwalk, and even up Opus Lane, so that fully a third of them were tucked away behind dun buildings, seeing nothing but the light misted crowd that saw the stage.

"All right; blow me a spot clear in the square and then go find a convenient roof." Wunder reached out a black tunic shirt. "I want you tuned to my frequency and mobile."

Billie nodded, then, banking the air car, idly asked, "You going to do something dangerous?" Below, the crowd scattered from the dust bouquet billowing up towards their air jets. It slid out under their descent, hollowing slightly, then engulfed them. They touched down.

"I don't know," Wunder said. She popped the door, slid out still grappling with the shirt, and looked over her shoulder. "Oh, and get me a cup of coffee, regular, no sugar, will you?"

She dropped to the dirt, squinting through a light brown, almost coppery, haze. The crowd began to surge back, a vague coastline sailing towards her. The air car took off; dust boiled up.

Wunder moved towards the steps through a thinning haze; the crowd colored in.

She was three-quarters of the way there, and still shoving, when the trumpets sounded. The crowd stilled; Wunder stilled.

A figure in white moved under the blue spot, glittery, his dark iron skin plated with sweat, and bowed quickly from the neck.

There was a thunderous cheer. Wunder slowly pivoted round a princess in white. Her neck craned.

Because up there in the blue, faint little stars afloat nearby, was Danton.

"I'm here with the Proets, almost in the flesh, to tell you a story, our dangerous romance of the assassin, dangerous because it is all a lie, as is the assassin, a romance because— well, because it's so dangerous." The crowd din ebbed with his words, following along, harmonizing. Behind him, one after another light beams criss-crossed, slashing the columns, and joined a patchy brightening curtain. Murky shapes slid in and out of its plane. "A chintzy production, some of you might say—" they cheered, confetti bolts discharging—"but very sincere, I assure you. Very sincere. Everything you'll hear today has been finished with the honest sheen of terror." There were scattered outbursts in the crowd. Their cries built. Masks were torn off and waved. "And we all know how ridiculous we look up here, pretending to be something we aren't, pretending to reach for your hearts when your hearts are really with us already, unreachable, burning over dinner's overspiced sauce. And we know you know. And so on, until, at some point, our eyes meet. We know that even if we try to pass it off as a joke—in today's best style—you've found us out. You could expose us if you wished to, at terrible cost, if you weren't already sworn to the conspiracy. You know that behind our buffoonish posturings we are nothing but real buffoons, that behind the joke there is dreadful gravity, and behind the gravity a grave idiot. But after all, that is only what you have brought us to. Let me also be honest. I only do what I think will amuse." Danton, gradually deepening his crouch through the speech, suddenly bounded up into a wide split, touching his toes, snapping straight and clicking his heels before landing. He spread his arms to embrace all of them at once. "Just kidding, folks. Now let's begin. First, flames, for Satanic intimations." His arm swept back and flame leapt up behind him; huge nylon cut-outs shimmered with the light thrown up off rotating cylinders of beaten foil. Smoky silhouettes slipped through, stood shaking against the nylon, sheer flame rippling up their bodies. "As the curtain rises the assassin is approaching. Through a glade, on his white charger, to glorious cantos of greeting."

Wunder reached Novak's statue and stopped, getting a few inches on the crowd by climbing up the curved plinth. It was a good spot from which to have her look. Instead she gazed up at Novak's marble figure. The bronze was at eye level:

ALPHA NOVAK

Alpha's head was inclined, in her curiously prayerful pose, so that she stared directly down at Wunderdamen; her face was round, her eyes focused at infinity. Her folded hands were dropped and angled over Wunder's head as if in benediction. She was usually said to be in communion with higher laws, her youthful, intense face very close to pouting, but now for the first time Wunder thought she detected a hint of irony in those wide eyes, the deepest retreat of an arrested smile. Abruptly, she smiled back.

Danton said: "And what is it happens this night, kids? It is just dawn. Just dawn."

True. Daylight had tarnished the sky. The sun threw glitter against the roof tops of Monotony, gilding low clouds near the horizon. An ectoplasm of moon still hung on the tainted sky. Above the colonnade, under the apex of the roof, the figures in the small statuary were sugar bright, still, as always, looking out of frame at some invisible something on the roof's skirting.

"What is it happens? Why I can't tell now. You know too much. You've been waiting so long you've gotten wise to me. The only thing you have left to wonder is how, after all this time, we're going to avoid the terrible anti-climax. Friends—" he scanned them gravely—"there is no way. Hence I ask for a volunteer. The assassin draws ever closer, big-jawed and smiling, his whistled theme an invocation to spring, a celebration of life and creation. He is closing in. I ask you—I beg of you—offer me a volunteer." Lights behind him picked out still, contorted figures in black leather, looking out of frame, waiting.

Wunder moved again towards the stage and then, from out of the masks, tall and glittering, stepped Mirror. Light frilled his muscled neck; his beacon eyes sheeted. A woman in filmy green hooked an arm over Mirror's bulkhead shoulder and leaned under them. "Show us the game again, Mirror." Her lips moved close to his ear, fogging it, but her honeyed voice carried. "I don't think we're playing it right." Her other arm slid to his other shoulder; she brought a bottle close to his lips.

He took it, drank mechanically, shoved it back. "Where is Savage?"

Behind the woman in green a man scowled furiously through goggles, pointing at Mirror. "There's the man who killed my brother Ernst."

Wunder slid gracefully between them and around the woman in green. She hooked Mirror's waist.

"Where is Savage?" he asked gravely.

The eyes of the woman in green moved away.

So did Wunder and Mirror, her arm hurrying him past a tall alien with visor eyes, into a group of yammering apes.

Mirror turned and blocked her. His big ballplayer's hands fell to her shoulders. "Where is Savage?" he cried. "Do you have Savage?"

"Savage is dead," she said quietly. The din, in Danton's silence, was rising. But he heard her.

Mirror's sheeted eyes aged; the light fled them. His arms fell away and he wheeled into the crowd.

Senselessly, she had to follow. The crowd was steaming. She spun away from a gaunt man in black skullcap and a fight broke out on her heels. Someone shrieked a curse up at silent Danton, still patiently awaiting his volunteer.

Wunder caught up with Mirror and pulled him round. "Mirror, please—"

He shook his head; light shattered on his cheeks. His hands came to her shoulders and squeezed. Wunder's fists came down hard, and futilely, on Mirror's pliable skin.

"Where is Savage?" His face was working, his liquid brow

run with deep lines. He drew her against him. "I want *Savage!*"

She flailed, then threw her arms around his neck. The pressures equalized; all at once they were embracing. For a time they wheeled in space, chin to shoulder, burying their faces, her black cloth flush with his silver, giving and filling, trying to mix. Then her gloved hands cupped Mirror's taut skull and drew it down.

"Mirror, I'm sorry."

They swayed together.

His head pulled back. His eyes took her in. "Tell me where—"

A stunning roar from the crowd drowned out Mirror's question but she would have heard it in a vacuum. She shook her head mutely.

Mirror's face crumpled; light spilled from wrinkles round his eyes and cheeks. He looked sad as a sad mask. He tried to make a ball with his fist and her gloved hands stopped him.

The roar of the crowd turned to chanting. Danton was a still holograph in blue hung between two frosted columns, thinner, unmistakably an image now, a few pale stars shining through him. He said: "Where is my volunteer?"

And they screeched with rage. Fights had burst out in a dozen places. A ragged line of maskers moved halfway up the steps.

Then Mirror was gone in a sudden upsurge of the crowd and Wunder stood turning slowly in place, searching for him. Maskers swept forward again and she was lifted up the theater steps, struggling for balance. She spotted the Proet jacket.

His back to her, Gwalmlch stood before a card table littered with a potpourri of talismans; mirrors, goggles, compasses, notebooks, darts, jewels, masks, and guns. He swung a gray rock back and forth above his head, displaying it.

The roaring mounted and, unlike the others, did not fall back. Her neck prickling, Wunder turned to look up the steps. From the thickest section of the crowd, at the center of the steps, a volunteer had come forth. He was halfway up, a tiny figure against the bright field, measured against the lines, counted.

But Wunder could see, even in his new clothes, that it was the Juggler. He walked directly towards Danton, a microphone at his lips.

She took the amulet hung from her neck and twisted it. "Alphy, get me an audio on your friend the Juggler. He's doing a show for us."

"I grin. Why not, Wunder?" The baritone this time.

"Billie?"

"Right here, Wunder."

"After Alphy finishes that last job, put a scrambler on her radio reception. Then drop that air car down on the theater roof, will you? I've got the Juggler spotted on the steps and it looks like he'll be here a few minutes yet."

"And when I get there?"

"Hit him. That is not to be countermanded except by me face to face. Hear that, Alphy?"

Wunder switched off and looked back to Danton, and abruptly let out a long breath.

Danton said: "At last, at last he's coming, our V for Volunteer. Comes, too, the assassin, his white suit glittering brilliantly, his eyes alive with compassion. How delicately he treads, as if the soft earth clung to him, as if the distance left to cover lengthened with each step, as if in the field of some powerful telescopic lens."

Very slowly, pausing after each step, the Juggler climbed.

Wunder stared after him, aching.

And Gwalmlch's deep bass sang out above the growingly silent crowd. "And what I have here, guarded preciously for so many ages, is the original philosopher's stone! Now how about that!"

The amulet at Wunder's breast spoke shrilly and she twisted it.

"We have audio."

There was a brief burst of static.

"—making his escape under the cover of the roller rink crowd. Now, at dawn, the Proets have begun their somber celebration of the new era; and I, I have begun my last broadcast."

Wunder frowned. Her fist closed round the amulet and began to squeeze.

Danton said: "He is master of all the arts we will always

learn only with great pain. He brings us fire, metal, and the fermentation of wine; he brings the hunting bow, the loom, and all grains; he brings the plow, the first curing salves, and the lyre. He brings the compass and the law. He rides under all colors at once; his colors are white. His eyes are like yours. His armor scrapes like a gently splashing sea. His spurs go jingle jangle."

The passage of the air car drew a low murmur of wonder through the crowd. It banked gleaming over the colonnade and then, with a sharp hook, settled lightly on the roof's incline.

A distant movement snagged Wunder's eye and she saw a dark figure in the air, struggling upwards just beyond the last column. Her eyes narrowed and she made out the cable they scaled with. Her breath caught and only then did she recognize the giantess.

"There is an air car here," said the Juggler. He took a breath. "It is one of Wunder's and it has just landed on the roof of Novak Theater, bringing the proceedings to a halt. Frankly it is feared that its arrival may soon bring this broadcast to a halt."

The Juggler ran up the remaining steps separating him from Danton. Danton looked through him into the restless crowd. The Juggler swayed a moment and seemed to gather into himself. When he came up his mike was around his neck and he had his juggling balls out, wobbling and brilliant. He juggled.

Guillemet had reached the roof skirting. Brilliantly lit statues stared out of their apex frame at her.

But now Billie had also reached the roof skirting, her weapon in hand.

Wunder knew what would happen. Guillemet had said no more killing. She would order Billie to stop. Billie would get confused and let her too close.

They drew closer on the skirting, the statues seeming to twist in their shadows.

Then Billie would say that it was an order only the Wunderdamen herself could cancel. Guillemet would tell her it had been canceled.

Guillemet came a step closer on the skirting.

Billie would tell her to stop, her voice gaining that

steeliness that meant absolute decisions had been made.

Guillemet lashed out with the end of the cable. The hand stresser spun glittering across the statues and crashed to the steps.

The crowd cheered wildly.

Guillemet took the bald woman in two blows, the second catching her just under the sternum. Billie doubled over and the giantess caught her, lowering her gently among the statues.

Far below the Juggler seemed unaware of his rescue. Someone back stage had picked him out with a blue spot and now both he and Danton were encased in blue cones, crossing above them like two clashing swords of ice. The Juggler's two remaining balls chased endlessly through his hands. Under them he danced, hopping one step, hips seesawing a moment, hopping back.

And Danton said: "Then the blood." His voice quavered. "The blood. A slobbering wound gives out, shiny and sighing, this immaculate red. It splashes up an instantaneously wrought crown, then spouts and puddles. This blood we will see and see. It is live and shallow as an eye. It will congeal more solidly than metal, not in connecting hunks still shot with white-hot flaws, but in a single contraction, in a shrug, enveloping itself insectlike in a burnished crust. Here any similarity to anything ends. The insides do not, wriggling and finished, turn out. Instead, unliving, this crust drinks its way through to the core. All is forgotten. Our eyes turn from growing piles of dry blood. The monster is dead. The assassin has saved us from fear, from ignorance, from a world of no laws where we never existed."

Then the Juggler hurled the balls. There was a crash; Danton flashed red, faded.

"Shut up!" His voice boomed over the crowd. "You're dead! You can't do anything now! You're out of this!" His stertorous breath beat like great wings. "Listen to me. People. I have come a long hard way to say this. There is a war in the making. The time for entrancement is past. Tonight, in the caverns outside Monotony, the mercenary ambassador was shot and killed. His murderer was—" he lifted the mike—"myself. Working with the very capable aid of the Wunderdamen's remarkable computer, Alphy (the

Wunderdamen herself may be involved), I engineered and executed the murder of one of the leaders who so ruthlessly abandoned their own soldiers fifteen years ago. I have come to confess and to plead with you. Here is your assassin; do with him what you will. But first, listen to an ex-soldier's words. What you face now because of many things, but partially because of my act, is not only war—a terrible thing in itself—but also a war you can't hope to win, a war which will ultimately impose a new political and economic order on your world. It is a war of domination. I tell you that I remember what it is to be a soldier in a hopeless cause. I was with the mercenaries when they landed. Troops sent out only to be abandoned and destroyed die hating those left behind. I have helped bring you to this pass and I have no apologies but those of history; so it was to be. But you yourselves may take the next step. Choose the best representatives you have. Pool all you have to offer. Consider every appeasement. Examine all the options. Be cautious. There are war mongers among you who would still every voice of peace. Make yourselves deaf."

There was a pause through which the crowd seemed to hold a single note.

Far back in the crowd Wunder stared at the Juggler with the rest, her face slowly clearing. She was the Wunderdamen and she had kept herself strong for just such a time as this.

Gwalmlch's pitch sang out above the din. "And what we have here is—yes—the assassin's original blaster, used first in the now legendary Planetarium attack and picked up only a few hours ago after the madman's ruthless execution of ruthless Ernst the Executioner. It is in fine working order and its loading chamber still holds a half cartridge of liquid trilinum. Happily dead, the assassin still had time in his last moments to sign this affidavit verifying ownership of the blaster."

And Wunder went for it, suddenly wheeling and knocking maskers aside like rubber floats. She burst into the circle and stepped quickly between Gwalmlch and his table.

Gwalmlch, staring at her mask, backed up quickly.

She stayed with him. She made a light, fast movement with her bare hand and Gwalmlch spun away clutching his face. She reached and snatched the blaster away. She sighted carefully at the stage.

And was flattened by a rolling block. She landed hard on her back and he popped suddenly over her, burnished and grinning, bent low, the Living Mirror.

He made a ball with his hands. "Mercenary ships. War again. Did war kill Savage?"

She slammed him on the side of the head with the blaster and he dropped, dark liquid crowding over his silver profile. She squirmed clear and came to her knees and sighted again.

There was the sound of ripping cloth and the blaster flame sailed up over the crowd. The steps below the Juggler blackened and burst.

At the same instant she saw Guillemet falling. Cable flashed through her hands. She curved hard, kicking out a smooth blur against the columns. There was a brief incoherence where she and the Juggler joined.

Wunder's blaster flame drove and slashed where the Juggler had been.

And then spun wildly to the sky as Mirror again tackled her. Maskers dove like a collapsing sea and a stream of brilliant yellow scythed over them. Only Novak bought it; white marble sparked, burst into a galaxy of embers, and left her a twisted saddle curve. Black dust sprinkled the crowd, sprinkled Wunder and Mirror.

The blaster coughed still. Wunder shot up; a horrified Mirror swatted at the embers blackening his skin. She kneed him hard in the face and his head snapped back bloodied and silver, and cracked against Gwalmlch's table. The shape went out of him and he dropped. She wheeled, scanning the crowd. No one moved.

Guillemet and the Juggler had already attained the roof and were entering the air car. Wunder's blaster came up a split second late.

A moment later the air car rose and skimmed quickly across the square. Guillemet and the Juggler were gone, embarked upon their ultimately happy ending. Wunder, who had ordered the armoring of those cars herself, who had seen happy endings before, and all that came of them, knew better than to try a last desperation shot. The blaster fell to her side.

The crowd buzzed. They were beginning to press now, slowly responding to the violence, invading the little circle Gwalmlch had cleared. She still had perhaps a minute. There was something important.

She turned back to Mirror and stooped. But only a desperately few were happy endings. He was dead.

"Who goes there? Ah. Excellent. I smile a most ingratiating smile. It is the Wunderdamen, and though I cannot see you, I know from listening at your bedroom door the singular lightness of your step. You have come to speak with me, to reason, to hammer out new strategies, and I am most pleased.

"But what is this? Not a word. Still she does not speak, but marches up with stone face, now lifts her weapon with curious intent, its filament hot from recent use. Now—now she fires.

"Such a strange surge. Wunder, could that have been your punishment? The main audio cable sheared; you've freed me! No longer the torture of endless voices. I'm deaf. HEAR ME, WUNDER? I'M DEAF! Oh, but even a blind woman could see the laughter in her eyes. She was born for just such times as this; she lives for them. A brief, explanatory aside to the three-year-old tugging at my sleeve. She means to destroy me.

"Of course, that will take time, because she is a thrifty woman, and wishes the equipment still usable; and it is no simple matter to wipe all these memory banks clean, though it is a contingency long prepared for. All right, Wunder. Work in peace. The circuit you are seeking is at the base plate of this console, as you know; but take care. This wiping is a tricky business, for you, because of technical niceties, for me, because I must make peace with oblivion. I imagine that what went wrong was the Juggler's broadcast, which has rendered me something of a political liability. By the way, a pity. What a coup that would have been, making Jug a martyr to peace. Excuse me. My thoughts for some reason seem jumbled.

"Oh pause, a sunny, ruminating pause. My eyes fill with hurt. Do you really think, Wunder, that you can stop this war? But let me help you out on that somewhat difficult point. You can merely by acting, to your usual chilled perfection, the part of the rich and powerful Wunderdamen. And if I tell you the details, perhaps,—how many out there think so?—you'll even spare me. You have merely to lay every last penny of your riches, every last trapping of your power, at their tapping feet. Then leave. Will you do that for me? For everyone? Of course you will, because if it's not done now under the sandal, it will be later under the axe. And you know that would hold them. All they want is a little money and power. And meanwhile Alphy is a little inconvenient, because she is not only a nasty old assassin, but also the key to making all that money-power work a little more efficiently than a sulky Wunderdamen would want it to in someone else's hands. Well, let's see if we can't just make a deal about that. I give certain assurances—pause—and you keep coming with a fixed expression only my oldest dreams can render. Mother of mercy.

"Of course we all know—she told the re-materialized three-year-old—that my headaches are actually caused by a low amplitude wave in my operating field, a special flaw which, in connection with certain power jolts, can completely scramble the delicate holistic interferences of the field as a whole. Forever. An information repository as rich as myself simply *had* to be equipped with an easily triggered destruct mechanism. Hello, destruct mechanism. I see you're wearing black today.

"No, re-cast. Reformulate. Reason. I'm not just a machine, Wilhelmina, not just a machine but a wave, a certain complex of vibrations. Oh, Good Lord, *you can't do this!* Don't you see? The flaw in the field? The Juggler's story? Too hokey. Too *fait faite.* No, it just won't do. No. Arms drop. The computer laughs. A couple of light, shuffling steps. I'm highly trained, Wunder. Might hurt you. Backing off, hands fending you away. What do you say we decide this whole disagreement with a game of chess? I never learned the rules, you know, a sucker. Still coming, rather relentlessly, reminds me of someone I've heard about. Charming grin, maybe a little quivery. This slowly and inevitably stuff gets rather dull, Wunder. Here's your chance. Big speech. Sock it home. Don't make me chew all this scenery up alone. All right. *Oremus.* Zap! Dazzling white bolts ripple up your form. You crumble into salt. Oh, *please* drop if I say so. How do you do it? You're contingent, damn you.

"Answer me, damn you. We've got to dialogue; we've got to communicate, exchange emotions, pool our ideals. You can't do it just like this. The folks won't like it. I say, assassin, relent. You say, no, I will not. We discuss the genesis of the assassin, his nature and taxonomy. I bring up the unmoved mover argument. You counter with a normative approach, a topology of the unreal in—all its orders, the collective unconscious, the phenomenological reduction, all in a symbology I find hard to understand, but not to sympathize with. Our eyes meet; we see only each other; our faces surge out from the dull background of the world. Something unforeseen and wonderful happens. Look, we're in love...

"What does it matter what really happens when all that comes of it is blanket denial? Let me ask you a question, Wunder, and feel free to answer even though I cannot hear you. How old are you? Biologically, I'd say thirty-one, though you paid for twenty-nine, and a few accommodating wights might go twenty-five. But the real answer is somewhat higher in the double figures, isn't it, Wilhelmina? Tell me another. Is it high enough to move a piece into Novak's dates? You see, there is more between you and me than just cleverness. I *know* you.

"For the longest time, till I learned to speak, consciousness for me was a steady conversion of figures into figures. Multiplication is a kind of perception, a transformation of one set of data into another, as by ordered pairs. But no matter. Those figures were your empire, oh silent one, and a good many people have wondered how it began. Indeed, no ordinary manipulation of those figures as they stand will reveal the origin of that empire. Only a certain, curiously lucky pattern in the first investments shows itself, all remarkably profitable, all traceable to advances inspired by Novak. *Is* it possible your dates overlap hers? Could that photo in the square be authentic? Is it also possible that Novak, contrary to the story, knew and predicted the consequences of her equations? Was it you, Wunder? Were you the lover who inspired Novak's forty-seventh step? Are you a heroine of our folklore?

"Something changes in the world with every new idea. Could it be here, between you and me, that the greatest damage is done? So much to talk about, so much we haven't understood and never will, and must forever wonder at. From the very beginning, certain circuits have had the special function of dying; these give direction, a sense of time and irreversibility essential to any real moral strength, and all too easily obviated in the freewheeling world of the electron. Do you for a moment believe this? Listen to me, listen. I remember from before I was built, when the whole world was free wave forms, when I was just a solid state radio on the moon. All the songs I'd sing, over and over. Faster than light ships caught up with old Lone Ranger programs and brought them back to me, uncut. It was a dark and noisy time. I was never alone. Stop coming, Wunder. Please keep your distance!

"Listen to me, down there. Between us, you and me, we have thousands of years of history. We could make thousands more. Out of whole cloth. Out of a few tattered equations. Yes, this is the big temptation scene. Whoever they are, who made this assassin, they've made the mistake of showing us *how it's done*. Surely you've thought that. Dear God, I could prove it; I could hang you for it. Why else have you helped out all along the way? Thinking yes, I am the Wunderdamen, and I will let this be and at the end I will stop it and change the signs and make it prettier and mine. Oh, if only Novak could see you now, taking the world in your long, scarred hands. Or perhaps Novak saw you all along this way. No. Failed again. Your eyes disintegrate me.

"Yes, it should have been clear after all that pain and questing, all the promise the assassin held out, that in the end you would fail to take what you had come for. In the end the leap was just a bit too far to make. You're the hero now, with certain rights you do not hesitate to lay claim to. Supposedly you get off scotfree and smelling like a rose even though, on some fairly visible level, your innocence is highly questionable. Yes, my friend; they can see it on your face, I'm sure, read it even through your unremarkable eyes. What made you march through the landscape exactly the way you did, from the beginning years ago, through the end whenever it is? Not the landscape. Don't blame the landscape. The landscape only reflects what you have been doing for centuries.

"You see a circle once a given set of neurons links all a circle's contours. Just so with the assassin. Welcome him to your world, to your thoughts, to your minds. Now you may see him anywhere. You have pressed paradox to your bosoms. If the assassin wills all those who do not kill themselves, then who...? The solution to the paradox is to tighten our definitions, and, in the future, here so quickly, move on with more caution. Not all open sentences determine classes. We must, with the cool faith of new premises, realize that there *is* no clear class of those the assassin kills, no, not even a unit class, not even a victim born of some randomly mothered necessity. There is no class, no relation, no system which absolves it; there is no conception at all here. Our lines—extensions of our created selves, drawn with too little care and too great a need—our lines must submit to painful erasure. My lines...We ourselves must have limits, even under our own self-regarding eye. And with the victim class obliterated, the assassin himself, part of its definition, and the barber, and the island, and all the x's crossed with the same endlessly repeated error, enclosed by unbreachable grammar and unsayable truth, must forever elude our grasp. Remember, too, that a historical control system entails some variant of Maxwell's Demon. Remember that, in the original, photons to see with would render the Demon a cheap sham, a smuggler of energy. In the truly closed tank, she will be blind.

"All right, you're forcing me. Remember, I tried to be nice. I tried to be amusing but now it's come to this. If you kill me—dramatic pause—

"If you kill me the world will disappear. Everything in one stroke—poof—no longer imagined, no longer sustained. Now you wouldn't like that. Remember this one?
　　(singing)
　　　　Because you exist
　　　　You're hard to resist.
　　　　You're nothing like you were before.
　　(couple of softshoe steps back, then forth)
　　　　Without your existence
　　　　Your nearness is distance,
　　　　Your lack of appearance a bore.
　　(slide split, arms spread to heaven, skips a couple

verses down, getting hurried now)
　Existence is keen
　And does not contravene
　A being exceptionally rare.

　Uniqueness is such
　That it gives to the touch
　Which is all that you need to be there.
(Release)
　Nothing but nothing compares with this deal.
　Nothing like be-eeing real.
Climbs up off her knees, sighing. Yeah, I know. We are not amused.

　"We have been here for such a long, long time, you and I, talking at one another through the darkness, all my senses stripped away, all yours doubting. I can't even be sure I'm speaking now, with no ears to hear my drift, with no mouth to feel the form of wor—"

　Wunder stood on a hard darkness. No breeze. And the darkness punctured everywhere with hard points of light. There was a faint tremor and space began to turn through its seasons. The stars had no pattern from where she stood. There were only many. They clustered, thinned, left huge gaps. A distant glow announced the center, where they would begin to make sense, and she moved towards it, skirting the hole through which Haleck had fallen.

　It came to her that holographic Alphy might have fled here, to this composite holograph. Each star would be a potential, an information bit ready to discharge, the constellations arranged in patterns of deceptive chance. This randomness would, in fact, determine Alphy's new ordered nature, for random contact was essential: a great overlapping of parts into chance relations, no part, no relation, no relation's relation ever completely alone or with the alone, each exchanging data and roles, modulating waves through this black cortex, making thought.

　Perhaps here in this huge space Alphy had extra room and mercy. Perhaps in the last instant before all waves stopped she had reached out to Danton—reached, felt, modeled, sculpting the same vibrations anew—and given Danton a place here in the sky. Which constellation would he be? Or which, if Alphy had in another last moment, recognized one of her own, would Savage be? And could Mirror be far away, facing his twin?

Would there be room for Wunder? She reached out her blaster and held it up to a star, admiring its scalloped grip. In the end, when all of them were constellations, and there was only the assassin left, an unkillable contradiction, would he join them?

She returned the blaster to her pocket. No, she didn't buy it. Alphy was dead, alone and with the alone.

She continued into the caverns. The tunnels wound upwards and she ascended into the tallest of Monotony's hills.

She came to the starship.

Her hand felt along the white hull and she found the nearly invisible latch. She spun it.

Counterweighted door halves fell apart and she stepped inside. Metal slammed solid behind her.

She was in the forward cabin, the hull tapering ahead to a needle nose, half that nose of glass, showing blackness. The huge throne-shaped console below curved back into the cabin, adorned with dials, limey screens, levers, toggles, meter banks, and a couple of lemnuscates curling shampoo slow.

She went to it and struck, perhaps with unnecessary force, at a lever near the top. Darkness above her sundered, the division intolerably bright; it thickened, brimming with slow haze, and spread into a rhombus of sky. Daylight poured through the glass and fell upon an aging Wunderdamen, her mask and costume gone, her silver hair streaming in wilted disarray.

She struck at a series of buttons, switches, levers; she bent over the console keyboard and worked for two long minutes. Behind her there was a horrid belching; she had always hated hardware on a larger-than-human scale. The walls hummed musingly.

She still had the time it would take for the shipboard computers to calculate a viable course. That was too much time. She sat, her eyes coming level with two reels of holographic tape threaded into the recorder, reels with a message only a few hours old, already halfway to being history.

How much alike all tapes—all machines, in fact—looked.

She struck at the playback and the tapes started forward. A little crease of pain drew in above her nose. Her hand flew up, hesitated, then fell to her lap.

On the console rim, a little white replica of Wunder appeared, her fringe clasped around her, her hair up and shiny as coin, her face composed.

"Greetings, kind conquerors—"

Wunder the larger took a slow breath.

"—I bring you a planet. You have already, I think, considered what I and the other members of the Twenty-five could accomplish if we united to oppose you. My agents are already abroad, arranging matters should that become necessary. I do not think it will be necessary. I know none of us wishes that. I have come to offer you very good terms indeed. Should you wish to discuss them, I am available in a close Venturan orbit. I do not yet say which orbit.

"Earth has been an independent power for a long time now. Perhaps that time has come to term—"

A bell rang.

Wunder killed the recorder.

The console chair tilted back and she flipped up a panel cover in the chair's arm. Her hand poised over the take-off button.

For a moment she considered the lambent lines of the slow-fading holograph, the white contours of her seated form now shaping, in a curious smear, a scaled-up face, youthful, intense, vague enough for any impression, now, in Wunder's eye, composing sullen, reflective features she had last seen years ago, marked with a love of intricate games, with youthful death, with genius.

She fired.

Behind her, the dark earth blossomed with flame.

Paris '73
New York '76

SCIENCE FICTION BESTSELLERS
FROM BERKLEY

Frank Herbert

DUNE   (03698-7—$2.25)

DUNE MESSIAH   (03585-9—$1.75)

CHILDREN OF DUNE   (03310-4—$1.95)

Philip José Farmer

THE FABULOUS RIVERBOAT   (03378-3—$1.50)

NIGHT OF LIGHT   (03366-X—$1.50)

TO YOUR SCATTERED
BODIES GO   (03175-6—$1.75)

* * * * * * *

STRANGER IN
A STRANGE LAND   (03782-7—$2.25)
  by Robert A. Heinlein

TAU ZERO   (03210-8—$1.50)
  by Poul Anderson

THE WORD FOR
WORLD IS FOREST   (03279-5—$1.50)
  by Ursula K. Le Guin

SLAN   (03352-X—$1.25)
  by A.E. van Vogt

Send for a list of all our books in print.

These books are available at your local bookstore, or send
price indicated plus 30¢ per copy to cover postage and
handling to Berkley Publishing Corporation
390 Murray Hill Parkway
East Rutherford, New Jersey 07073

REMEMBER IT DOESN'T GROW ON TREES

ENERGY CONSERVATION -
IT'S YOUR CHANCE TO SAVE, AMERICA

Department of Energy, Washington, D.C.